The Golden Slipper

And Other Problems for Violet Strange

Anna Katharine Green

The Golden Slipper and Other Problems for Violet Strange

ISBN: 979-8-88942-532-8

CONTENTS

Problem I   The Golden Slipper 1
Problem II   The Second Bullet 12
Problem III   An Intangible Clue 25
Problem IV   The Grotto Spectre 39
Problem V   The Dreaming Lady 54
Problem VI   The House of Clocks 71
Problem VII   The Doctor, His Wife, and the Clock 95
Problem VIII   Missing: Page Thirteen 128
Problem IX   Violet's Own 152

PROBLEM I

THE GOLDEN SLIPPER

"She's here! I thought she would be. She's one of the three young ladies you see in the right-hand box near the proscenium."

The gentleman thus addressed—a man of middle age and a member of the most exclusive clubs—turned his opera glass toward the spot designated, and in some astonishment retorted:

"She? Why those are the Misses Pratt and—"

"Miss Violet Strange; no other."

"And do you mean to say—"

"I do—"

"That yon silly little chit, whose father I know, whose fortune I know, who is seen everywhere, and who is called one of the season's belles is an agent of yours; a—a—"

"No names here, please. You want a mystery solved. It is not a matter for the police—that is, as yet,—and so you come to me, and when I ask for the facts, I find that women and only women are involved, and that these women are not only young but one and all of the highest society. Is it a man's work to go to the bottom of a combination like this? No. Sex against sex, and, if possible, youth against youth. Happily, I know such a person—a girl of gifts and extraordinarily well placed for the purpose. Why she uses her talents in this direction—why, with means enough to play the part natural to her as a successful debutante, she consents to occupy herself with social and other mysteries, you must ask her, not me. Enough that I promise you her aid if you want it. That is, if you can interest her. She will not work otherwise."

Mr. Driscoll again raised his opera glass.

"But it's a comedy face," he commented. "It's hard to associate intellectuality with such quaintness of expression. Are you sure of her discretion?"

"Whom is she with?"

"Abner Pratt, his wife, and daughters."

"Is he a man to entrust his affairs unadvisedly?"

"Abner Pratt! Do you mean to say that she is anything more to him than his daughters' guest?"

"Judge. You see how merry they are. They were in deep trouble yesterday. You are witness to a celebration."

"And she?"

"Don't you observe how they are loading her with attentions? She's too young to rouse such interest in a family of notably unsympathetic temperament for any other reason than that of gratitude."

"It's hard to believe. But if what you hint is true, secure me an opportunity at once of talking to this youthful marvel. My affair is serious. The dinner I have mentioned comes off in three days and—"

"I know. I recognize your need; but I think you had better enter Mr. Pratt's box without my intervention. Miss Strange's value to us will be impaired the moment her connection with us is discovered."

"Ah, there's Ruthven! He will take me to Mr. Pratt's box," remarked Driscoll as the curtain fell on the second act. "Any suggestions before I go?"

"Yes, and an important one. When you make your bow, touch your left shoulder with your right hand. It is a signal. She may respond to it; but if she does not, do not be discouraged. One of her idiosyncrasies is a theoretical dislike of her work. But once she gets interested, nothing will hold her back. That's all, except this. In no event give away her secret. That's part of the compact, you remember."

Driscoll nodded and left his seat for Ruthven's box. When the curtain rose for the third time he could be seen sitting with the Misses Pratt and their vivacious young friend. A widower and still on the right side of fifty, his presence there did not pass unnoted, and curiosity was rife among certain onlookers as to which of the twin belles was responsible for this change in his well-known habits. Unfortunately, no opportunity was given him for showing. Other and younger men had followed his lead into the box, and they saw him forced upon the good graces of the fascinating but inconsequent Miss Strange whose rapid fire of talk he was hardly of a temperament to appreciate.

Did he appear dissatisfied? Yes; but only one person in the opera house knew why. Miss Strange had shown no comprehension of or sympathy with his errand. Though she chatted amiably enough between duets and trios, she gave him no opportunity to express his wishes though she knew them well enough, owing to the signal he had given her.

This might be in character but it hardly suited his views; and, being a man of resolution, he took advantage of an absorbing minute on the stage to lean forward and whisper in her ear:

"It's my daughter for whom I request your services; as fine a girl as any in this house. Give me a hearing. You certainly can manage it."

She was a small, slight woman whose naturally quaint appearance was accentuated by the extreme simplicity of her attire. In the tier upon tier of boxes rising before his eyes, no other personality could vie with hers in strangeness, or in the illusive quality of her ever-changing expression. She was vivacity incarnate and, to the ordinary observer, light as thistledown in fibre and in feeling. But not to all. To those who watched her long, there came moments—say when the music rose to heights of greatness—when the mouth so given over to laughter took on curves of the rarest sensibility, and a woman's lofty soul shone through her odd, bewildering features.

Driscoll had noted this, and consequently awaited her reply in secret hope.

It came in the form of a question and only after an instant's display of displeasure or possibly of pure nervous irritability.

"What has she done?"

"Nothing. But slander is in the air, and any day it may ripen into public accusation."

"Accusation of what?" Her tone was almost pettish.

"Of—of theft," he murmured. "On a great scale," he emphasized, as the music rose to a crash.

"Jewels?"

"Inestimable ones. They are always returned by somebody. People say, by me."

"Ah!" The little lady's hands grew steady,—they had been fluttering all over her lap. "I will see you to-morrow morning at my father's house," she presently observed; and turned her full attention to the stage.

Some three days after this Mr. Driscoll opened his house on the Hudson to notable guests. He had not desired the publicity of such an event, nor the opportunity it gave for an increase of the scandal secretly in circulation against his daughter. But the Ambassador and his wife were foreign and any evasion of the promised hospitality would be sure to be misunderstood; so the scheme was carried forward though with less eclat than possibly was expected.

Among the lesser guests, who were mostly young and well acquainted with the house and its hospitality, there was one unique figure,—that of the lively Miss Strange, who, if personally unknown to Miss Driscoll, was so gifted with the qualities which tell on an occasion of this kind, that the stately young hostess hailed her presence with very obvious gratitude.

The manner of their first meeting was singular, and of great interest to one of them at least. Miss Strange had come in an automobile and had been shown her room; but there was nobody to accompany her down-stairs afterward, and, finding herself alone in the great hall, she naturally moved toward the library, the door of which stood ajar. She had pushed this door half open before she noticed that the room was already occupied. As a consequence, she was made the unexpected observer of a beautiful picture of youth and love.

A young man and a young woman were standing together in the glow of a blazing wood-fire. No word was to be heard, but in their faces, eloquent with passion, there shone something so deep and true that the chance intruder hesitated on the threshold, eager to lay this picture away in her mind with the other lovely and tragic memories now fast accumulating there. Then she drew back, and readvancing with a less noiseless foot, came into the full presence of Captain Holliday drawn up in all the pride of his military rank beside Alicia, the accomplished daughter of the house, who, if under a shadow as many whispered, wore that shadow as some women wear a crown.

Miss Strange was struck with admiration, and turned upon them the brightest facet of her vivacious nature all the time she was saying to herself: "Does she know why I am here? Or does she look upon me only as an additional guest foisted upon her by a thoughtless parent?"

There was nothing in the manner of her cordial but composed young hostess to show, and Miss Strange, with but one thought in mind since she had caught the light of feeling on the two faces confronting her, took the first opportunity that offered of running over the facts given her by Mr. Driscoll, to see if any reconcilement were possible between them and an innocence in which she must henceforth believe.

They were certainly of a most damaging nature.

Miss Driscoll and four other young ladies of her own station in life had formed themselves, some two years before, into a coterie of five, called The Inseparables. They lunched together, rode together, visited together. So close was the bond and their mutual dependence so evident, that it came to be the custom to invite the whole five whenever the size of the function warranted it. In fact, it was far from an uncommon occurrence to see them grouped at receptions or following one another down the aisles of churches or through the mazes of the dance at balls or assemblies. And no one demurred at this, for they were all handsome and attractive girls, till it began to be noticed that, coincident with their presence, some article of value was found missing from the dressing-room or from the tables where wedding gifts were displayed. Nothing was safe where they went, and though, in the course of time, each article found its way back to its owner in a manner as mysterious as its previous abstraction, the scandal grew and, whether with good reason or bad, finally settled about the person of Miss Driscoll, who was the showiest, least pecuniarily tempted, and most dignified in manner and speech of them all.

Some instances had been given by way of further enlightenment. This is one: A theatre party was in progress. There were twelve in the party, five of whom were the Inseparables. In the course of the last act, another lady—in fact, their chaperon—missed her handkerchief, an almost priceless bit of lace. Positive that she had brought it with her into the box, she caused a careful search, but without the least success. Recalling certain whispers she had heard, she noted which of the five girls were with her in the box. They were Miss Driscoll, Miss Hughson, Miss Yates, and Miss Benedict. Miss West sat in the box adjoining.

A fortnight later this handkerchief reappeared—and where? Among the cushions of a yellow satin couch in her own drawing-room. The Inseparables had just made their call and the three who had sat on the couch were Miss Driscoll, Miss Hughson, and Miss Benedict.

The next instance seemed to point still more insistently toward the lady already named. Miss Yates had an expensive present to buy, and the whole five Inseparables went in an imposing group to Tiffany's. A tray of rings was set before them. All examined and eagerly fingered the stock out of which Miss Yates presently chose a finely set emerald. She was leading her friends away when the clerk suddenly whispered in her ear, "I miss one of the rings." Dismayed beyond speech, she turned and consulted the faces of her four companions who stared back at her with immovable serenity. But one of them was paler than usual, and this lady (it was Miss Driscoll) held her hands in her muff and did not offer to take them out. Miss Yates, whose father had completed a big "deal" the week before, wheeled round upon the clerk. "Charge it! charge it at its full value," said she. "I buy both the rings."

And in three weeks the purloined ring came back to her, in a box of violets with no name attached.

The third instance was a recent one, and had come to Mr. Driscoll's ears directly from the lady suffering the loss. She was a woman of uncompromising integrity, who felt it her duty to make known to this gentleman the following facts: She had just left a studio reception, and was standing at the curb waiting for a taxicab to draw up, when a small boy—a street arab—darted toward her from the other side of the street, and thrusting into her hand something small and hard, cried breathlessly as he slipped away, "It's yours, ma'am; you dropped it." Astonished, for she had not been conscious of any loss, she looked down at her treasure trove and found it to be a small medallion which she sometimes wore on a chain at her belt. But she had not worn it that day, nor any day for weeks. Then she remembered. She had worn it a month before to a similar reception at this same studio. A number of young girls had stood about her admiring it—she remembered well who they were; the Inseparables, of course, and to please them she had slipped it from its chain. Then something had happened,—something which diverted her attention entirely,—and she had gone home without the medallion; had, in fact, forgotten it, only to recall its loss now. Placing it in her bag, she looked hastily about her. A crowd was at her back; nothing to be distinguished there. But in front, on the opposite side of the street, stood a club-house, and in one of its windows she perceived a solitary figure looking out. It was that of Miss Driscoll's father. He could imagine her conclusion.

In vain he denied all knowledge of the matter. She told him other stories which had come to her ears of thefts as mysterious, followed by restorations as peculiar as this one, finishing with, "It is your daughter, and people are beginning to say so."

And Miss Strange, brooding over these instances, would have said the same, but for Miss Driscoll's absolute serenity of demeanour and complete abandonment to love. These seemed incompatible with guilt; these, whatever the appearances, proclaimed innocence—an innocence she was here to prove if fortune favoured and the really guilty person's madness should again break forth.

For madness it would be and nothing less, for any hand, even the most experienced, to draw attention to itself by a repetition of old tricks on an occasion so marked. Yet because it would take madness, and madness knows no law, she prepared herself for the contingency under a mask of girlish smiles which made her at once the delight and astonishment of her watchful and uneasy host.

With the exception of the diamonds worn by the Ambassadress, there was but one jewel of consequence to be seen at the dinner that night; but how great was that consequence and with what splendour it invested the snowy neck it adorned!

Miss Strange, in compliment to the noble foreigners, had put on one of her family heirlooms—a filigree pendant of extraordinary sapphires which had once belonged to Marie Antoinette. As its beauty flashed upon the women, and its value struck the host, the latter could not restrain himself from casting an anxious eye about the board in search of some token of the cupidity with which one person there must welcome this unexpected sight.

Naturally his first glance fell upon Alicia, seated opposite to him at the other end of the table. But her eyes were elsewhere, and her smile for Captain Holliday, and the father's gaze travelled on, taking up each young girl's face in turn. All were contemplating Miss Strange and her jewels, and the cheeks of one were flushed and those of the others pale, but whether with dread or longing who could tell. Struck with foreboding, but alive to his duty as host, he forced his glances away, and did not even allow himself to question the motive or the wisdom of the temptation thus offered.

Two hours later and the girls were all in one room. It was a custom of the Inseparables to meet for a chat before retiring, but always alone and in the room of one of their number. But this was a night of innovations; Violet was not only included, but the meeting was held in her room. Her way with girls was even more fruitful of result than her way with men. They might laugh at her, criticize her or even call her names significant of disdain, but they never left her long to herself or missed an opportunity to make the most of her irrepressible chatter.

Her satisfaction at entering this charmed circle did not take from her piquancy, and story after story fell from her lips, as she fluttered about, now here now there, in her endless preparations for retirement. She had taken off her historic pendant after it had been duly admired and handled by all present, and, with the careless confidence of an assured ownership, thrown it down upon the end of her dresser, which, by the way, projected very close to the open window.

"Are you going to leave your jewel there?" whispered a voice in her ear as a burst of laughter rang out in response to one of her sallies.

Turning, with a simulation of round-eyed wonder, she met Miss Hughson's earnest gaze with the careless rejoinder, "What's the harm?" and went on with her story with all the reckless ease of a perfectly thoughtless nature.

Miss Hughson abandoned her protest. How could she explain her reasons for it to one apparently uninitiated in the scandal associated with their especial clique.

Yes, she left the jewel there; but she locked her door and quickly, so that they must all have heard her before reaching their rooms. Then she crossed to the window, which, like all on this side, opened on a balcony running the length of the house. She was aware of this balcony, also of the fact that only young ladies slept in the corridor communicating with it. But she was not quite sure that this one corridor accommodated them all. If one of them should room elsewhere! (Miss Driscoll, for instance). But no! the anxiety displayed for the safety of her jewel precluded that supposition. Their hostess, if none of the others, was within access of this room and its open window. But how about the rest? Perhaps the lights would tell. Eagerly the little schemer looked forth, and let her glances travel down the full length of the balcony. Two separate beams of light shot across it as she looked, and presently another, and, after some waiting, a fourth. But the fifth failed to appear. This troubled her, but not seriously. Two of the girls might be sleeping in one bed.

Drawing her shade, she finished her preparations for the night; then with her kimono on, lifted the pendant and thrust it into a small box she had taken from her trunk. A curious smile, very unlike any she had shown to man or woman that day, gave a sarcastic lift to her lips, as with a slow and thoughtful manipulation of her dainty fingers she moved the jewel about in this small receptacle and then returned it, after one quick examining glance, to the very spot on the dresser from which she had taken it. "If only the madness is great enough!" that smile seemed to say. Truly, it was much to hope for, but a chance is a chance; and comforting herself with the thought, Miss Strange put out her light, and, with a hasty raising of the shade she had previously pulled down, took a final look at the prospect.

Its aspect made her shudder. A low fog was rising from the meadows in the far distance, and its ghostliness under the moon woke all sorts of uncanny images in her excited mind. To escape them she crept into bed where she lay with her eyes on the end of her dresser. She had closed that half of the French window over which she had drawn the shade; but she had left ajar the one giving free access to the jewels; and when she was not watching the scintillation of her sapphires in the moonlight, she was dwelling in fixed attention on this narrow opening.

But nothing happened, and two o'clock, then three o'clock struck, without a dimming of the blue scintillations on the end of her dresser. Then she suddenly sat up. Not that she heard anything new, but that a thought had come to her. "If an attempt is made," so she murmured softly to herself, "it will be by—" She did not finish. Something—she could not call it sound—set her heart beating tumultuously, and listening—listening—watching—watching—she followed in her imagination the approach down the balcony of an almost inaudible step, not daring to move herself, it seemed so near, but waiting with eyes fixed, for the shadow which must fall across the shade she had failed to raise over that half of the swinging window she had so carefully left shut.

At length she saw it projecting slowly across the slightly illuminated surface. Formless, save for the outreaching hand, it passed the casement's edge, nearing with pauses and hesitations the open gap beyond through which the neglected sapphires beamed with steady lustre. Would she ever see the hand itself appear between the dresser and the window frame? Yes, there it comes,—small, delicate, and startlingly white, threading that gap—darting with the suddenness of a serpent's tongue toward the dresser and disappearing again with the pendant in its clutch.

As she realizes this,—she is but young, you know,—as she sees her bait taken and the hardly expected event fulfilled, her pent-up breath sped forth in a sigh which sent the intruder flying, and so startled herself that she sank back in terror on her pillow.

The breakfast-call had sounded its musical chimes through the halls. The Ambassador and his wife had responded, so had most of the young gentlemen and ladies, but the daughter of the house was not amongst them, nor Miss Strange, whom one would naturally expect to see down first of all.

These two absences puzzled Mr. Driscoll. What might they not portend? But his suspense, at least in one regard, was short. Before his guests were well seated, Miss Driscoll entered from the terrace in company with Captain Holliday. In her arms she carried a huge bunch of roses and was looking very beautiful. Her father's heart warmed at the sight. No shadow from the night rested upon her.

But Miss Strange!—where was she? He could not feel quite easy till he knew.

"Have any of you seen Miss Strange?" he asked, as they sat down at table. And his eyes sought the Inseparables.

Five lovely heads were shaken, some carelessly, some wonderingly, and one, with a quick, forced smile. But he was in no mood to discriminate, and he had beckoned one of the servants to him, when a step was heard at the door and the delinquent slid in and took her place, in a shamefaced manner suggestive of a cause deeper than mere tardiness. In fact, she had what might be called a frightened air, and stared into her plate, avoiding every eye, which was certainly not natural to her. What did it mean? and why, as she made a poor attempt at eating, did four of the Inseparables exchange glances of doubt and dismay and then concentrate their looks upon his daughter? That Alicia failed to notice this, but sat abloom above her roses now fastened in a great bunch upon her breast, offered him some comfort, yet, for all the volubility of his chief guests, the meal was a great trial to his patience, as well as a poor preparation for the hour when, the noble pair gone, he stepped into the library to find Miss Strange awaiting him with one hand behind her back and a piteous look on her infantile features.

"O, Mr. Driscoll," she began,—and then he saw that a group of anxious girls hovered in her rear—"my pendant! my beautiful pendant! It is gone! Somebody reached in from the balcony and took it from my dresser in the night. Of course, it was to frighten me; all of the girls told me not to leave it there. But I—I cannot make them give it back, and papa is so particular about this jewel that I'm afraid to go home. Won't you tell them it's no joke, and see that I get it again. I won't be so careless another time."

Hardly believing his eyes, hardly believing his ears,—she was so perfectly the spoiled child detected in a fault—he looked sternly about upon the girls and bade them end the jest and produce the gems at once.

But not one of them spoke, and not one of them moved; only his daughter grew pale until the roses seemed a mockery, and the steady stare of her large eyes was almost too much for him to bear.

The anguish of this gave asperity to his manner, and in a strange, hoarse tone he loudly cried:

"One of you did this. Which? If it was you, Alicia, speak. I am in no mood for nonsense. I want to know whose foot traversed the balcony and whose hand abstracted these jewels."

A continued silence, deepening into painful embarrassment for all. Mr. Driscoll eyed them in ill-concealed anguish, then turning to Miss Strange was still further thrown off his balance by seeing her pretty head droop and her gaze fall in confusion.

"Oh! it's easy enough to tell whose foot traversed the balcony," she murmured. "It left this behind." And drawing forward her hand, she held out to view a small gold-coloured slipper. "I found it outside my window," she explained. "I hoped I should not have to show it."

A gasp of uncontrollable feeling from the surrounding group of girls, then absolute stillness.

"I fail to recognize it," observed Mr. Driscoll, taking it in his hand. "Whose slipper is this?" he asked in a manner not to be gainsaid.

Still no reply, then as he continued to eye the girls one after another a voice—the last he expected to hear—spoke and his daughter cried:

"It is mine. But it was not I who walked in it down the balcony."

"Alicia!"

A month's apprehension was in that cry. The silence, the pent-up emotion brooding in the air was intolerable. A fresh young laugh broke it.

"Oh," exclaimed a roguish voice, "I knew that you were all in it! But the especial one who wore the slipper and grabbed the pendant cannot hope to hide herself. Her finger-tips will give her away."

Amazement on every face and a convulsive movement in one half-hidden hand.

"You see," the airy little being went on, in her light way, "I have some awfully funny tricks. I am always being scolded for them, but somehow I don't improve. One is to keep my jewelry bright with a strange foreign paste an old Frenchwoman once gave me in Paris. It's of a vivid red, and stains the fingers dreadfully if you don't take care. Not even water will take it off, see mine. I used that paste on my pendant last night just after you left me, and being awfully sleepy I didn't stop to rub it off. If your finger-tips are not red, you never touched the pendant, Miss Driscoll. Oh, see! They are as white as milk.

"But some one took the sapphires, and I owe that person a scolding, as well as myself. Was it you, Miss Hughson? You, Miss Yates? or—" and here she paused before Miss West, "Oh, you have your gloves on! You are the guilty one!" and her laugh rang out like a peal of bells, robbing her next sentence of even a suggestion of sarcasm. "Oh, what a sly-boots!" she cried. "How you have deceived me! Whoever would have thought you to be the one to play the mischief!"

Who indeed! Of all the five, she was the one who was considered absolutely immune from suspicion ever since the night Mrs. Barnum's handkerchief had been taken, and she not in the box. Eyes which had surveyed Miss Driscoll askance now rose in wonder toward hers, and failed to fall again because of the stoniness into which her delicately-carved features had settled.

"Miss West, I know you will be glad to remove your gloves; Miss Strange certainly has a right to know her special tormentor," spoke up her host in as natural a voice as his great relief would allow.

But the cold, half-frozen woman remained without a movement. She was not deceived by the banter of the moment. She knew that to all of the others, if not to Peter Strange's odd little daughter, it was the thief who was being spotted and brought thus hilariously to light. And her eyes grew hard, and her lips grey, and she failed to unglove the hands upon which all glances were concentrated.

"You do not need to see my hands; I confess to taking the pendant."

"Caroline!"

A heart overcome by shock had thrown up this cry. Miss West eyed her bosom-friend disdainfully.

"Miss Strange has called it a jest," she coldly commented. "Why should you suggest anything of a graver character?"

Alicia brought thus to bay, and by one she had trusted most, stepped quickly forward, and quivering with vague doubts, aghast before unheard-of possibilities, she tremulously remarked:

"We did not sleep together last night. You had to come into my room to get my slippers. Why did you do this? What was in your mind, Caroline?"

A steady look, a low laugh choked with many emotions answered her.

"Do you want me to reply, Alicia? Or shall we let it pass?"

"Answer!"

It was Mr. Driscoll who spoke. Alicia had shrunk back, almost to where a little figure was cowering with wide eyes fixed in something like terror on the aroused father's face.

"Then hear me," murmured the girl, entrapped and suddenly desperate. "I wore Alicia's slippers and I took the jewels, because it was time that an end should come to your mutual dissimulation. The love I once felt for her she has herself deliberately killed. I had a lover—she took him. I had faith in life, in honour, and in friendship. She destroyed all. A thief—she has dared to aspire to him! And you condoned her fault. You, with your craven restoration of her

9

booty, thought the matter cleared and her a fit mate for a man of highest honour."

"Miss West,"—no one had ever heard that tone in Mr. Driscoll's voice before, "before you say another word calculated to mislead these ladies, let me say that this hand never returned any one's booty or had anything to do with the restoration of any abstracted article. You have been caught in a net, Miss West, from which you cannot escape by slandering my innocent daughter."

"Innocent!" All the tragedy latent in this peculiar girl's nature blazed forth in the word. "Alicia, face me. Are you innocent? Who took the Dempsey corals, and that diamond from the Tiffany tray?"

"It is not necessary for Alicia to answer," the father interposed with not unnatural heat. "Miss West stands self-convicted."

"How about Lady Paget's scarf? I was not there that night."

"You are a woman of wiles. That could be managed by one bent on an elaborate scheme of revenge."

"And so could the abstraction of Mrs. Barnum's five-hundred-dollar handkerchief by one who sat in the next box," chimed in Miss Hughson, edging away from the friend to whose honour she would have pinned her faith an hour before. "I remember now seeing her lean over the railing to adjust the old lady's shawl."

With a start, Caroline West turned a tragic gaze upon the speaker.

"You think me guilty of all because of what I did last night?"

"Why shouldn't I?"

"And you, Anna?"

"Alicia has my sympathy," murmured Miss Benedict.

Yet the wild girl persisted.

"But I have told you my provocation. You cannot believe that I am guilty of her sin; not if you look at her as I am looking now."

But their glances hardly followed her pointing finger. Her friends—the comrades of her youth, the Inseparables with their secret oath—one and all held themselves aloof, struck by the perfidy they were only just beginning to take in. Smitten with despair, for these girls were her life, she gave one wild leap and sank on her knees before Alicia.

"O speak!" she began. "Forgive me, and—"

A tremble seized her throat; she ceased to speak and let fall her partially uplifted hands. The cheery sound of men's voices had drifted in from the terrace, and the figure of Captain Holliday could be seen passing by. The shudder which shook Caroline West communicated itself to Alicia Driscoll, and the former rising quickly, the two women surveyed each other, possibly for the first time, with open soul and a complete understanding.

"Caroline!" murmured the one.

"Alicia!" pleaded the other.

"Caroline, trust me," said Alicia Driscoll in that moving voice of hers, which more than her beauty caught and retained all hearts. "You have served me ill, but it was not all undeserved. Girls," she went on, eyeing both them and her father with the wistfulness of a breaking heart, "neither Caroline nor myself are worthy of Captain Holliday's love. Caroline has told you her fault, but mine is perhaps a worse one. The ring—the scarf—the diamond pins—I took them all—took them if I did not retain them. A curse has been over my life—

the curse of a longing I could not combat. But love was working a change in me. Since I have known Captain Holliday—but that's all over. I was mad to think I could be happy with such memories in my life. I shall never marry now—or touch jewels again—my own or another's. Father, father, you won't go back on your girl! I couldn't see Caroline suffer for what I have done. You will pardon me and help—help—"

Her voice choked. She flung herself into her father's arms; his head bent over hers, and for an instant not a soul in the room moved. Then Miss Hughson gave a spring and caught her by the hand. "We are inseparable," said she, and kissed the hand, murmuring, "Now is our time to show it."

Then other lips fell upon those cold and trembling fingers, which seemed to warm under these embraces. And then a tear. It came from the hard eye of Caroline, and remained a sacred secret between the two.

"You have your pendant?"

Mr. Driscoll's suffering eye shone down on Violet Strange's uplifted face as she advanced to say good-bye preparatory to departure.

"Yes," she acknowledged, "but hardly, I fear, your gratitude."

And the answer astonished her.

"I am not sure that the real Alicia will not make her father happier than the unreal one has ever done."

"And Captain Holliday?"

"He may come to feel the same."

"Then I do not quit in disgrace?"

"You depart with my thanks."

When a certain personage was told of the success of Miss Strange's latest manoeuvre, he remarked: "The little one progresses. We shall have to give her a case of prime importance next."

END OF PROBLEM I

PROBLEM II

THE SECOND BULLET

"You must see her."

"No. No."

"She's a most unhappy woman. Husband and child both taken from her in a moment; and now, all means of living as well, unless some happy thought of yours—some inspiration of your genius—shows us a way of re-establishing her claims to the policy voided by this cry of suicide."

But the small wise head of Violet Strange continued its slow shake of decided refusal.

"I'm sorry," she protested, "but it's quite out of my province. I'm too young to meddle with so serious a matter."

"Not when you can save a bereaved woman the only possible compensation left her by untoward fate?"

"Let the police try their hand at that."

"They have had no success with the case."

"Or you?"

"Nor I either."

"And you expect—"

"Yes, Miss Strange. I expect you to find the missing bullet which will settle the fact that murder and not suicide ended George Hammond's life. If you cannot, then a long litigation awaits this poor widow, ending, as such litigation usually does, in favour of the stronger party. There's the alternative. If you once saw her—"

"But that's what I'm not willing to do. If I once saw her I should yield to her importunities and attempt the seemingly impossible. My instincts bid me say no. Give me something easier."

"Easier things are not so remunerative. There's money in this affair, if the insurance company is forced to pay up. I can offer you—"

"What?"

There was eagerness in the tone despite her effort at nonchalance. The other smiled imperceptibly, and briefly named the sum.

It was larger than she had expected. This her visitor saw by the way her eyelids fell and the peculiar stillness which, for an instant, held her vivacity in check.

"And you think I can earn that?"

Her eyes were fixed on his in an eagerness as honest as it was unrestrained.

He could hardly conceal his amazement, her desire was so evident and the cause of it so difficult to understand. He knew she wanted money—that was her avowed reason for entering into this uncongenial work. But to want it so much! He glanced at her person; it was simply clad but very expensively—how expensively it was his business to know. Then he took in the room in which they sat. Simplicity again, but the simplicity of high art—the drawing-room of one rich enough to indulge in the final luxury of a highly cultivated taste, viz.:

unostentatious elegance and the subjection of each carefully chosen ornament to the general effect.

What did this favoured child of fortune lack that she could be reached by such a plea, when her whole being revolted from the nature of the task he offered her? It was a question not new to him; but one he had never heard answered and was not likely to hear answered now. But the fact remained that the consent he had thought dependent upon sympathetic interest could be reached much more readily by the promise of large emolument,—and he owned to a feeling of secret disappointment even while he recognized the value of the discovery.

But his satisfaction in the latter, if satisfaction it were, was of very short duration. Almost immediately he observed a change in her. The sparkle which had shone in the eye whose depths he had never been able to penetrate, had dissipated itself in something like a tear and she spoke up in that vigorous tone no one but himself had ever heard, as she said:

"No. The sum is a good one and I could use it; but I will not waste my energy on a case I do not believe in. The man shot himself. He was a speculator, and probably had good reason for his act. Even his wife acknowledges that he has lately had more losses than gains."

"See her. She has something to tell you which never got into the papers."

"You say that? You know that?"

"On my honour, Miss Strange."

Violet pondered; then suddenly succumbed.

"Let her come, then. Prompt to the hour. I will receive her at three. Later I have a tea and two party calls to make."

Her visitor rose to leave. He had been able to subdue all evidence of his extreme gratification, and now took on a formal air. In dismissing a guest, Miss Strange was invariably the society belle and that only. This he had come to recognize.

The case (well known at the time) was, in the fewest possible words, as follows:

On a sultry night in September, a young couple living in one of the large apartment houses in the extreme upper portion of Manhattan were so annoyed by the incessant crying of a child in the adjoining suite, that they got up, he to smoke, and she to sit in the window for a possible breath of cool air. They were congratulating themselves upon the wisdom they had shown in thus giving up all thought of sleep—for the child's crying had not ceased— when (it may have been two o'clock and it may have been a little later) there came from somewhere near, the sharp and somewhat peculiar detonation of a pistol-shot.

He thought it came from above; she, from the rear, and they were staring at each other in the helpless wonder of the moment, when they were struck by the silence. The baby had ceased to cry. All was as still in the adjoining apartment as in their own—too still—much too still. Their mutual stare turned to one of horror. "It came from there!" whispered the wife. "Some accident has occurred to Mr. or Mrs. Hammond—we ought to go—"

Her words—very tremulous ones—were broken by a shout from below. They were standing in their window and had evidently been seen by a passing policeman. "Anything wrong up there?" they heard him cry. Mr. Saunders

immediately looked out. "Nothing wrong here," he called down. (They were
but two stories from the pavement.) "But I'm not so sure about the rear
apartment. We thought we heard a shot. Hadn't you better come up, officer?
My wife is nervous about it. I'll meet you at the stair-head and show you the
way."

The officer nodded and stepped in. The young couple hastily donned some
wraps, and, by the time he appeared on their floor, they were ready to
accompany him.

Meanwhile, no disturbance was apparent anywhere else in the house, until
the policeman rang the bell of the Hammond apartment. Then, voices began
to be heard, and doors to open above and below, but not the one before which
the policeman stood.

Another ring, and this time an insistent one;—and still no response. The
officer's hand was rising for the third time when there came a sound of
fluttering from behind the panels against which he had laid his ear, and finally
a choked voice uttering unintelligible words. Then a hand began to struggle
with the lock, and the door, slowly opening, disclosed a woman clad in a
hastily donned wrapper and giving every evidence of extreme fright.

"Oh!" she exclaimed, seeing only the compassionate faces of her neighbours.
"You heard it, too! a pistol-shot from there—there—my husband's room. I
have not dared to go—I—I—O, have mercy and see if anything is wrong! It is
so still—so still, and only a moment ago the baby was crying. Mrs. Saunders,
Mrs. Saunders, why is it so still?"

She had fallen into her neighbour's arms. The hand with which she had
pointed out a certain door had sunk to her side and she appeared to be on the
verge of collapse.

The officer eyed her sternly, while noting her appearance, which was that of
a woman hastily risen from bed.

"Where were you?" he asked. "Not with your husband and child, or you
would know what had happened there."

"I was sleeping down the hall," she managed to gasp out. "I'm not well—I—
Oh, why do you all stand still and do nothing? My baby's in there. Go! go!"
and, with sudden energy, she sprang upright, her eyes wide open and burning,
her small well featured face white as the linen she sought to hide.

The officer demurred no longer. In another instant he was trying the door at
which she was again pointing.

It was locked.

Glancing back at the woman, now cowering almost to the floor, he pounded
at the door and asked the man inside to open.

No answer came back.

With a sharp turn he glanced again at the wife.

"You say that your husband is in this room?"

She nodded, gasping faintly, "And the child!"

He turned back, listened, then beckoned to Mr. Saunders. "We shall have to
break our way in," said he. "Put your shoulder well to the door. Now!"

The hinges of the door creaked; the lock gave way (this special officer
weighed two hundred and seventy-five, as he found out, next day), and a
prolonged and sweeping crash told the rest.

Mrs. Hammond gave a low cry; and, straining forward from where she crouched in terror on the floor, searched the faces of the two men for some hint of what they saw in the dimly-lighted space beyond. Something dreadful, something which made Mr. Saunders come rushing back with a shout:

"Take her away! Take her to our apartment, Jennie. She must not see—"

Not see! He realized the futility of his words as his gaze fell on the young woman who had risen up at his approach and now stood gazing at him without speech, without movement, but with a glare of terror in her eyes, which gave him his first realization of human misery.

His own glance fell before it. If he had followed his instinct he would have fled the house rather than answer the question of her look and the attitude of her whole frozen body.

Perhaps in mercy to his speechless terror, perhaps in mercy to herself, she was the one who at last found the word which voiced their mutual anguish.

"Dead?"

No answer. None was needed.

"And my baby?"

O, that cry! It curdled the hearts of all who heard it. It shook the souls of men and women both inside and outside the apartment; then all was forgotten in the wild rush she made. The wife and mother had flung herself upon the scene, and, side by side with the not unmoved policeman, stood looking down upon the desolation made in one fatal instant in her home and heart.

They lay there together, both past help, both quite dead. The child had simply been strangled by the weight of his father's arm which lay directly across the upturned little throat. But the father was a victim of the shot they had heard. There was blood on his breast, and a pistol in his hand.

Suicide! The horrible truth was patent. No wonder they wanted to hold the young widow back. Her neighbour, Mrs. Saunders, crept in on tiptoe and put her arms about the swaying, fainting woman; but there was nothing to say— absolutely nothing.

At least, they thought not. But when they saw her throw herself down, not by her husband, but by the child, and drag it out from under that strangling arm and hug and kiss it and call out wildly for a doctor, the officer endeavoured to interfere and yet could not find the heart to do so, though he knew the child was dead and should not, according to all the rules of the coroner's office, be moved before that official arrived. Yet because no mother could be convinced of a fact like this, he let her sit with it on the floor and try all her little arts to revive it, while he gave orders to the janitor and waited himself for the arrival of doctor and coroner.

She was still sitting there in wide-eyed misery, alternately fondling the little body and drawing back to consult its small set features for some sign of life, when the doctor came, and, after one look at the child, drew it softly from her arms and laid it quietly in the crib from which its father had evidently lifted it but a short time before. Then he turned back to her, and found her on her feet, upheld by her two friends. She had understood his action, and without a groan had accepted her fate. Indeed, she seemed incapable of any further speech or action. She was staring down at her husband's body, which she, for the first time, seemed fully to see. Was her look one of grief or of resentment for the part he had played so unintentionally in her child's death? It was hard to tell; and when, with slowly rising finger, she pointed to the pistol so tightly clutched in the other outstretched hand, no one there—and by this time the room was full—could foretell what her words would be when her tongue regained its usage and she could speak.

What she did say was this:

"Is there a bullet gone? Did he fire off that pistol?" A question so manifestly one of delirium that no one answered it, which seemed to surprise her, though she said nothing till her glance had passed all around the walls of the room to where a window stood open to the night,—its lower sash being entirely raised. "There! look there!" she cried, with a commanding accent, and, throwing up her hands, sank a dead weight into the arms of those supporting her.

No one understood; but naturally more than one rushed to the window. An open space was before them. Here lay the fields not yet parcelled out into lots and built upon; but it was not upon these they looked, but upon the strong trellis which they found there, which, if it supported no vine, formed a veritable ladder between this window and the ground.

Could she have meant to call attention to this fact; and were her words expressive of another idea than the obvious one of suicide?

If so, to what lengths a woman's imagination can go! Or so their combined looks seemed to proclaim, when to their utter astonishment they saw the officer, who had presented a calm appearance up till now, shift his position and with a surprised grunt direct their eyes to a portion of the wall just visible beyond the half-drawn curtains of the bed. The mirror hanging there showed a star-shaped breakage, such as follows the sharp impact of a bullet or a fiercely projected stone.

"He fired two shots. One went wild; the other straight home."

It was the officer delivering his opinion.

Mr. Saunders, returning from the distant room where he had assisted in carrying Mrs. Hammond, cast a look at the shattered glass, and remarked forcibly:

"I heard but one; and I was sitting up, disturbed by that poor infant. Jennie, did you hear more than one shot?" he asked, turning toward his wife.

"No," she answered, but not with the readiness he had evidently expected. "I heard only one, but that was not quite usual in its tone. I'm used to guns," she explained, turning to the officer. "My father was an army man, and he taught me very early to load and fire a pistol. There was a prolonged sound to this shot; something like an echo of itself, following close upon the first ping. Didn't you notice that, Warren?"

"I remember something of the kind," her husband allowed.

"He shot twice and quickly," interposed the policeman, sententiously. "We shall find a spent bullet back of that mirror."

But when, upon the arrival of the coroner, an investigation was made of the mirror and the wall behind, no bullet was found either there or any where else in the room, save in the dead man's breast. Nor had more than one been shot from his pistol, as five full chambers testified. The case which seemed so simple had its mysteries, but the assertion made by Mrs. Saunders no longer carried weight, nor was the evidence offered by the broken mirror considered as indubitably establishing the fact that a second shot had been fired in the room.

Yet it was equally evident that the charge which had entered the dead speculator's breast had not been delivered at the close range of the pistol found clutched in his hand. There were no powder-marks to be discerned on his pajama-jacket, or on the flesh beneath. Thus anomaly confronted anomaly, leaving open but one other theory: that the bullet found in Mr. Hammond's breast came from the window and the one he shot went out of it. But this would necessitate his having shot his pistol from a point far removed from where he was found; and his wound was such as made it difficult to believe that he would stagger far, if at all, after its infliction.

Yet, because the coroner was both conscientious and alert, he caused a most rigorous search to be made of the ground overlooked by the above mentioned window; a search in which the police joined, but which was without any result save that of rousing the attention of people in the neighbourhood and leading to a story being circulated of a man seen some time the night before crossing the fields in a great hurry. But as no further particulars were forthcoming, and not even a description of the man to be had, no emphasis would have been laid upon this story had it not transpired that the moment a report of it had come to Mrs. Hammond's ears (why is there always some one to carry these reports?) she roused from the torpor into which she had fallen, and in wild fashion exclaimed:

"I knew it! I expected it! He was shot through the window and by that wretch. He never shot himself." Violent declarations which trailed off into the one continuous wail, "O, my baby! my poor baby!"

Such words, even though the fruit of delirium, merited some sort of attention, or so this good coroner thought, and as soon as opportunity offered and she was sufficiently sane and quiet to respond to his questions, he asked her whom she had meant by that wretch, and what reason she had, or thought she had, of attributing her husband's death to any other agency than his own disgust with life.

And then it was that his sympathies, although greatly roused in her favour began to wane. She met the question with a cold stare followed by a few ambiguous words out of which he could make nothing. Had she said wretch? She did not remember. They must not be influenced by anything she might have uttered in her first grief. She was well-nigh insane at the time. But of one thing they might be sure: her husband had not shot himself; he was too much afraid of death for such an act. Besides, he was too happy. Whatever folks might say he was too fond of his family to wish to leave it.

Nor did the coroner or any other official succeed in eliciting anything further from her. Even when she was asked, with cruel insistence, how she explained the fact that the baby was found lying on the floor instead of in its crib, her only answer was: "His father was trying to soothe it. The child was crying dreadfully, as you have heard from those who were kept awake by him that night, and my husband was carrying him about when the shot came which caused George to fall and overlay the baby in his struggles."

"Carrying a baby about with a loaded pistol in his hand?" came back in stern retort.

She had no answer for this. She admitted when informed that the bullet extracted from her husband's body had been found to correspond exactly with those remaining in the five chambers of the pistol taken from his hand, that he was not only the owner of this pistol but was in the habit of sleeping with it under his pillow; but, beyond that, nothing; and this reticence, as well as her manner which was cold and repellent, told against her.

A verdict of suicide was rendered by the coroner's jury, and the life-insurance company, in which Mr. Hammond had but lately insured himself for a large sum, taking advantage of the suicide clause embodied in the policy, announced its determination of not paying the same.

Such was the situation, as known to Violet Strange and the general public, on the day she was asked to see Mrs. Hammond and learn what might alter her opinion as to the justice of this verdict and the stand taken by the Shuler Life Insurance Company.

The clock on the mantel in Miss Strange's rose-coloured boudoir had struck three, and Violet was gazing in some impatience at the door, when there came a gentle knock upon it, and the maid (one of the elderly, not youthful, kind) ushered in her expected visitor.

"You are Mrs. Hammond?" she asked, in natural awe of the too black figure outlined so sharply against the deep pink of the sea-shell room.

The answer was a slow lifting of the veil which shadowed the features she knew only from the cuts she had seen in newspapers.

"You are—Miss Strange?" stammered her visitor; "the young lady who—"

"I am," chimed in a voice as ringing as it was sweet. "I am the person you have come here to see. And this is my home. But that does not make me less interested in the unhappy, or less desirous of serving them. Certainly you have met with the two greatest losses which can come to a woman—I know your story well enough to say that—; but what have you to tell me in proof that you should not lose your anticipated income as well? Something vital, I hope, else I cannot help you; something which you should have told the coroner's jury— and did not."

The flush which was the sole answer these words called forth did not take from the refinement of the young widow's expression, but rather added to it; Violet watched it in its ebb and flow and, seriously affected by it (why, she did not know, for Mrs. Hammond had made no other appeal either by look or gesture), pushed forward a chair and begged her visitor to be seated.

"We can converse in perfect safety here," she said. "When you feel quite equal to it, let me hear what you have to communicate. It will never go any further. I could not do the work I do if I felt it necessary to have a confidant."

"But you are so young and so—so—"

"So inexperienced you would say and so evidently a member of what New Yorkers call 'society.' Do not let that trouble you. My inexperience is not likely to last long and my social pleasures are more apt to add to my efficiency than to detract from it."

With this Violet's face broke into a smile. It was not the brilliant one so often seen upon her lips, but there was something in its quality which carried encouragement to the widow and led her to say with obvious eagerness:

"You know the facts?"

"I have read all the papers."

"I was not believed on the stand."

"It was your manner—"

"I could not help my manner. I was keeping something back, and, being unused to deceit, I could not act quite naturally."

"Why did you keep something back? When you saw the unfavourable impression made by your reticence, why did you not speak up and frankly tell your story?"

"Because I was ashamed. Because I thought it would hurt me more to speak than to keep silent. I do not think so now; but I did then—and so made my great mistake. You must remember not only the awful shock of my double loss, but the sense of guilt accompanying it; for my husband and I had quarreled that night, quarreled bitterly—that was why I had run away into another room and not because I was feeling ill and impatient of the baby's fretful cries."

"So people have thought." In saying this, Miss Strange was perhaps cruelly emphatic. "You wish to explain that quarrel? You think it will be doing any good to your cause to go into that matter with me now?"

"I cannot say; but I must first clear my conscience and then try to convince you that quarrel or no quarrel, he never took his own life. He was not that kind. He had an abnormal fear of death. I do not like to say it but he was a physical coward. I have seen him turn pale at the least hint of danger. He could no more have turned that muzzle upon his own breast than he could have turned it upon his baby. Some other hand shot him, Miss Strange. Remember the open window, the shattered mirror; and I think I know that hand."

Her head had fallen forward on her breast. The emotion she showed was not so eloquent of grief as of deep personal shame.

"You think you know the man?" In saying this, Violet's voice sunk to a whisper. It was an accusation of murder she had just heard.

"To my great distress, yes. When Mr. Hammond and I were married," the widow now proceeded in a more determined tone, "there was another man—a very violent one—who vowed even at the church door that George and I should never live out two full years together. We have not. Our second anniversary would have been in November."

"But—"

"Let me say this: the quarrel of which I speak was not serious enough to occasion any such act of despair on his part. A man would be mad to end his life on account of so slight a disagreement. It was not even on account of the person of whom I've just spoken, though that person had been mentioned between us earlier in the evening, Mr. Hammond having come across him face to face that very afternoon in the subway. Up to this time neither of us had seen or heard of him since our wedding-day."

"And you think this person whom you barely mentioned, so mindful of his old grudge that he sought out your domicile, and, with the intention of murder, climbed the trellis leading to your room and turned his pistol upon the shadowy figure which was all he could see in the semi-obscurity of a much lowered gas-jet?"

"A man in the dark does not need a bright light to see his enemy when he is intent upon revenge."

Miss Strange altered her tone.

"And your husband? You must acknowledge that he shot off his pistol whether the other did or not."

"It was in self-defence. He would shoot to save his own life—or the baby's."

"Then he must have heard or seen—"

"A man at the window."

"And would have shot there?"

"Or tried to."

"Tried to?"

"Yes; the other shot first—oh, I've thought it all out—causing my husband's bullet to go wild. It was his which broke the mirror."

Violet's eyes, bright as stars, suddenly narrowed.

"And what happened then?" she asked. "Why cannot they find the bullet?"

"Because it went out of the window;—glanced off and went out of the window."

Mrs. Hammond's tone was triumphant; her look spirited and intense.

Violet eyed her compassionately.

"Would a bullet glancing off from a mirror, however hung, be apt to reach a window so far on the opposite side?"

"I don't know; I only know that it did," was the contradictory, almost absurd, reply.

"What was the cause of the quarrel you speak of between your husband and yourself? You see, I must know the exact truth and all the truth to be of any assistance to you."

"It was—it was about the care I gave, or didn't give, the baby. I feel awfully to have to say it, but George did not think I did my full duty by the child. He said there was no need of its crying so; that if I gave it the proper attention it would not keep the neighbours and himself awake half the night. And I—I got angry and insisted that I did the best I could; that the child was naturally fretful and that if he wasn't satisfied with my way of looking after it, he might try his. All of which was very wrong and unreasonable on my part, as witness the awful punishment which followed."

"And what made you get up and leave him?"

"The growl he gave me in reply. When I heard that, I bounded out of bed and said I was going to the spare room to sleep; and if the baby cried he might just try what he could do himself to stop it."

"And he answered?"

"This, just this—I shall never forget his words as long as I live—'If you go, you need not expect me to let you in again no matter what happens.'"

"He said that?"

"And locked the door after me. You see I could not tell all that."

"It might have been better if you had. It was such a natural quarrel and so unprovocative of actual tragedy."

Mrs. Hammond was silent. It was not difficult to see that she had no very keen regrets for her husband personally. But then he was not a very estimable man nor in any respect her equal.

"You were not happy with him," Violet ventured to remark.

"I was not a fully contented woman. But for all that he had no cause to complain of me except for the reason I have mentioned. I was not a very intelligent mother. But if the baby were living now—O, if he were living now—with what devotion I should care for him."

She was on her feet, her arms were raised, her face impassioned with feeling. Violet, gazing at her, heaved a little sigh. It was perhaps in keeping with the situation, perhaps extraneous to it, but whatever its source, it marked a change in her manner. With no further check upon her sympathy, she said very softly:

"It is well with the child."

The mother stiffened, swayed, and then burst into wild weeping.

"But not with me," she cried, "not with me. I am desolate and bereft. I have not even a home in which to hide my grief and no prospect of one."

"But," interposed Violet, "surely your husband left you something? You cannot be quite penniless?"

"My husband left nothing," was the answer, uttered without bitterness, but with all the hardness of fact. "He had debts. I shall pay those debts. When these and other necessary expenses are liquidated, there will be but little left. He made no secret of the fact that he lived close up to his means. That is why he was induced to take on a life insurance. Not a friend of his but knows his improvidence. I—I have not even jewels. I have only my determination and an absolute conviction as to the real nature of my husband's death."

"What is the name of the man you secretly believe to have shot your husband from the trellis?"

Mrs. Hammond told her.

It was a new one to Violet. She said so and then asked:

"What else can you tell me about him?"

"Nothing, but that he is a very dark man and has a club-foot."

"Oh, what a mistake you've made."

"Mistake? Yes, I acknowledge that."

"I mean in not giving this last bit of information at once to the police. A man can be identified by such a defect. Even his footsteps can be traced. He might have been found that very day. Now, what have we to go upon?"

"You are right, but not expecting to have any difficulty about the insurance money I thought it would be generous in me to keep still. Besides, this is only surmise on my part. I feel certain that my husband was shot by another hand than his own, but I know of no way of proving it. Do you?"

Then Violet talked seriously with her, explaining how their only hope lay in the discovery of a second bullet in the room which had already been ransacked for this very purpose and without the shadow of a result.

A tea, a musicale, and an evening dance kept Violet Strange in a whirl for the remainder of the day. No brighter eye nor more contagious wit lent brilliance to these occasions, but with the passing of the midnight hour no one who had seen her in the blaze of electric lights would have recognized this favoured child of fortune in the earnest figure sitting in the obscurity of an up-town apartment, studying the walls, the ceilings, and the floors by the dim light of a lowered gas-jet. Violet Strange in society was a very different person from Violet Strange under the tension of her secret and peculiar work.

She had told them at home that she was going to spend the night with a friend; but only her old coachman knew who that friend was. Therefore a very natural sense of guilt mingled with her emotions at finding herself alone on a scene whose gruesome mystery she could solve only by identifying herself with the place and the man who had perished there.

Dismissing from her mind all thought of self, she strove to think as he thought, and act as he acted on the night when he found himself (a man of but little courage) left in this room with an ailing child.

At odds with himself, his wife, and possibly with the child screaming away in its crib, what would he be apt to do in his present emergency? Nothing at first, but as the screaming continued he would remember the old tales of fathers walking the floor at night with crying babies, and hasten to follow suit. Violet, in her anxiety to reach his inmost thought, crossed to where the crib had stood, and, taking that as a start, began pacing the room in search of the spot from which a bullet, if shot, would glance aside from the mirror in the direction of the window. (Not that she was ready to accept this theory of Mrs. Hammond, but that she did not wish to entirely dismiss it without putting it to the test.)

She found it in an unexpected quarter of the room and much nearer the bed-head than where his body was found. This, which might seem to confuse matters, served, on the contrary to remove from the case one of its most serious difficulties. Standing here, he was within reach of the pillow under which his pistol lay hidden, and if startled, as his wife believed him to have been by a noise at the other end of the room, had but to crouch and reach behind him in order to find himself armed and ready for a possible intruder.

Imitating his action in this as in other things, she had herself crouched low at the bedside and was on the point of withdrawing her hand from under the pillow, when a new surprise checked her movement and held her fixed in her position, with eyes staring straight at the adjoining wall. She had seen there what he must have seen in making this same turn—the dark bars of the opposite window-frame outlined in the mirror—and understood at once what had happened. In the nervousness and terror of the moment, George Hammond had mistaken this reflection of the window for the window itself, and shot impulsively at the man he undoubtedly saw covering him from the trellis without. But while this explained the shattering of the mirror, how about the other and still more vital question, of where the bullet went afterward? Was the angle at which it had been fired acute enough to send it out of a window diagonally opposed? No; even if the pistol had been held closer to the man firing it than she had reason to believe, the angle still would be oblique enough to carry it on to the further wall.

But no sign of any such impact had been discovered on this wall. Consequently, the force of the bullet had been expended before reaching it, and when it fell—

Here, her glance, slowly traveling along the floor, impetuously paused. It had reached the spot where the two bodies had been found, and unconsciously her eyes rested there, conjuring up the picture of the bleeding father and the strangled child. How piteous and how dreadful it all was. If she could only understand—Suddenly she rose straight up, staring and immovable in the dim light. Had the idea—the explanation—the only possible explanation covering the whole phenomena come to her at last?

It would seem so, for as she so stood, a look of conviction settled over her features, and with this look, evidences of a horror which for all her fast accumulating knowledge of life and its possibilities made her appear very small and very helpless.

A half-hour later, when Mrs. Hammond, in her anxiety at hearing nothing more from Miss Strange, opened the door of her room, it was to find, lying on the edge of the sill, the little detective's card with these words hastily written across it:

I do not feel as well as I could wish, and so have telephoned to my own coachman to come and take me home. I will either see or write you within a few days. But do not allow yourself to hope. I pray you do not allow yourself the least hope; the outcome is still very problematical.

When Violet's employer entered his office the next morning it was to find a veiled figure awaiting him which he at once recognized as that of his little deputy. She was slow in lifting her veil and when it finally came free he felt a momentary doubt as to his wisdom in giving her just such a matter as this to investigate. He was quite sure of his mistake when he saw her face, it was so drawn and pitiful.

"You have failed," said he.

"Of that you must judge," she answered; and drawing near she whispered in his ear.

"No!" he cried in his amazement.

"Think," she murmured, "think. Only so can all the facts be accounted for."

"I will look into it; I will certainly look into it," was his earnest reply. "If you are right—But never mind that. Go home and take a horseback ride in the Park. When I have news in regard to this I will let you know. Till then forget it all. Hear me, I charge you to forget everything but your balls and your parties."

And Violet obeyed him.

Some few days after this, the following statement appeared in all the papers:

"Owing to some remarkable work done by the firm of —— & ——, the well-known private detective agency, the claim made by Mrs. George Hammond against the Shuler Life Insurance Company is likely to be allowed without further litigation. As our readers will remember, the contestant has insisted from the first that the bullet causing her husband's death came from another pistol than the one found clutched in his own hand. But while reasons were not lacking to substantiate this assertion, the failure to discover more than the disputed track of a second bullet led to a verdict of suicide, and a refusal of the company to pay.

"But now that bullet has been found. And where? In the most startling place in the world, viz.: in the larynx of the child found lying dead upon the floor beside his father, strangled as was supposed by the weight of that father's arm. The theory is, and there seems to be none other, that the father, hearing a suspicious noise at the window, set down the child he was endeavouring to soothe and made for the bed and his own pistol, and, mistaking a reflection of the assassin for the assassin himself, sent his shot sidewise at a mirror just as the other let go the trigger which drove a similar bullet into his breast. The course of the one was straight and fatal and that of the other deflected. Striking the mirror at an oblique angle, the bullet fell to the floor where it was picked up by the crawling child, and, as was most natural, thrust at once into his mouth. Perhaps it felt hot to the little tongue; perhaps the child was simply frightened by some convulsive movement of the father who evidently spent his last moment in an endeavour to reach the child, but, whatever the cause, in the quick gasp it gave, the bullet was drawn into the larynx, strangling him.

"That the father's arm, in his last struggle, should have fallen directly across the little throat is one of those anomalies which confounds reason and misleads justice by stopping investigation at the very point where truth lies and mystery disappears.

"Mrs. Hammond is to be congratulated that there are detectives who do not give too much credence to outward appearances."

We expect soon to hear of the capture of the man who sped home the death-dealing bullet.

END OF PROBLEM II

PROBLEM III

AN INTANGIBLE CLUE

"Have you studied the case?"

"Not I."

"Not studied the case which for the last few days has provided the papers with such conspicuous headlines?"

"I do not read the papers. I have not looked at one in a whole week."

"Miss Strange, your social engagements must be of a very pressing nature just now?"

"They are."

"And your business sense in abeyance?"

"How so?"

"You would not ask if you had read the papers."

To this she made no reply save by a slight toss of her pretty head. If her employer felt nettled by this show of indifference, he did not betray it save by the rapidity of his tones as, without further preamble and possibly without real excuse, he proceeded to lay before her the case in question. "Last Tuesday night a woman was murdered in this city; an old woman, in a lonely house where she has lived for years. Perhaps you remember this house? It occupies a not inconspicuous site in Seventeenth Street—a house of the olden time?"

"No, I do not remember."

The extreme carelessness of Miss Strange's tone would have been fatal to her socially; but then, she would never have used it socially. This they both knew, yet he smiled with his customary indulgence.

"Then I will describe it."

She looked around for a chair and sank into it. He did the same.

"It has a fanlight over the front door."

She remained impassive.

"And two old-fashioned strips of parti-coloured glass on either side."

"And a knocker between its panels which may bring money some day."

"Oh, you do remember! I thought you would, Miss Strange."

"Yes. Fanlights over doors are becoming very rare in New York."

"Very well, then. That house was the scene of Tuesday's tragedy. The woman who has lived there in solitude for years was foully murdered. I have since heard that the people who knew her best have always anticipated some such violent end for her. She never allowed maid or friend to remain with her after five in the afternoon; yet she had money—some think a great deal—always in the house."

"I am interested in the house, not in her."

"Yet, she was a character—as full of whims and crotchets as a nut is of meat. Her death was horrible. She fought—her dress was torn from her body in rags. This happened, you see, before her hour for retiring; some think as early as six in the afternoon. And"—here he made a rapid gesture to catch Violet's wandering attention—"in spite of this struggle; in spite of the fact that she was dragged from room to room—that her person was searched—and everything in the house searched—that drawers were pulled out of bureaus—doors wrenched off of cupboards—china smashed upon the floor—whole shelves denuded and not a spot from cellar to garret left unransacked, no direct clue to the perpetrator has been found—nothing that gives any idea of his personality save his display of strength and great cupidity. The police have even deigned to consult me,—an unusual procedure—but I could find nothing, either. Evidences of fiendish purpose abound—of relentless search—but no clue to the man himself. It's uncommon, isn't it, not to have any clue?"

"I suppose so." Miss Strange hated murders and it was with difficulty she could be brought to discuss them. But she was not going to be let off; not this time.

"You see," he proceeded insistently, "it's not only mortifying to the police but disappointing to the press, especially as few reporters believe in the No-thoroughfare business. They say, and we cannot but agree with them, that no such struggle could take place and no such repeated goings to and fro through the house without some vestige being left by which to connect this crime with its daring perpetrator."

Still she stared down at her hands—those little hands so white and fluttering, so seemingly helpless under the weight of their many rings, and yet so slyly capable.

"She must have queer neighbours," came at last, from Miss Strange's reluctant lips. "Didn't they hear or see anything of all this?"

"She has no neighbours—that is, after half-past five o'clock. There's a printing establishment on one side of her, a deserted mansion on the other side, and nothing but warehouses back and front. There was no one to notice what took place in her small dwelling after the printing house was closed. She was the most courageous or the most foolish of women to remain there as she did. But nothing except death could budge her. She was born in the room where she died; was married in the one where she worked; saw husband, father, mother, and five sisters carried out in turn to their graves through the door with the fanlight over the top—and these memories held her."

"You are trying to interest me in the woman. Don't."

"No, I'm not trying to interest you in her, only trying to explain her. There was another reason for her remaining where she did so long after all residents had left the block. She had a business."

"Oh!"

"She embroidered monograms for fine ladies."

"She did? But you needn't look at me like that. She never embroidered any for me."

"No? She did first-class work. I saw some of it. Miss Strange, if I could get you into that house for ten minutes—not to see her but to pick up the loose intangible thread which I am sure is floating around in it somewhere—wouldn't you go?"

Violet slowly rose—a movement which he followed to the letter.

"Must I express in words the limit I have set for myself in our affair?" she asked. "When, for reasons I have never thought myself called upon to explain, I consented to help you a little now and then with some matter where a woman's tact and knowledge of the social world might tell without offence to herself or others, I never thought it would be necessary for me to state that temptation must stop with such cases, or that I should not be asked to touch the sordid or the bloody. But it seems I was mistaken, and that I must stoop to be explicit. The woman who was killed on Tuesday might have interested me greatly as an embroiderer, but as a victim, not at all. What do you see in me, or miss in me, that you should drag me into an atmosphere of low-down crime?"

"Nothing, Miss Strange. You are by nature, as well as by breeding, very far removed from everything of the kind. But you will allow me to suggest that no crime is low-down which makes imperative demand upon the intellect and intuitive sense of its investigator. Only the most delicate touch can feel and hold the thread I've just spoken of, and you have the most delicate touch I know."

"Do not attempt to flatter me. I have no fancy for handling befouled spider webs. Besides, if I had—if such elusive filaments fascinated me—how could I, well-known in person and name, enter upon such a scene without prejudice to our mutual compact?"

"Miss Strange"—she had reseated herself, but so far he had failed to follow her example (an ignoring of the subtle hint that her interest might yet be caught, which seemed to annoy her a trifle), "I should not even have suggested such a possibility had I not seen a way of introducing you there without risk to your position or mine. Among the boxes piled upon Mrs. Doolittle's table—boxes of finished work, most of them addressed and ready for delivery—was one on which could be seen the name of—shall I mention it?"

"Not mine? You don't mean mine? That would be too odd—too ridiculously odd. I should not understand a coincidence of that kind; no, I should not, notwithstanding the fact that I have lately sent out such work to be done."

"Yet it was your name, very clearly and precisely written—your whole name, Miss Strange. I saw and read it myself."

"But I gave the order to Madame Pirot on Fifth Avenue. How came my things to be found in the house of this woman of whose horrible death we have been talking?"

"Did you suppose that Madame Pirot did such work with her own hands?—or even had it done in her own establishment? Mrs. Doolittle was universally employed. She worked for a dozen firms. You will find the biggest names on most of her packages. But on this one—I allude to the one addressed to you—there was more to be seen than the name. These words were written on it in another hand. Send without opening. This struck the police as suspicious; sufficiently so, at least, for them to desire your presence at the house as soon as you can make it convenient."

"To open the box?"

"Exactly."

The curl of Miss Strange's disdainful lip was a sight to see.

"You wrote those words yourself," she coolly observed. "While someone's back was turned, you whipped out your pencil and—"

"Resorted to a very pardonable subterfuge highly conducive to the public's good. But never mind that. Will you go?"

Miss Strange became suddenly demure.

"I suppose I must," she grudgingly conceded. "However obtained, a summons from the police cannot be ignored even by Peter Strange's daughter."

Another man might have displayed his triumph by smile or gesture; but this one had learned his role too well. He simply said:

"Very good. Shall it be at once? I have a taxi at the door."

But she failed to see the necessity of any such hurry. With sudden dignity she replied:

"That won't do. If I go to this house it must be under suitable conditions. I shall have to ask my brother to accompany me."

"Your brother!"

"Oh, he's safe. He—he knows."

"Your brother knows?" Her visitor, with less control than usual, betrayed very openly his uneasiness.

"He does and—approves. But that's not what interests us now, only so far as it makes it possible for me to go with propriety to that dreadful house."

A formal bow from the other and the words:

"They may expect you, then. Can you say when?"

"Within the next hour. But it will be a useless concession on my part," she pettishly complained. "A place that has been gone over by a dozen detectives is apt to be brushed clean of its cobwebs, even if such ever existed."

"That's the difficulty," he acknowledged; and did not dare to add another word; she was at that particular moment so very much the great lady, and so little his confidential agent.

He might have been less impressed, however, by this sudden assumption of manner, had he been so fortunate as to have seen how she employed the three quarters of an hour's delay for which she had asked.

She read those neglected newspapers, especially the one containing the following highly coloured narration of this ghastly crime:

"A door ajar—an empty hall—a line of sinister looking blotches marking a guilty step diagonally across the flagging—silence—and an unmistakable odour repugnant to all humanity,—such were the indications which met the eyes of Officer O'Leary on his first round last night, and led to the discovery of a murder which will long thrill the city by its mystery and horror.

"Both the house and the victim are well known." Here followed a description of the same and of Mrs. Doolittle's manner of life in her ancient home, which Violet hurriedly passed over to come to the following:

"As far as one can judge from appearances, the crime happened in this wise: Mrs. Doolittle had been in her kitchen, as the tea-kettle found singing on the stove goes to prove, and was coming back through her bedroom, when the wretch, who had stolen in by the front door which, to save steps, she was unfortunately in the habit of leaving on the latch till all possibility of customers for the day was over, sprang upon her from behind and dealt her a swinging blow with the poker he had caught up from the hearthstone.

"Whether the struggle which ensued followed immediately upon this first attack or came later, it will take medical experts to determine. But, whenever it did occur, the fierceness of its character is shown by the grip taken upon her throat and the traces of blood which are to be seen all over the house. If the wretch had lugged her into her workroom and thence to the kitchen, and thence back to the spot of first assault, the evidences could not have been more ghastly. Bits of her clothing torn off by a ruthless hand, lay scattered over all these floors. In her bedroom, where she finally breathed her last, there could be seen mingled with these a number of large but worthless glass beads; and close against one of the base-boards, the string which had held them, as shown by the few remaining beads still clinging to it. If in pulling the string from her neck he had hoped to light upon some valuable booty, his fury at his disappointment is evident. You can almost see the frenzy with which he flung the would-be necklace at the wall, and kicked about and stamped upon its rapidly rolling beads.

"Booty! That was what he was after; to find and carry away the poor needlewoman's supposed hoardings. If the scene baffles description—if, as some believe, he dragged her yet living from spot to spot, demanding information as to her places of concealment under threat of repeated blows, and, finally baffled, dealt the finishing stroke and proceeded on the search alone, no greater devastation could have taken place in this poor woman's house or effects. Yet such was his precaution and care for himself that he left no finger-print behind him nor any other token which could lead to personal identification. Even though his footsteps could be traced in much the order I have mentioned, they were of so indeterminate and shapeless a character as to convey little to the intelligence of the investigator.

"That these smears (they could not be called footprints) not only crossed the hall but appeared in more than one place on the staircase proves that he did not confine his search to the lower storey; and perhaps one of the most interesting features of the case lies in the indications given by these marks of the raging course he took through these upper rooms. As the accompanying diagram will show [we omit the diagram] he went first into the large front chamber, thence to the rear where we find two rooms, one unfinished and filled with accumulated stuff most of which he left lying loose upon the floor, and the other plastered, and containing a window opening upon an alley-way at the side, but empty of all furniture and without even a carpet on the bare boards.

"Why he should have entered the latter place, and why, having entered he should have crossed to the window, will be plain to those who have studied the conditions. The front chamber windows were tightly shuttered, the attic ones cumbered with boxes and shielded from approach by old bureaus and discarded chairs. This one only was free and, although darkened by the proximity of the house neighbouring it across the alley, was the only spot on the storey where sufficient light could be had at this late hour for the examination of any object of whose value he was doubtful. That he had come across such an object and had brought it to this window for some such purpose is very satisfactorily demonstrated by the discovery of a worn out wallet of ancient make lying on the floor directly in front of this window—a proof of his cupidity but also proof of his ill-luck. For this wallet, when lifted and opened, was found to contain two hundred or more dollars in old bills, which, if not the full hoard of their industrious owner, was certainly worth the taking by one who had risked his neck for the sole purpose of theft.

"This wallet, and the flight of the murderer without it, give to this affair, otherwise simply brutal, a dramatic interest which will be appreciated not only by the very able detectives already hot upon the chase, but by all other inquiring minds anxious to solve a mystery of which so estimable a woman has been the unfortunate victim. A problem is presented to the police—"

There Violet stopped.

When, not long after, the superb limousine of Peter Strange stopped before the little house in Seventeenth Street, it caused a veritable sensation, not only in the curiosity-mongers lingering on the sidewalk, but to the two persons within—the officer on guard and a belated reporter.

Though dressed in her plainest suit, Violet Strange looked much too fashionable and far too young and thoughtless to be observed, without emotion, entering a scene of hideous and brutal crime. Even the young man who accompanied her promised to bring a most incongruous element into this atmosphere of guilt and horror, and, as the detective on guard whispered to the man beside him, might much better have been left behind in the car.

But Violet was great for the proprieties and young Arthur followed her in.

Her entrance was a coup du theatre. She had lifted her veil in crossing the sidewalk and her interesting features and general air of timidity were very fetching. As the man holding open the door noted the impression made upon his companion, he muttered with sly facetiousness:

"You think you'll show her nothing; but I'm ready to bet a fiver that she'll want to see it all and that you'll show it to her."

The detective's grin was expressive, notwithstanding the shrug with which he tried to carry it off.

And Violet? The hall into which she now stepped from the most vivid sunlight had never been considered even in its palmiest days as possessing cheer even of the stately kind. The ghastly green light infused through it by the coloured glass on either side of the doorway seemed to promise yet more dismal things beyond.

"Must I go in there?" she asked, pointing, with an admirable simulation of nervous excitement, to a half-shut door at her left. "Is there where it happened? Arthur, do you suppose that there is where it happened?"

"No, no, Miss," the officer made haste to assure her. "If you are Miss Strange" (Violet bowed), "I need hardly say that the woman was struck in her bedroom. The door beside you leads into the parlour, or as she would have called it, her work-room. You needn't be afraid of going in there. You will see nothing but the disorder of her boxes. They were pretty well pulled about. Not all of them though," he added, watching her as closely as the dim light permitted. "There is one which gives no sign of having been tampered with. It was done up in wrapping paper and is addressed to you, which in itself would not have seemed worthy of our attention had not these lines been scribbled on it in a man's handwriting: 'Send without opening.'"

"How odd!" exclaimed the little minx with widely opened eyes and an air of guileless innocence. "Whatever can it mean? Nothing serious I am sure, for the woman did not even know me. She was employed to do this work by Madame Pirot."

"Didn't you know that it was to be done here?"

"No. I thought Madame Pirot's own girls did her embroidery for her."

"So that you were surprised—"

"Wasn't I!"

"To get our message."

"I didn't know what to make of it."

The earnest, half-injured look with which she uttered this disclaimer, did its appointed work. The detective accepted her for what she seemed and, oblivious to the reporter's satirical gesture, crossed to the work-room door, which he threw wide open with the remark:

"I should be glad to have you open that box in our presence. It is undoubtedly all right, but we wish to be sure. You know what the box should contain?"

"Oh, yes, indeed; pillow-cases and sheets, with a big S embroidered on them."

"Very well. Shall I undo the string for you?"

"I shall be much obliged," said she, her eye flashing quickly about the room before settling down upon the knot he was deftly loosening.

Her brother, gazing indifferently in from the doorway, hardly noticed this look; but the reporter at his back did, though he failed to detect its penetrating quality.

"Your name is on the other side," observed the detective as he drew away the string and turned the package over.

The smile which just lifted the corner of her lips was not in answer to this remark, but to her recognition of her employer's handwriting in the words under her name: Send without opening. She had not misjudged him.

"The cover you may like to take off yourself," suggested the officer, as he lifted the box out of its wrapper.

"Oh, I don't mind. There's nothing to be ashamed of in embroidered linen. Or perhaps that is not what you are looking for?"

No one answered. All were busy watching her whip off the lid and lift out the pile of sheets and pillow-cases with which the box was closely packed.

"Shall I unfold them?" she asked.

The detective nodded.

Taking out the topmost sheet, she shook it open. Then the next and the next till she reached the bottom of the box. Nothing of a criminating nature came to light. The box as well as its contents was without mystery of any kind. This was not an unexpected result of course, but the smile with which she began to refold the pieces and throw them back into the box, revealed one of her dimples which was almost as dangerous to the casual observer as when it revealed both.

"There," she exclaimed, "you see! Household linen exactly as I said. Now may I go home?"

"Certainly, Miss Strange."

The detective stole a sly glance at the reporter. She was not going in for the horrors then after all.

But the reporter abated nothing of his knowing air, for while she spoke of going, she made no move towards doing so, but continued to look about the room till her glances finally settled on a long dark curtain shutting off an adjoining room.

"There's where she lies, I suppose," she feelingly exclaimed. "And not one of you knows who killed her. Somehow, I cannot understand that. Why don't you know when that's what you're hired for?" The innocence with which she uttered this was astonishing. The detective began to look sheepish and the reporter turned aside to hide his smile. Whether in another moment either would have spoken no one can say, for, with a mock consciousness of having said something foolish, she caught up her parasol from the table and made a start for the door.

But of course she looked back.

"I was wondering," she recommenced, with a half wistful, half speculative air, "whether I should ask to have a peep at the place where it all happened."

The reporter chuckled behind the pencil-end he was chewing, but the officer maintained his solemn air, for which act of self-restraint he was undoubtedly grateful when in another minute she gave a quick impulsive shudder not altogether assumed, and vehemently added: "But I couldn't stand the sight; no, I couldn't! I'm an awful coward when it comes to things like that. Nothing in all the world would induce me to look at the woman or her room. But I should like—" here both her dimples came into play though she could not be said exactly to smile—"just one little look upstairs, where he went poking about so long without any fear it seems of being interrupted. Ever since I've read about it I have seen, in my mind, a picture of his wicked figure sneaking from room to room, tearing open drawers and flinging out the contents of closets just to find a little money—a little, little money! I shall not sleep to-night just for wondering how those high up attic rooms really look."

Who could dream that back of this display of mingled childishness and audacity there lay hidden purpose, intellect, and a keen knowledge of human nature. Not the two men who listened to this seemingly irresponsible chatter. To them she was a child to be humoured and humour her they did. The dainty feet which had already found their way to that gloomy staircase were allowed to ascend, followed it is true by those of the officer who did not dare to smile back at the reporter because of the brother's watchful and none too conciliatory eye.

At the stair head she paused to look back.

"I don't see those horrible marks which the papers describe as running all along the lower hall and up these stairs."

"No, Miss Strange; they have gradually been rubbed out, but you will find some still showing on these upper floors."

"Oh! oh! where? You frighten me—frighten me horribly! But—but—if you don't mind, I should like to see."

Why should not a man on a tedious job amuse himself? Piloting her over to the small room in the rear, he pointed down at the boards. She gave one look and then stepped gingerly in.

"Just look!" she cried; "a whole string of marks going straight from door to window. They have no shape, have they,—just blotches? I wonder why one of them is so much larger than the rest?"

This was no new question. It was one which everybody who went into the room was sure to ask, there was such a difference in the size and appearance of the mark nearest the window. The reason—well, minds were divided about that, and no one had a satisfactory theory. The detective therefore kept discreetly silent.

This did not seem to offend Miss Strange. On the contrary it gave her an opportunity to babble away to her heart's content.

"One, two, three, four, five, six," she counted, with a shudder at every count. "And one of them bigger than the others." She might have added, "It is the trail of one foot, and strangely, intermingled at that," but she did not, though we may be quite sure that she noted the fact. "And where, just where did the old wallet fall? Here? or here?"

She had moved as she spoke, so that in uttering the last "here," she stood directly before the window. The surprise she received there nearly made her forget the part she was playing. From the character of the light in the room, she had expected, on looking out, to confront a near-by wall, but not a window in that wall. Yet that was what she saw directly facing her from across the old-fashioned alley separating this house from its neighbour; twelve unshuttered and uncurtained panes through which she caught a darkened view of a room almost as forlorn and devoid of furniture as the one in which she then stood.

When quite sure of herself, she let a certain portion of her surprise appear. "Why, look!" she cried, "if you can't see right in next door! What a lonesome-looking place! From its desolate appearance I should think the house quite empty."

"And it is. That's the old Shaffer homestead. It's been empty for a year."

"Oh, empty!" And she turned away, with the most inconsequent air in the world, crying out as her name rang up the stair, "There's Arthur calling. I suppose he thinks I've been here long enough. I'm sure I'm very much obliged to you, officer. I really shouldn't have slept a wink to-night, if I hadn't been given a peep at these rooms, which I had imagined so different." And with one additional glance over her shoulder, that seemed to penetrate both windows and the desolate space beyond, she ran quickly out and down in response to her brother's reiterated call.

"Drive quickly!—as quickly as the law allows, to Hiram Brown's office in Duane Street."

Arrived at the address named, she went in alone to see Mr. Brown. He was her father's lawyer and a family friend.

Hardly waiting for his affectionate greeting, she cried out quickly. "Tell me how I can learn anything about the old Shaffer house in Seventeenth Street. Now, don't look so surprised. I have very good reasons for my request and—and—I'm in an awful hurry."

"But—"

"I know, I know; there's been a dreadful tragedy next door to it; but it's about the Shaffer house itself I want some information. Has it an agent, a—"

"Of course it has an agent, and here is his name."

Mr. Brown presented her with a card on which he had hastily written both name and address.

She thanked him, dropped him a mocking curtsey full of charm, whispered "Don't tell father," and was gone.

Her manner to the man she next interviewed was very different. As soon as she saw him she subsided into her usual society manner. With just a touch of the conceit of the successful debutante, she announced herself as Miss Strange of Seventy-second Street. Her business with him was in regard to the possible renting of the Shaffer house. She had an old lady friend who was desirous of living downtown.

In passing through Seventeenth Street, she had noticed that the old Shaffer house was standing empty and had been immediately struck with the advantages it possessed for her elderly friend's occupancy. Could it be that the house was for rent? There was no sign on it to that effect, but—etc.

His answer left her nothing to hope for.

"It is going to be torn down," he said.

"Oh, what a pity!" she exclaimed. "Real colonial, isn't it! I wish I could see the rooms inside before it is disturbed. Such doors and such dear old-fashioned mantelpieces as it must have! I just dote on the Colonial. It brings up such pictures of the old days; weddings, you know, and parties;—all so different from ours and so much more interesting."

Is it the chance shot that tells? Sometimes. Violet had no especial intention in what she said save as a prelude to a pending request, but nothing could have served her purpose better than that one word, wedding. The agent laughed and giving her his first indulgent look, remarked genially:

"Romance is not confined to those ancient times. If you were to enter that house to-day you would come across evidences of a wedding as romantic as any which ever took place in all the seventy odd years of its existence. A man and a woman were married there day before yesterday who did their first courting under its roof forty years ago. He has been married twice and she once in the interval; but the old love held firm and now at the age of sixty and over they have come together to finish their days in peace and happiness. Or so we will hope."

"Married! married in that house and on the day that—"

She caught herself up in time. He did not notice the break.

"Yes, in memory of those old days of courtship, I suppose. They came here about five, got the keys, drove off, went through the ceremony in that empty house, returned the keys to me in my own apartment, took the steamer for Naples, and were on the sea before midnight. Do you not call that quick work as well as highly romantic?"

"Very." Miss Strange's cheek had paled. It was apt to when she was greatly excited. "But I don't understand," she added, the moment after. "How could they do this and nobody know about it? I should have thought it would have got into the papers."

"They are quiet people. I don't think they told their best friends. A simple announcement in the next day's journals testified to the fact of their marriage, but that was all. I would not have felt at liberty to mention the circumstances myself, if the parties were not well on their way to Europe."

"Oh, how glad I am that you did tell me! Such a story of constancy and the hold which old associations have upon sensitive minds! But—"

"Why, Miss? What's the matter? You look very much disturbed."

"Don't you remember? Haven't you thought? Something else happened that very day and almost at the same time on that block. Something very dreadful—"

"Mrs. Doolittle's murder?"

"Yes. It was as near as next door, wasn't it? Oh, if this happy couple had known—"

"But fortunately they didn't. Nor are they likely to, till they reach the other side. You needn't fear that their honeymoon will be spoiled that way."

"But they may have heard something or seen something before leaving the street. Did you notice how the gentleman looked when he returned you the keys?"

"I did, and there was no cloud on his satisfaction."

"Oh, how you relieve me!" One—two dimples made their appearance in Miss Strange's fresh, young cheeks. "Well! I wish them joy. Do you mind telling me their names? I cannot think of them as actual persons without knowing their names."

"The gentleman was Constantin Amidon; the lady, Marian Shaffer. You will have to think of them now as Mr. and Mrs. Amidon."

"And I will. Thank you, Mr. Hutton, thank you very much. Next to the pleasure of getting the house for my friend, is that of hearing this charming bit of news its connection."

She held out her hand and, as he took it, remarked:

"They must have had a clergyman and witnesses."

"Undoubtedly."

"I wish I had been one of the witnesses," she sighed sentimentally.

"They were two old men."

"Oh, no! Don't tell me that."

"Fogies; nothing less."

"But the clergyman? He must have been young. Surely there was some one there capable of appreciating the situation?"

"I can't say about that; I did not see the clergyman."

"Oh, well! it doesn't matter." Miss Strange's manner was as nonchalant as it was charming. "We will think of him as being very young."

And with a merry toss of her head she flitted away.

But she sobered very rapidly upon entering her limousine.

"Hello!"

"Ah, is that you?"

"Yes, I want a Marconi sent."

"A Marconi?"

"Yes, to the Cretic, which left dock the very night in which we are so deeply interested."

"Good. Whom to? The Captain?"

"No, to a Mrs. Constantin Amidon. But first be sure there is such a passenger."

"Mrs.! What idea have you there?"

"Excuse my not stating over the telephone. The message is to be to this effect. Did she at any time immediately before or after her marriage to Mr. Amidon get a glimpse of any one in the adjoining house? No remarks, please. I use the telephone because I am not ready to explain myself. If she did, let her send a written description to you of that person as soon as she reaches the Azores."

"You surprise me. May I not call or hope for a line from you early to-morrow?"

"I shall be busy till you get your answer."

He hung up the receiver. He recognized the resolute tone.

But the time came when the pending explanation was fully given to him. An answer had been returned from the steamer, favourable to Violet's hopes. Mrs. Amidon had seen such a person and would send a full description of the same at the first opportunity. It was news to fill Violet's heart with pride; the filament of a clue which had led to this great result had been so nearly invisible and had felt so like nothing in her grasp.

To her employer she described it as follows:

"When I hear or read of a case which contains any baffling features, I am apt to feel some hidden chord in my nature thrill to one fact in it and not to any of the others. In this case the single fact which appealed to my imagination was the dropping of the stolen wallet in that upstairs room. Why did the guilty man drop it? and why, having dropped it, did he not pick it up again? but one answer seemed possible. He had heard or seen something at the spot where it fell which not only alarmed him but sent him in flight from the house."

"Very good; and did you settle to your own mind the nature of that sound or that sight?"

"I did." Her manner was strangely businesslike. No show of dimples now. "Satisfied that if any possibility remained of my ever doing this, it would have to be on the exact place of this occurrence or not at all, I embraced your suggestion and visited the house."

"And that room no doubt."

"And that room. Women, somehow, seem to manage such things."

"So I've noticed, Miss Strange. And what was the result of your visit? What did you discover there?"

"This: that one of the blood spots marking the criminal's steps through the room was decidedly more pronounced than the rest; and, what was even more important, that the window out of which I was looking had its counterpart in the house on the opposite side of the alley. In gazing through the one I was gazing through the other; and not only that, but into the darkened area of the room beyond. Instantly I saw how the latter fact might be made to explain the former one. But before I say how, let me ask if it is quite settled among you that the smears on the floor and stairs mark the passage of the criminal's footsteps!"

"Certainly; and very bloody feet they must have been too. His shoes—or rather his one shoe—for the proof is plain that only the right one left its mark—must have become thoroughly saturated to carry its traces so far."

"Do you think that any amount of saturation would have done this? Or, if you are not ready to agree to that, that a shoe so covered with blood could have failed to leave behind it some hint of its shape, some imprint, however faint, of heel or toe? But nowhere did it do this. We see a smear—and that is all."

"You are right, Miss Strange; you are always right. And what do you gather from this?"

She looked to see how much he expected from her, and, meeting an eye not quite as free from ironic suggestion as his words had led her to expect, faltered a little as she proceeded to say:

"My opinion is a girl's opinion, but such as it is you have the right to have it. From the indications mentioned I could draw but this conclusion: that the blood which accompanied the criminal's footsteps was not carried through the house by his shoes;—he wore no shoes; he did not even wear stockings; probably he had none. For reasons which appealed to his judgment, he went about his wicked work barefoot; and it was the blood from his own veins and not from those of his victim which made the trail we have followed with so much interest. Do you forget those broken beads;—how he kicked them about and stamped upon them in his fury? One of them pierced the ball of his foot, and that so sharply that it not only spurted blood but kept on bleeding with every step he took. Otherwise, the trail would have been lost after his passage up the stairs."

"Fine!" There was no irony in the bureau-chief's eye now. "You are progressing, Miss Strange. Allow me, I pray, to kiss your hand. It is a liberty I have never taken, but one which would greatly relieve my present stress of feeling."

She lifted her hand toward him, but it was in gesture, not in recognition of his homage.

"Thank you," said she, "but I claim no monopoly on deductions so simple as these. I have not the least doubt that not only yourself but every member of the force has made the same. But there is a little matter which may have escaped the police, may even have escaped you. To that I would now call your attention since through it I have been enabled, after a little necessary groping, to reach the open. You remember the one large blotch on the upper floor where the man dropped the wallet? That blotch, more or less commingled with a fainter one, possessed great significance for me from the first moment I saw it. How came his foot to bleed so much more profusely at that one spot than at any other? There could be but one answer: because here a surprise met him—a surprise so startling to him in his present state of mind, that he gave a quick spring backward, with the result that his wounded foot came down suddenly and forcibly instead of easily as in his previous wary tread. And what was the surprise? I made it my business to find out, and now I can tell you that it was the sight of a woman's face staring upon him from the neighbouring house which he had probably been told was empty. The shock disturbed his judgment. He saw his crime discovered—his guilty secret read, and fled in unreasoning panic. He might better have held on to his wits. It was this display of fear which led me to search after its cause, and consequently to discover that at this especial hour more than one person had been in the Shaffer house; that, in fact, a marriage had been celebrated there under circumstances as romantic as any we read of in books, and that this marriage, privately carried out, had been followed by an immediate voyage of the happy couple on one of the White Star steamers. With the rest you are conversant. I do not need to say anything about what has followed the sending of that Marconi."

"But I am going to say something about your work in this matter, Miss Strange. The big detectives about here will have to look sharp if—"

"Don't, please! Not yet." A smile softened the asperity of this interruption. "The man has yet to be caught and identified. Till that is done I cannot enjoy any one's congratulations. And you will see that all this may not be so easy. If no one happened to meet the desperate wretch before he had an opportunity to retie his shoe-laces, there will be little for you or even for the police to go upon but his wounded foot, his undoubtedly carefully prepared alibi, and later, a woman's confused description of a face seen but for a moment only and that under a personal excitement precluding minute attention. I should not be surprised if the whole thing came to nothing."

But it did not. As soon as the description was received from Mrs. Amidon (a description, by the way, which was unusually clear and precise, owing to the peculiar and contradictory features of the man), the police were able to recognize him among the many suspects always under their eye. Arrested, he pleaded, just as Miss Strange had foretold, an alibi of a seemingly unimpeachable character; but neither it, nor the plausible explanation with which he endeavoured to account for a freshly healed scar amid the callouses of his right foot, could stand before Mrs. Amidon's unequivocal testimony that he was the same man she had seen in Mrs. Doolittle's upper room on the afternoon of her own happiness and of that poor woman's murder.

The moment when, at his trial, the two faces again confronted each other across a space no wider than that which had separated them on the dread occasion in Seventeenth Street, is said to have been one of the most dramatic in the annals of that ancient court room.

END OF PROBLEM III

THE GROTTO SPECTRE

Miss Strange was not often pensive—at least not at large functions or when under the public eye. But she certainly forgot herself at Mrs. Provost's musicale and that, too, without apparent reason. Had the music been of a high order one might have understood her abstraction; but it was of a decidedly mediocre quality, and Violet's ear was much too fine and her musical sense too cultivated for her to be beguiled by anything less than the very best.

Nor had she the excuse of a dull companion. Her escort for the evening was a man of unusual conversational powers; but she seemed to be almost oblivious of his presence; and when, through some passing courteous impulse, she did turn her ear his way, it was with just that tinge of preoccupation which betrays the divided mind.

Were her thoughts with some secret problem yet unsolved? It would scarcely seem so from the gay remark with which she had left home. She was speaking to her brother and her words were: "I am going out to enjoy myself. I've not a care in the world. The slate is quite clean." Yet she had never seemed more out of tune with her surroundings nor shown a mood further removed from trivial entertainment. What had happened to becloud her gaiety in the short time which had since elapsed?

We can answer in a sentence.

She had seen, among a group of young men in a distant doorway, one with a face so individual and of an expression so extraordinary that all interest in the people about her had stopped as a clock stops when the pendulum is held back. She could see nothing else, think of nothing else. Not that it was so very handsome—though no other had ever approached it in its power over her imagination—but because of its expression of haunting melancholy,—a melancholy so settled and so evidently the result of long-continued sorrow that her interest had been reached and her heartstrings shaken as never before in her whole life.

She would never be the same Violet again.

Yet moved as she undoubtedly was, she was not conscious of the least desire to know who the young man was, or even to be made acquainted with his story. She simply wanted to dream her dream undisturbed.

It was therefore with a sense of unwelcome shock that, in the course of the reception following the programme, she perceived this fine young man approaching herself, with his right hand touching his left shoulder in the peculiar way which committed her to an interview with or without a formal introduction.

Should she fly the ordeal? Be blind and deaf to whatever was significant in his action, and go her way before he reached her; thus keeping her dream intact? Impossible. His eye prevented that. His glance had caught hers and she felt forced to await his advance and give him her first spare moment.

It came soon, and when it came she greeted him with a smile. It was the first she had ever bestowed in welcome of a confidence of whose tenor she was entirely ignorant.

To her relief he showed his appreciation of the dazzling gift though he made no effort to return it. Scorning all preliminaries in his eagerness to discharge himself of a burden which was fast becoming intolerable, he addressed her at once in these words:

"You are very good, Miss Strange, to receive me in this unconventional fashion. I am in that desperate state of mind which precludes etiquette. Will you listen to my petition? I am told—you know by whom—"(and he again touched his shoulder) "that you have resources of intelligence which especially fit you to meet the extraordinary difficulties of my position. May I beg you to exercise them in my behalf? No man would be more grateful if—But I see that you do not recognize me. I am Roger Upjohn. That I am admitted to this gathering is owing to the fact that our hostess knew and loved my mother. In my anxiety to meet you and proffer my plea, I was willing to brave the cold looks you have probably noticed on the faces of the people about us. But I have no right to subject you to criticism. I—"

"Remain." Violet's voice was troubled, her self-possession disturbed; but there was a command in her tone which he was only too glad to obey. "I know the name" (who did not!) "and possibly my duty to myself should make me shun a confidence which may burden me without relieving you. But you have been sent to me by one whose behests I feel bound to respect and—"

Mistrusting her voice, she stopped. The suffering which made itself apparent in the face before her appealed to her heart in a way to rob her of her judgment. She did not wish this to be seen, and so fell silent.

He was quick to take advantage of her obvious embarrassment. "Should I have been sent to you if I had not first secured the confidence of the sender? You know the scandal attached to my name, some of it just, some of it very unjust. If you will grant me an interview to-morrow, I will make an endeavour to refute certain charges which I have hitherto let go unchallenged. Will you do me this favour? Will you listen in your own house to what I have to say?"

Instinct cried out against any such concession on her part, bidding her beware of one who charmed without excellence and convinced without reason. But compassion urged compliance and compassion won the day. Though conscious of weakness,—she, Violet Strange on whom strong men had come to rely in critical hours calling for well-balanced judgment,—she did not let this concern her, or allow herself to indulge in useless regrets even after the first effect of his presence had passed and she had succeeded in recalling the facts which had cast a cloud about his name.

Roger Upjohn was a widower, and the scandal affecting him was connected with his wife's death.

Though a degenerate in some respects, lacking the domineering presence, the strong mental qualities, and inflexible character of his progenitors, the wealthy Massachusetts Upjohns whose great place on the coast had a history as old as the State itself, he yet had gifts and attractions of his own which would have made him a worthy representative of his race, if only he had not fixed his affections on a woman so cold and heedless that she would have inspired universal aversion instead of love, had she not been dowered with the beauty and physical fascination which sometimes accompany a hard heart and a scheming brain. It was this beauty which had caught the lad; and one day, just as the careful father had mapped out a course of study calculated to make a man of his son, that son drove up to the gates with this lady whom he introduced as his wife.

The shock, not of her beauty, though that was of the dazzling quality which catches a man in the throat and makes a slave of him while the first surprise lasts, but of the overthrow of all his hopes and plans, nearly prostrated Homer Upjohn. He saw, as most men did the moment judgment returned, that for all her satin skin and rosy flush, the wonder of her hair and the smile which pierced like arrows and warmed like wine, she was more likely to bring a curse into the house than a blessing.

And so it proved. In less than a year the young husband had lost all his ambitions and many of his best impulses. No longer inclined to study, he spent his days in satisfying his wife's whims and his evenings in carousing with the friends with which she had provided him. This in Boston whither they had fled from the old gentleman's displeasure; but after their little son came the father insisted upon their returning home, which led to great deceptions, and precipitated a tragedy no one ever understood. They were natural gamblers—this couple—as all Boston society knew; and as Homer Upjohn loathed cards, they found life slow in the great house and grew correspondingly restless till they made a discovery—or shall I say a rediscovery—of the once famous grotto hidden in the rocks lining their portion of the coast. Here they found a retreat where they could hide themselves (often when they were thought to be abed and asleep) and play together for money or for a supper in the city or for anything else that foolish fancy suggested. This was while their little son remained an infant; later, they were less easily satisfied. Both craved company, excitement, and gambling on a large scale; so they took to inviting friends to meet them in this grotto which, through the agency of one old servant devoted to Roger to the point of folly, had been fitted up and lighted in a manner not only comfortable but luxurious. A small but sheltered haven hidden in the curve of the rocks made an approach by boat feasible at high tide; and at low the connection could be made by means of a path over the promontory in which this grotto lay concealed. The fortune which Roger had inherited from his mother made these excesses possible, but many thousands, let alone the few he could call his, soon disappeared under the witchery of an irresponsible woman, and the half-dozen friends who knew his secret had to stand by and see his ruin, without daring to utter a word to the one who alone could stay it. For Homer Upjohn was not a man to be approached lightly, nor was he one to listen to charges without ocular proof to support them; and this called for courage, more courage than was possessed by any one who knew them both.

He was a hard man was Homer Upjohn, but with a heart of gold for those he loved. This, even his wary daughter-in-law was wise enough to detect, and for a long while after the birth of her child she besieged him with her coaxing ways and bewitching graces. But he never changed his first opinion of her, and once she became fully convinced of the folly of her efforts, she gave up all attempt to please him and showed an open indifference. This in time gradually extended till it embraced not only her child but her husband as well. Yes, it had come to that. His love no longer contented her. Her vanity had grown by what it daily fed on, and now called for the admiration of the fast men who sometimes came up from Boston to play with them in their unholy retreat. To win this, she dressed like some demon queen or witch, though it drove her husband into deeper play and threatened an exposure which would mean disaster not only to herself but to the whole family.

In all this, as any one could see, Roger had been her slave and the willing victim of all her caprices. What was it, then, which so completely changed him that a separation began to be talked of and even its terms discussed? One rumour had it that the father had discovered the secret of the grotto and exacted this as a penalty from the son who had dishonoured him. Another, that Roger himself was the one to take the initiative in this matter: That, on returning unexpectedly from New York one evening and finding her missing from the house, he had traced her to the grotto where he came upon her playing a desperate game with the one man he had the greatest reason to distrust.

But whatever the explanation of this sudden change in their relations, there is but little doubt that a legal separation between this ill-assorted couple was pending, when one bleak autumn morning she was discovered dead in her bed under circumstances peculiarly open to comment.

The physicians who made out the certificate ascribed her death to heart-disease, symptoms of which had lately much alarmed the family doctor; but that a personal struggle of some kind had preceded the fatal attack was evident from the bruises which blackened her wrists. Had there been the like upon her throat it might have gone hard with the young husband who was known to be contemplating her dismissal from the house. But the discoloration of her wrists was all, and as bruised wrists do not kill and there was besides no evidence forthcoming of the two having spent one moment together for at least ten hours preceding the tragedy but rather full and satisfactory testimony to the contrary, the matter lapsed and all criminal proceedings were avoided.

But not the scandal which always follows the unexplained. As time passed and the peculiar look which betrays the haunted soul gradually became visible in the young widower's eyes, doubts arose and reports circulated which cast strange reflections upon the tragic end of his mistaken marriage. Stories of the disreputable use to which the old grotto had been put were mingled with vague hints of conjugal violence never properly investigated. The result was his general avoidance not only by the social set dominated by his high-minded father, but by his own less reputable coterie, which, however lax in its moral code, had very little use for a coward.

Such was the gossip which had reached Violet's ears in connection with this new client, prejudicing her altogether against him till she caught that beam of deep and concentrated suffering in his eye and recognized an innocence which ensured her sympathy and led her to grant him the interview for which he so earnestly entreated.

He came prompt to the hour, and when she saw him again with the marks of a sleepless night upon him and all the signs of suffering intensified in his unusual countenance, she felt her heart sink within her in a way she failed to understand. A dread of what she was about to hear robbed her of all semblance of self-possession, and she stood like one in a dream as he uttered his first greetings and then paused to gather up his own moral strength before he began his story. When he did speak it was to say:

"I find myself obliged to break a vow I have made to myself. You cannot understand my need unless I show you my heart. My trouble is not the one with which men have credited me. It has another source and is infinitely harder to bear. Personal dishonour I have deserved in a greater or less degree, but the trial which has come to me now involves a person more dear to me than myself, and is totally without alleviation unless you—" He paused, choked, then recommenced abruptly: "My wife"—Violet held her breath—"was supposed to have died from heart-disease or—or some strange species of suicide. There were reasons for this conclusion—reasons which I accepted without serious question till some five weeks ago when I made a discovery which led me to fear—"

The broken sentence hung suspended. Violet, notwithstanding his hurried gesture, could not restrain herself from stealing a look at his face. It was set in horror and, though partially turned aside, made an appeal to her compassion to fill the void made by his silence, without further suggestion from him.

She did this by saying tentatively and with as little show of emotion as possible:

"You feared that the event called for vengeance and that vengeance would mean increased suffering to yourself as well as to another?"

"Yes; great suffering. But I may be under a most lamentable mistake. I am not sure of my conclusions. If my doubts have no real foundation—if they are simply the offspring of my own diseased imagination, what an insult to one I revere! What a horror of ingratitude and misunderstanding—"

"Relate the facts," came in startled tones from Violet. "They may enlighten us."

He gave one quick shudder, buried his face for one moment in his hands, then lifted it and spoke up quickly and with unexpected firmness:

"I came here to do so and do so I will. But where begin? Miss Strange, you cannot be ignorant of the circumstances, open and avowed, which attended my wife's death. But there were other and secret events in its connection which happily have been kept from the world, but which I must now disclose to you at any cost to my pride and so-called honour. This is the first one: On the morning preceding the day of Mrs. Upjohn's death, an interview took place between us at which my father was present. You do not know my father, Miss Strange. A strong man and a stern one, with a hold upon old traditions which nothing can shake. If he has a weakness it is for my little boy Roger in whose promising traits he sees the one hope which has survived the shipwreck of all for which our name has stood. Knowing this, and realizing what the child's presence in the house meant to his old age, I felt my heart turn sick with apprehension, when in the midst of the discussion as to the terms on which my wife would consent to a permanent separation, the little fellow came dancing into the room, his curls atoss and his whole face beaming with life and joy.

"She had not mentioned the child, but I knew her well enough to be sure that at the first show of preference on his part for either his grandfather or myself, she would raise a claim to him which she would never relinquish. I dared not speak, but I met his eager looks with my most forbidding frown and hoped by this show of severity to hold him back. But his little heart was full and, ignoring her outstretched arms, he bounded towards mine with his most affectionate cry. She saw and uttered her ultimatum. The child should go with her or she would not consent to a separation. It was useless for us to talk; she had said her last word. The blow struck me hard, or so I thought, till I looked at my father. Never had I beheld such a change as that one moment had made in him. He stood as before; he faced us with the same silent reprobation; but his heart had run from him like water.

"It was a sight to call up all my resources. To allow her to remain now, with my feelings towards her all changed and my father's eyes fully opened to her stony nature, was impossible. Nor could I appeal to law. An open scandal was my father's greatest dread and divorce proceedings his horror. The child would have to go unless I could find a way to influence her through her own nature. I knew of but one—do not look at me, Miss Strange. It was dishonouring to us both, and I'm horrified now when I think of it. But to me at that time it was natural enough as a last resort. There was but one debt which my wife ever paid, but one promise she ever kept. It was that made at the gaming-table. I offered, as soon as my father, realizing the hopelessness of the situation, had gone tottering from the room, to gamble with her for the child.

"And she accepted."

The shame and humiliation expressed in this final whisper; the sudden darkness—for a storm was coming up—shook Violet to the soul. With strained gaze fixed on the man before her, now little more than a shadow in the prevailing gloom, she waited for him to resume, and waited in vain. The minutes passed, the darkness became intolerable, and instinctively her hand crept towards the electric button beneath which she was sitting. But she failed to press it. A tale so dark called for an atmosphere of its own kind. She would cast no light upon it. Yet she shivered as the silence continued, and started in uncontrollable dismay when at length her strange visitor rose, and still, without speaking, walked away from her to the other end of the room. Only so could he go on with the shameful tale; and presently she heard his voice once more in these words:

"Our house is large and its rooms many; but for such work as we two contemplated there was but one spot where we could command absolute seclusion. You may have heard of it, a famous natural grotto hidden in our own portion of the coast and so fitted up as to form a retreat for our miserable selves when escape from my father's eye seemed desirable. It was not easy of access, and no one, so far as we knew, had ever followed us there.

"But to ensure ourselves against any possible interruption, we waited till the whole house was abed before we left it for the grotto. We went by boat and oh! the dip of those oars! I hear them yet. And the witchery of her face in the moonlight; and the mockery of her low fitful laugh! As I caught the sinister note in its silvery rise and fall, I knew what was before me if I failed to retain my composure. And I strove to hold it and to meet her calmness with stoicism and the taunt of her expression with a mask of immobility. But the effort was hopeless, and when the time came for dealing out the cards, my eyes were burning in their sockets and my hands shivering like leaves in a rising gale.

"We played one game—and my wife lost. We played another—and my wife won. We played the third—and the fate I had foreseen from the first became mine. The luck was with her, and I had lost my boy!"

A gasp—a pause, during which the thunder spoke and the lightning flashed,—then a hurried catching of his breath and the tale went on.

"A burst of laughter, rising gaily above the boom of the sea, announced her victory—her laugh and the taunting words: 'You play badly, Roger. The child is mine. Never fear that I shall fail to teach him to revere his father.' Had I a word to throw back? No. When I realized anything but my dishonoured manhood, I found myself in the grotto's mouth staring helplessly out upon the sea. The boat which had floated us in at high tide lay stranded but a few feet away, but I did not reach for it. Escape was quicker over the rocks, and I made for the rocks.

"That it was a cowardly act to leave her there to find her way back alone at midnight by the same rough road I was taking, did not strike my mind for an instant. I was in flight from my own past; in flight from myself and the haunting dread of madness. When I awoke to reality again it was to find the small door, by which we had left the house, standing slightly ajar. I was troubled by this, for I was sure of having closed it. But the impression was brief, and entering, I went stumbling up to my room, leaving the way open behind me more from sheer inability to exercise my will than from any thought of her.

"'Miss Strange' (he had come out of the shadows and was standing now directly before her), 'I must ask you to trust implicitly in what I tell you of my further experiences that fatal night. It was not necessary for me to pass my little son's door in order to reach the room I was making for; but anguish took me there and held me glued to the panels for what seemed a long, long time. When I finally crept away it was to go to the room I had chosen in the top of the house, where I had my hour of hell and faced my desolated future. Did I hear anything meantime in the halls below? No. Did I even listen for the sound of her return? No. I was callous to everything, dead to everything but my own misery. I did not even heed the approach of morning, till suddenly, with a shrillness no ear could ignore, there rose, tearing through the silence of the house, that great scream from my wife's room which announced the discovery of her body lying stark and cold in her bed.

"'They said I showed little feeling.' He had moved off again and spoke from somewhere in the shadows. 'Do you wonder at this after such a manifest stroke by a benevolent Providence? My wife being dead, Roger was saved to us! It was the one song of my still undisciplined soul, and I had to assume coldness lest they should see the greatness of my joy. A wicked and guilty rejoicing you will say, and you are right. But I had no memory then of the part I had played in this fatality. I had forgotten my reckless flight from the grotto, which left her with no aid but that of her own triumphant spirit to help her over those treacherous rocks. The necessity for keeping secret this part of our disgraceful story led me to exert myself to keep it out of my own mind. It has only come back to me in all its force since a new horror, a new suspicion, has driven me to review carefully every incident of that awful night.

"'I was never a man of much logic, and when they came to me on that morning of which I have just spoken and took me in where she lay and pointed to her beautiful cold body stretched out in seeming peace under the satin coverlet, and then to the pile of dainty clothes lying neatly folded on a chair with just one fairy slipper on top, I shuddered at her fate but asked no questions, not even when one of the women of the house mentioned the circumstance of the single slipper and said that a search should be made for its mate. Nor was I as much impressed as one would naturally expect by the whisper dropped in my ear that something was the matter with her wrists. It is true that I lifted the lace they had carefully spread over them and examined the discoloration which extended like a ring about each pearly arm; but having no memories of any violence offered her (I had not so much as laid hand upon her in the grotto), these marks failed to rouse my interest. But—and now I must leap a year in my story—there came a time when both of these facts recurred to my mind with startling distinctness and clamoured for explanation.

"I had risen above the shock which such a death following such events would naturally occasion even in one of my blunted sensibilities, and was striving to live a new life under the encouragement of my now fully reconciled father, when accident forced me to re-enter the grotto where I had never stepped foot since that night. A favourite dog in chase of some innocent prey had escaped the leash and run into its dim recesses and would not come out at my call. As I needed him immediately for the hunt, I followed him over the promontory and, swallowing my repugnance, slid into the grotto to get him. Better a plunge to my death from the height of the rocks towering above it. For there in a remote corner, lighted up by a reflection from the sea, I beheld my setter crouched above an object which in another moment I recognized as my dead wife's missing slipper. Here! Not in the waters of the sea or in the interstices of the rocks outside, but here! Proof that she had never walked back to the house where she was found lying quietly in her bed; proof positive; for I knew the path too well and the more than usual tenderness of her feet.

"How then, did she get there; and by whose agency? Was she living when she went, or was she already dead? A year had passed since that delicate shoe had borne her from the boat into these dim recesses; but it might have been only a day, so vividly did I live over in this moment of awful enlightenment all the events of the hour in which we sat there playing for the possession of our child. Again I saw her gleaming eyes, her rosy, working mouth, her slim, white hand, loaded with diamonds, clutching the cards. Again I heard the lap of the sea on the pebbles outside and smelt the odour of the wine she had poured out for us both. The bottle which had held it; the glass from which she had drunk lay now in pieces on the rocky floor. The whole scene was mine again and as I followed the event to its despairing close, I seemed to see my own wild figure springing away from her to the grotto's mouth and so over the rocks. But here fancy faltered, caught by a quick recollection to which I had never given a thought till now. As I made my way along those rocks, a sound had struck my ear from where some stunted bushes made a shadow in the moonlight. The wind might have caused it or some small night creature hustling away at my approach; and to some such cause I must at the time have attributed it. But now, with brain fired by suspicion, it seemed more like the quick intake of a human breath. Some one had been lying there in wait, listening at the one loophole in the rocks where it was possible to hear what was said and done in the heart of the grotto. But who? who? and for what purpose this listening; and to what end did it lead?

"Though I no longer loved even the memory of my wife, I felt my hair lift, as I asked myself these questions. There seemed to be but one logical answer to the last, and it was this: A struggle followed by death. The shoe fallen from her foot, the clothes found folded in her room (my wife was never orderly), and the dimly blackened wrists which were snow-white when she dealt the cards— all seemed to point to such a conclusion. She may have died from heart-failure, but a struggle had preceded her death, during which some man's strong fingers had been locked about her wrists. And again the question rose, Whose?

"If any place was ever hated by mortal man that grotto was hated by me. I loathed its walls, its floor, its every visible and invisible corner. To linger there—to look—almost tore my soul from my body; yet I did linger and did look and this is what I found by way of reward.

"Behind a projecting ledge of stone from which a tattered rug still hung, I came upon two nails driven a few feet apart into a fissure of the rock. I had driven those nails myself long before for a certain gymnastic attachment much in vogue at the time, and on looking closer, I discovered hanging from them the rope-ends by which I was wont to pull myself about. So far there was nothing to rouse any but innocent reminiscences. But when I heard the dog's low moan and saw him leap at the curled-up ends, and nose them with an eager look my way, I remembered the dark marks circling the wrists about which I had so often clasped my mother's bracelets, and the world went black before me.

"When consciousness returned—when I could once more move and see and think, I noted another fact. Cards were strewn about the floor, face up and in a fixed order as if laid in a mocking mood to be looked upon by reluctant eyes; and near the ominous half-circle they made, a cushion from the lounge, stained horribly with what I then thought to be blood, but which I afterwards found to be wine. Vengeance spoke in those ropes and in the carefully spread-out cards, and murder in the smothering pillow. The vengeance of one who had watched her corroding influence eat the life out of my honour and whose love for our little Roger was such that any deed which ensured his continued presence in the home appeared not only warrantable but obligatory. Alas! I knew of but one person in the whole world who could cherish feeling to this extent or possess sufficient will power to carry her lifeless body back to the house and lay it in her bed and give no sign of the abominable act from that day on to this.

"Miss Strange, there are men who have a peculiar conception of duty. My father—"

"You need not go on." How gently, how tenderly our Violet spoke. "I understand your trouble—"

Did she? She paused to ask herself if this were so, and he, deaf perhaps to her words, caught up his broken sentence and went on:

"My father was in the hall the day I came staggering in from my visit to the grotto. No words passed, but our eyes met and from that hour I have seen death in his countenance and he has seen it in mine, like two opponents, each struck to the heart, who stand facing each other with simulated smiles till they fall. My father will drop first. He is old—very old since that day five weeks ago; and to see him die and not be sure—to see the grave close over a possible innocence, and I left here in ignorance of the blissful fact till my own eyes close forever, is more than I can hold up under; more than any son could. Cannot you help me then to a positive knowledge? Think! think! A woman's mind is strangely penetrating, and yours, I am told, has an intuitive faculty more to be relied upon than the reasoning of men. It must suggest some means of confirming my doubts or of definitely ending them."

Then Violet stirred and looked about at him and finally found voice.

"Tell me something about your father's ways. What are his habits? Does he sleep well or is he wakeful at night?"

"He has poor nights. I do not know how poor because I am not often with him. His valet, who has always been in our family, shares his room and acts as his constant nurse. He can watch over him better than I can; he has no distracting trouble on his mind."

"And little Roger? Does your father see much of little Roger? Does he fondle him and seem happy in his presence?"

"Yes; yes. I have often wondered at it, but he does. They are great chums. It is a pleasure to see them together."

"And the child clings to him—shows no fear—sits on his lap or on the bed and plays as children do play with his beard or with his watch-chain?"

"Yes. Only once have I seen my little chap shrink, and that was when my father gave him a look of unusual intensity,—looking for his mother in him perhaps."

"Mr. Upjohn, forgive me the question; it seems necessary. Does your father—or rather did your father before he fell ill—ever walk in the direction of the grotto or haunt in any way the rocks which surround it?"

"I cannot say. The sea is there; he naturally loves the sea. But I have never seen him standing on the promontory."

"Which way do his windows look?"

"Towards the sea."

"Therefore towards the promontory?"

"Yes."

"Can he see it from his bed?"

"No. Perhaps that is the cause of a peculiar habit he has."

"What habit?"

"Every night before he retires (he is not yet confined to his bed) he stands for a few minutes in his front window looking out. He says it's his good-night to the ocean. When he no longer does this, we shall know that his end is very near."

The face of Violet began to clear. Rising, she turned on the electric light, and then, reseating herself, remarked with an aspect of quiet cheer:

"I have two ideas; but they necessitate my presence at your place. You will not mind a visit? My brother will accompany me."

Roger Upjohn did not need to speak, hardly to make a gesture; his expression was so eloquent.

She thanked him as if he had answered in words, adding with an air of gentle reserve: "Providence assists us in this matter. I am invited to Beverly next week to attend a wedding. I was intending to stay two days, but I will make it three and spend the extra one with you."

"What are your requirements, Miss Strange? I presume you have some."

Violet turned from the imposing portrait of Mr. Upjohn which she had been gravely contemplating, and met the troubled eye of her young host with an enigmatical flash of her own. But she made no answer in words. Instead, she lifted her right hand and ran one slender finger thoughtfully up the casing of the door near which they stood till it struck a nick in the old mahogany almost on a level with her head.

"Is your son Roger old enough to reach so far?" she asked with another short look at him as she let her finger rest where it had struck the roughened wood. "I thought he was a little fellow."

"He is. That cut was made by—by my wife; a sample of her capricious willfulness. She wished to leave a record of herself in the substance of our house as well as in our lives. That nick marks her height. She laughed when she made it. 'Till the walls cave in or burn,' is what she said. And I thought her laugh and smile captivating."

Cutting short his own laugh which was much too sardonic for a lady's ears, he made a move as if to lead the way into another portion of the room. But Violet failed to notice this, and lingering in quiet contemplation of this suggestive little nick,—the only blemish in a room of ancient colonial magnificence,—she thoughtfully remarked:

"Then she was a small woman?" adding with seeming irrelevance—"like myself."

Roger winced. Something in the suggestion hurt him, and in the nod he gave there was an air of coldness which under ordinary circumstances would have deterred her from pursuing this subject further. But the circumstances were not ordinary, and she allowed herself to say:

"Was she so very different from me,—in figure, I mean?"

"No. Why do you ask? Shall we not join your brother on the terrace?"

"Not till I have answered the question you put me a moment ago. You wished to know my requirements. One of the most important you have already fulfilled. You have given your servants a half-holiday and by so doing ensured to us full liberty of action. What else I need in the attempt I propose to make, you will find listed in this memorandum." And taking a slip of paper from her bag, she offered it to him with a hand, the trembling of which he would have noted had he been freer in mind.

As he read, she watched him, her fingers nervously clutching her throat.

"Can you supply what I ask?" she faltered, as he failed to raise his eyes or make any move or even to utter the groan she saw surging up to his lips. "Will you?" she impetuously urged, as his fingers closed spasmodically on the paper, in evidence that he understood at last the trend of her daring purpose.

The answer came slowly, but it came. "I will. But what—"

Her hand rose in a pleading gesture.

"Do not ask me, but take Arthur and myself into the garden and show us the flowers. Afterwards, I should like a glimpse of the sea."

He bowed and they joined Arthur who had already begun to stroll through the grounds.

Violet was seldom at a loss for talk even at the most critical moments. But she was strangely tongue-tied on this occasion, as was Roger himself. Save for a few observations casually thrown out by Arthur, the three passed in a disquieting silence through pergola after pergola, and around beds gorgeous with every variety of fall flowers, till they turned a sharp corner and came in full view of the sea.

"Ah!" fell in an admiring murmur from Violet's lips as her eyes swept the horizon. Then as they settled on a mass of rock jutting out from the shore in a great curve, she leaned towards her host and softly whispered:

"The promontory?"

He nodded, and Violet ventured no farther, but stood for a little while gazing at the tumbled rocks. Then, with a quick look back at the house, she asked him to point out his father's window.

He did so, and as she noted how openly it faced the sea, her expression relaxed and her manner lost some of its constraint. As they turned to re-enter the house, she noticed an old man picking flowers from a vine clambering over one end of the piazza.

"Who is that?" she asked.

"Our oldest servant, and my father's own man," was Roger's reply. "He is picking my father's favourite flowers, a few late honeysuckles."

"How fortunate! Speak to him, Mr. Upjohn. Ask him how your father is this evening."

"Accompany me and I will; and do not be afraid to enter into conversation with him. He is the mildest of creatures and devoted to his patient. He likes nothing better than to talk about him."

Violet, with a meaning look at her brother, ran up the steps at Roger's side. As she did so, the old man turned and Violet was astonished at the wistfulness with which he viewed her.

"What a dear old creature!" she murmured. "See how he stares this way. You would think he knew me."

"He is glad to see a woman about the place. He has felt our isolation—Good evening, Abram. Let this young lady have a spray of your sweetest honeysuckle. And, Abram, before you go, how is Father to-night? Still sitting up?"

"Yes, sir. He is very regular in his ways. Nine is his hour; not a minute before and not a minute later. I don't have to look at the clock when he says: 'There, Abram, I've sat up long enough.'"

"When my father retires before his time or goes to bed without a final look at the sea, he will be a very sick man, Abram."

"That he will, Mr. Roger; that he will. But he's very feeble to-night, very feeble. I noticed that he gave the boy fewer kisses than usual. Perhaps he was put out because the child was brought in a half-hour earlier than the stated time. He don't like changes; you know that, Mr. Roger; he don't like changes. I hardly dared to tell him that the servants were all going out in a bunch to-night."

"I'm sorry," muttered Roger. "But he'll forget it by to-morrow. I couldn't bear to keep a single one from the concert. They'll be back in good season and meantime we have you. Abram is worth half a dozen of them, Miss Strange. We shall miss nothing."

"Thank you, Mr. Roger, thank you," faltered the old man. "I try to do my duty." And with another wistful glance at Violet, who looked very sweet and youthful in the half-light, he pottered away.

The silence which followed his departure was as painful to her as to Roger Upjohn. When she broke it it was with this decisive remark:

"That man must not speak of me to your father. He must not even mention that you have a guest to-night. Run after him and tell him so. It is necessary that your father's mind should not be taken up with present happenings. Run."

Roger made haste to obey her. When he came back she was on the point of joining her brother but stopped to utter a final injunction:

"I shall leave the library, or wherever we may be sitting, just as the clock strikes half-past eight. Arthur will do the same, as by that time he will feel like smoking on the terrace. Do not follow either him or myself, but take your stand here on the piazza where you can get a full view of the right-hand wing without attracting any attention to yourself. When you hear the big clock in the hall strike nine, look up quickly at your father's window. What you see may determine—oh, Arthur! still admiring the prospect? I do not wonder. But I find it chilly. Let us go in."

Roger Upjohn, sitting by himself in the library, was watching the hands of the mantel clock slowly approaching the hour of nine.

Never had silence seemed more oppressive nor his sense of loneliness greater. Yet the boom of the ocean was distinct to the ear, and human presence no farther away than the terrace where Arthur Strange could be seen smoking out his cigar in solitude. The silence and the loneliness were in Roger's own soul; and, in face of the expected revelation which would make or unmake his future, the desolation they wrought was measureless.

To cut his suspense short, he rose at length and hurried out to the spot designated by Miss Strange as the best point from which to keep watch upon his father's window. It was at the end of the piazza where the honeysuckle hung, and the odour of the blossoms, so pleasing to his father, well-nigh overpowered him not only by its sweetness but by the many memories it called up. Visions of that father as he looked at all stages of their relationship passed in a bewildering maze before him. He saw him as he appeared to his childish eyes in those early days of confidence when the loss of the mother cast them in mutual dependence upon each other. Then a sterner picture of the relentless parent who sees but one straight course to success in this world and the next. Then the teacher and the matured adviser; and then—oh, bitter change! the man whose hopes he had crossed—whose life he had undone, and all for her who now came stealing upon the scene with her slim, white, jewelled hand forever lifted up between them. And she! Had he ever seen her more clearly? Once more the dainty figure stepped from fairy-land, beauteous with every grace that can allure and finally destroy a man. And as he saw, he trembled and wished that these moments of awful waiting might pass and the test be over which would lay bare his father's heart and justify his fears or dispel them forever.

But the crisis, if crisis it was, was one of his own making and not to be hastened or evaded. With one quick glance at his father's window, he turned in his impatience towards the sea whose restless and continuous moaning had at length struck his ear. What was in its call to-night that he should thus sway towards it as though drawn by some dread magnetic force? He had been born to the dashing of its waves and knew its every mood and all the passion of its song from frolicsome ripple to melancholy dirge. But there was something odd and inexplicable in its effect upon his spirit as he faced it at this hour. Grim and implacable—a sound rather than a sight—it seemed to hold within its invisible distances the image of his future fate. What this image was and why he should seek for it in this impenetrable void, he did not know. He felt himself held and was struggling with this influence as with an unknown enemy when there rang out, from the hall within, the preparatory chimes for which his ear was waiting, and then the nine slow strokes which signalized the moment when he was to look for his father's presence at the window.

Had he wished, he could not have forborne that look. Had his eyes been closing in death, or so he felt, the trembling lids would have burst apart at this call and the revelations it promised.

And what did he see? What did that window hold for him?

Nothing that he might not have seen there any night at this hour. His father's figure drawn up behind the panes in wistful contemplation of the night. No visible change in his attitude, nothing forced or unusual in his manner. Even the hand, lifted to pull down the shade, moves with its familiar hesitation. In a moment more that shade will be down and—But no! the lifted hand falls back; the easy attitude becomes strained, fixed. He is staring now—not merely gazing out upon the wastes of sky and sea; and Roger, following the direction of his glance, stares also in breathless emotion at what those distances, but now so impenetrable, are giving to the eye.

A spectre floating in the air above the promontory! The spectre of a woman—of his wife, clad, as she had been clad that fatal night! Outlined in supernatural light, it faces them with lifted arms showing the ends of rope dangling from either wrist. A sight awful to any eye, but to the man of guilty heart—

Ah! it comes—the cry for which the agonized son had been listening! An old man's shriek, hoarse with the remorse of sleepless nights and days of unimaginable regret and foreboding! It cuts the night. It cuts its way into his heart. He feels his senses failing him, yet he must glance once more at the window and see with his last conscious look—But what is this! a change has taken place in the picture and he beholds, not the distorted form of his father sinking back in shame and terror before this visible image of his secret sin, but that of another weak, old man falling to the floor behind his back! Abram! the attentive, seemingly harmless, guardian of the household! Abram! who had never spoken a word or given a look in any way suggestive of his having played any other part in the hideous drama of their lives than that of the humble and sympathetic servant!

The shock was too great, the relief too absolute for credence. He, the listener at the grotto? He, the avenger of the family's honour? He, the insurer of little Roger's continuance with the family at a cost the one who loved him best would rather have died himself than pay? Yes! there is no misdoubting this old servitor's attitude of abject appeal, or the meaning of Homer Upjohn's joyfully uplifted countenance and outspreading arms. The servant begs for mercy from man, and the master is giving thanks to Heaven. Why giving thanks? Has he been the prey of cankering doubts also? Has the father dreaded to discover that in the son which the son has dreaded to discover in the father?

It might easily be; and as Roger recognizes this truth and the full tragedy of their mutual lives, he drops to his knees amid the honeysuckles.

"Violet, you are a wonder. But how did you dare?"

This from Arthur as the two rode to the train in the early morning.

The answer came a bit waveringly.

"I do not know. I am astonished yet, at my own daring. Look at my hands. They have not ceased trembling since the moment you threw the light upon me on the rocks. The figure of old Mr. Upjohn in the window looked so august."

Arthur, with a short glance at the little hands she held out, shrugged his shoulders imperceptibly. It struck him that the tremulousness she complained of was due more to some parting word from their young host, than from prolonged awe at her own daring. But he made no remark to this effect, only observed:

"Abram has confessed his guilt, I hear."

"Yes, and will die of it. The master will bury the man, and not the man the master."

"And Roger? Not the little fellow, but the father?"

"We will not talk of him," said she, her eyes seeking the sea where the sun in its rising was battling with a troop of lowering clouds and slowly gaining the victory.

END OF PROBLEM IV

53

PROBLEM V

THE DREAMING LADY

"And this is all you mean to tell me?"

"I think you will find it quite enough, Miss Strange."

"Just the address—"

"And this advice: that your call be speedy. Distracted nerves cannot wait."

Violet, across whose wonted piquancy there lay an indefinable shadow, eyed her employer with a doubtful air before turning away toward the door. She had asked him for a case to investigate (something she had never done before), and she had even gone so far as to particularize the sort of case she desired: "It must be an interesting one," she had stipulated, "but different, quite different from the last one. It must not involve death or any kind of horror. If you have a case of subtlety without crime, one to engage my powers without depressing my spirits, I beg you to let me have it. I—I have not felt quite like myself since I came from Massachusetts." Whereupon, without further comment, but with a smile she did not understand, he had handed her a small slip of paper on which he had scribbled an address. She should have felt satisfied, but for some reason she did not. She regarded him as capable of plunging her into an affair quite the reverse of what she felt herself in a condition to undertake.

"I should like to know a little more," she pursued, making a move to unfold the slip he had given her.

But he stopped her with a gesture.

"Read it in your limousine," said he. "If you are disappointed then, let me know. But I think you will find yourself quite ready for your task."

"And my father?"

"Would approve if he could be got to approve the business at all. You do not even need to take your brother with you."

"Oh, then, it's with women only I have to deal?"

"Read the address after you are headed up Fifth Avenue."

But when, with her doubts not yet entirely removed, she opened the small slip he had given her, the number inside suggested nothing but the fact that her destination lay somewhere near Eightieth Street. It was therefore with the keenest surprise she beheld her motor stop before the conspicuous house of the great financier whose late death had so affected the money-market. She had not had any acquaintance with this man herself, but she knew his house. Everyone knew that. It was one of the most princely in the whole city. C. Dudley Brooks had known how to spend his millions. Indeed, he had known how to do this so well that it was of him her father, also a financier of some note, had once said he was the only successful American he envied.

She was expected; that she saw the instant the door was opened. This made her entrance easy—an entrance further brightened by the delightful glimpse of a child's cherubic face looking at her from a distant doorway. It was an instantaneous vision, gone as soon as seen; but its effect was to rob the pillared spaces of the wonderful hallway of some of their chill, and to modify in some slight degree the formality of a service which demanded three men to usher her into a small reception-room not twenty feet from the door of entrance.

Left in this secluded spot, she had time to ask herself what member of the household she would be called upon to meet, and was surprised to find that she did not even know of whom the household consisted. She was sure of the fact that Mr. Brooks had been a widower for many years before his death, but beyond that she knew nothing of his domestic life. His son—but was there a son? She had never heard any mention made of a younger Mr. Brooks, yet there was certainly some one of his connection who enjoyed the rights of an heir. Him she must be prepared to meet with a due composure, whatever astonishment he might show at the sight of a slip of a girl instead of the experienced detective he had every right to expect.

But when the door opened to admit the person she was awaiting, the surprise was hers. It was a woman who stood before her, a woman and an oddity. Yet, in just what her oddity lay, Violet found it difficult to decide. Was it in the smoothness of her white locks drawn carefully down over her ears, or in the contrast afforded by her eager eyes and her weak and tremulous mouth? She was dressed in the heaviest of mourning and very expensively, but there was that in her bearing and expression which made it impossible to believe that she took any interest in her garments or even knew in which of her dresses she had been attired.

"I am the person you have come here to see," she said. "Your name is not unfamiliar to me, but you may not know mine. It is Quintard; Mrs. Quintard. I am in difficulty. I need assistance—secret assistance. I did not know where to go for it except to a detective agency; so I telephoned to the first one I saw advertised; and—and I was told to expect Miss Strange. But I didn't think it would be you though I suppose it's all right. You have come here for this purpose, haven't you, though it does seem a little queer?"

"Certainly, Mrs. Quintard; and if you will tell me—"

"My dear, it's just this—yes, I will sit down. Last week my brother died. You have heard of him no doubt, C. Dudley Brooks?"

"Oh, yes; my father knew him—we all knew him by reputation. Do not hurry, Mrs. Quintard. I have sent my car away. You can take all the time you wish."

"No, no, I cannot. I'm in desperate haste. He—but let me go on with my story. My brother was a widower, with no children to inherit. That everybody knows. But his wife left behind her a son by a former husband, and this son of hers my brother had in a measure adopted, and even made his sole heir in a will he drew up during the lifetime of his wife. But when he found, as he very soon did, that this young man was not developing in a way to meet such great responsibilities, he made a new will—though unhappily without the knowledge of the family, or even of his most intimate friends—in which he gave the bulk of his great estate to his nephew Clement, who has bettered the promise of his youth and who besides has children of great beauty whom my brother had learned to love. And this will—this hoarded scrap of paper which means so much to us all, is lost! lost! and I—" here her voice which had risen almost to a scream, sank to a horrified whisper, "am the one who lost it."

"But there's a copy of it somewhere—there is always a copy—"

"Oh, but you haven't heard all. My nephew is an invalid; has been an invalid for years—that's why so little is known about him. He's dying of consumption. The doctors hold out no hope for him, and now, with the fear preying upon him of leaving his wife and children penniless, he is wearing away so fast that any hour may see his end. And I have to meet his eyes—such pitiful eyes—and the look in them is killing me. Yet, I was not to blame. I could not help—Oh, Miss Strange," she suddenly broke in with the inconsequence of extreme feeling, "the will is in the house! I never carried it off the floor where I sleep. Find it; find it, I pray, or—"

The moment had come for Violet's soft touch, for Violet's encouraging word.

"I will try," she answered her.

Mrs. Quintard grew calmer.

"But, first," the young girl continued, "I must know more about the conditions. Where is this nephew of yours—the man who is ill?"

"In this house, where he has been for the last eight months."

"Was the child his of whom I caught a glimpse in the hall as I came in?"

"Yes, and—"

"I will fight for that child!" Violet cried out impulsively. "I am sure his father's cause is good. Where is the other claimant—the one you designate as Carlos?"

"Oh, there's where the trouble is! Carlos is on the Mauretania, and she is due here in a couple of days. He comes from the East where he has been touring with his wife. Miss Strange, the lost will must be found before then, or the other will be opened and read and Carlos made master of this house, which would mean our quick departure and Clement's certain death."

"Move a sick man?—a relative as low as you say he is? Oh no, Mrs. Quintard; no one would do that, were the house a cabin and its owners paupers."

"You do not know Carlos; you do not know his wife. We should not be given a week in which to pack. They have no children and they envy Clement who has. Our only hope lies in discovering the paper which gives us the right to remain here in face of all opposition. That or penury. Now you know my trouble."

"And it is trouble; one from which I shall make every effort to relieve you. But first let me ask if you are not worrying unnecessarily about this missing document? If it was drawn up by Mr. Brooks's lawyer—"

"But it was not," that lady impetuously interrupted. "His lawyer is Carlos's near relative, and has never been told of the change in my brother's intentions. Clement (I am speaking now of my brother and not of my nephew) was a great money-getter, but when it came to standing up for his rights in domestic matters, he was more timid than a child. He was subject to his wife while she lived, and when she was gone, to her relatives, who are all of a dominating character. When he finally made up his mind to do us justice and eliminate Carlos, he went out of town—I wish I could remember where—and had this will drawn up by a stranger, whose name I cannot recall."

Her shaking tones, her nervous manner betrayed a weakness equalling, if not surpassing, that of the brother who dared in secret what he had not strength to acknowledge openly, and it was with some hesitation Violet prepared to ask those definite questions which would elucidate the cause and manner of a loss seemingly so important. She dreaded to hear some commonplace tale of inexcusable carelessness. Something subtler than this— the presence of some unsuspected agency opposed to young Clement's interest; some partisan of Carlos; some secret undermining force in a house full of servants and dependants, seemed necessary for the development of so ordinary a situation into a drama justifying the exercise of her special powers.

"I think I understand now your exact position in the house, as well as the value of the paper which you say you have lost. The next thing for me to hear is how you came to have charge of this paper, and under what circumstances you were led to mislay it. Do you not feel quite ready to tell me?"

"Is—is that necessary?" Mrs. Quintard faltered.

"Very," replied Violet, watching her curiously.

"I didn't expect—that is, I hoped you would be able to point out, by some power we cannot of course explain, just the spot where the paper lies, without having to tell all that. Some people can, you know."

"Ah, I understand. You regarded me as unfit for practical work, and so credited me with occult powers. But that is where you made a mistake, Mrs. Quintard; I'm nothing if not practical. And let me add, that I'm as secret as the grave concerning what my clients tell me. If I am to be of any help to you, I must be made acquainted with every fact involved in the loss of this valuable paper. Relate the whole circumstance or dismiss me from the case. You can have done nothing more foolish or wrong than many—"

"Oh, don't say things like that!" broke in the poor woman in a tone of great indignation. "I have done nothing anyone could call either foolish or wicked. I am simply very unfortunate, and being sensitive—But this isn't telling the story. I'll try to make it all clear; but if I do not, and show any confusion, stop me and help me out with questions. I—I—oh, where shall I begin?"

"With your first knowledge of this second will."

"Thank you, thank you; now I can go on. One night, shortly after my brother had been given up by the physicians, I was called to his bedside for a confidential talk. As he had received that day a very large amount of money from the bank, I thought he was going to hand it over to me for Clement, but it was for something much more serious than this he had summoned me. When he was quite sure that we were alone and nobody anywhere within hearing, he told me that he had changed his mind as to the disposal of his property and that it was to Clement and his children, and not to Carlos, he was going to leave this house and the bulk of his money. That he had had a new will drawn up which he showed me—"

"Showed you?"

"Yes; he made me bring it to him from the safe where he kept it; and, feeble as he was, he was so interested in pointing out certain portions of it that he lifted himself in bed and was so strong and animated that I thought he was getting better. But it was a false strength due to the excitement of the moment, as I saw next day when he suddenly died."

"You were saying that you brought the will to him from his safe. Where was the safe?"

"In the wall over his head. He gave me the key to open it. This key he took from under his pillow. I had no trouble in fitting it or in turning the lock."

"And what happened after you looked at the will?"

"I put it back. He told me to. But the key I kept. He said I was not to part with it again till the time came for me to produce the will."

"And when was that to be?"

"Immediately after the funeral, if it so happened that Carlos had arrived in time to attend it. But if for any reason he failed to be here, I was to let it lie till within three days of his return, when I was to take it out in the presence of a Mr. Delahunt who was to have full charge of it from that time. Oh, I remember all that well enough! and I meant most earnestly to carry out his wishes, but-"

"Go on, Mrs. Quintard, pray go on. What happened? Why couldn't you do what he asked?"

"Because the will was gone when I went to take it out. There was nothing to show Mr. Delahunt but the empty shelf."

"Oh, a theft! just a common theft! Someone overheard the talk you had with your brother. But how about the key? You had that?"

"Yes, I had that."

"Then it was taken from you and returned? You must have been careless as to where you kept it—"

"No, I wore it on a chain about my neck. Though I had no reason to mistrust any one in the house, I felt that I could not guard this key too carefully. I even kept it on at night. In fact it never left me. It was still on my person when I went into the room with Mr. Delahunt. But the safe had been opened for all that."

"There were two keys to it, then?"

"No; in giving me the key, my brother had strictly warned me not to lose it, as it had no duplicate."

"Mrs. Quintard, have you a special confidant or maid?"

"Yes, my Hetty."

"How much did she know about this key?"

"Nothing, but that it didn't help the fit of my dress. Hetty has cared for me for years. There's no more devoted woman in all New York, nor one who can be more relied upon to tell the truth. She is so honest with her tongue that I am bound to believe her even when she says—"

"What?"

"That it was I and nobody else who took the will out of the safe last night. That she saw me come from my brother's room with a folded paper in my hand, pass with it into the library, and come out again without it. If this is so, then that will is somewhere in that great room. But we've looked in every conceivable place except the shelves, where it is useless to search. It would take days to go through them all, and meanwhile Carlos—"

"We will not wait for Carlos. We will begin work at once. But just one other question. How came Hetty to see you in your walk through the rooms? Did she follow you?"

"Yes. It's—it's not the first time I have walked in my sleep. Last night—but she will tell you. It's a painful subject to me. I will send for her to meet us in the library."

"Where you believe this document to lie hidden?"

"Yes."

"I am anxious to see the room. It is upstairs, I believe."

"Yes."

She had risen and was moving rapidly toward the door. Violet eagerly followed her.

Let us accompany her in her passage up the palatial stairway, and realize the effect upon her of a splendour whose future ownership possibly depended entirely upon herself.

It was a cold splendour. The merry voices of children were lacking in these great halls. Death past and to come infused the air with solemnity and mocked the pomp which yet appeared so much a part of the life here that one could hardly imagine the huge pillared spaces without it.

To Violet, more or less accustomed to fine interiors, the chief interest of this one lay in its connection with the mystery then occupying her. Stopping for a moment on the stair, she inquired of Mrs. Quintard if the loss she so deplored had been made known to the servants, and was much relieved to find that, with the exception of Mr. Delahunt, she had not spoken of it to any one but Clement. "And he will never mention it," she declared, "not even to his wife. She has troubles enough to bear without knowing how near she stood to a fortune."

"Oh, she will have her fortune!" Violet confidently replied. "In time, the lawyer who drew up the will will appear. But what you want is an immediate triumph over the cold Carlos, and I hope you may have it. Ah!"

This expletive was a sigh of sheer surprise.

Mrs. Quintard had unlocked the library door and Violet had been given her first glimpse of this, the finest room in New York.

She remembered now that she had often heard it so characterized, and, indeed, had it been taken bodily from some historic abbey of the old world, it could not have expressed more fully, in structure and ornamentation, the Gothic idea at its best. All that it lacked were the associations of vanished centuries, and these, in a measure, were supplied to the imagination by the studied mellowness of its tints and the suggestion of age in its carvings.

So much for the room itself, which was but a shell for holding the great treasure of valuable books ranged along every shelf. As Violet's eyes sped over their ranks and thence to the five windows of deeply stained glass which faced her from the southern end, Mrs. Quintard indignantly exclaimed:

"And Carlos would turn this into a billiard room!"

"I do not like Carlos," Violet returned hotly; then remembering herself, hastened to ask whether Mrs. Quintard was quite positive as to this room being the one in which she had hidden the precious document.

"You had better talk to Hetty," said that lady, as a stout woman of most prepossessing appearance entered their presence and paused respectfully just inside the doorway. "Hetty, you will answer any questions this young lady may put. If anyone can help us, she can. But first, what news from the sick-room?"

"Nothing good. The doctor has just come for the third time today. Mrs. Brooks is crying and even the children are dumb with fear."

"I will go. I must see the doctor. I must tell him to keep Clement alive by any means till—"

She did not wait to say what; but Violet understood and felt her heart grow heavy. Could it be that her employer considered this the gay and easy task she had asked for?

The next minute she was putting her first question:

"Hetty, what did you see in Mrs. Quintard's action last night, to make you infer that she left the missing document in this room?"

The woman's eyes, which had been respectfully studying her face, brightened with a relief which made her communicative. With the self-possession of a perfectly candid nature, she inquiringly remarked:

"My mistress has spoken of her infirmity?"

"Yes, and very frankly."

"She walks in her sleep."

"So she said."

"And sometimes when others are asleep, and she is not."

"She did not tell me that."

"She is a very nervous woman and cannot always keep still when she rouses up at night. When I hear her rise, I get up too; but, never being quite sure whether she is sleeping or not, I am careful to follow her at a certain distance. Last night I was so far behind her that she had been to her brother's room and left it before I saw her face."

"Where is his room and where is hers?"

"Hers is in front on this same floor. Mr. Brooks's is in the rear, and can be reached either by the hall or by passing through this room into a small one beyond, which we called his den."

"Describe your encounter. Where were you standing when you saw her first?"

"In the den I have just mentioned. There was a bright light in the hall behind me and I could see her figure quite plainly. She was holding a folded paper clenched against her breast, and her movement was so mechanical that I was sure she was asleep. She was coming this way, and in another moment she entered this room. The door, which had been open, remained so, and in my anxiety I crept to it and looked in after her. There was no light burning here at that hour, but the moon was shining in in long rays of variously coloured light. If I had followed her—but I did not. I just stood and watched her long enough to see her pass through a blue ray, then through a green one, and then into, if not through, a red one. Expecting her to walk straight on, and having some fears of the staircase once she got into the hall, I hurried around to the door behind you there to head her off. But she had not yet left this room. I waited and waited and still she did not come. Fearing some accident, I finally ventured to approach the door and try it. It was locked. This alarmed me. She had never locked herself in anywhere before and I did not know what to make of it. Some persons would have shouted her name, but I had been warned against doing that, so I simply stood where I was, and eventually I heard the key turn in the lock and saw her come out. She was still walking stiffly, but her hands were empty and hanging at her side."

"And then?"

"She went straight to her room and I after her. I was sure she was dead asleep by this time."

"And she was?"

"Yes, Miss; but still full of what was on her mind. I know this because she stopped when she reached the bedside and began fumbling with the waist of her wrapper. It was for the key she was searching, and when her fingers encountered it hanging on the outside, she opened her wrapper and thrust it in on her bare skin."

"You saw her do all that?"

"As plainly as I see you now. The light in her room was burning brightly."

"And after that?"

"She got into bed. It was I who turned off the light."

"Has that wrapper of hers a pocket?"

"No, Miss."

"Nor her gown?"

"No, Miss."

"So she could not have brought the paper into her room concealed about her person?"

"No, Miss; she left it here. It never passed beyond this doorway."

"But might she not have carried it back to some place of concealment in the rooms she had left?"

The woman's face changed and a slight flush showed through the natural brown of her cheeks.

"No," she disclaimed; "she could not have done that. I was careful to lock the library door behind her before I ran out into the hall."

"Then," concluded Violet, with all the emphasis of conviction, "it is here, and nowhere else we must look for that document till we find it."

Thus assured of the first step in the task she had before her, Miss Strange settled down to business.

The room, which towered to the height of two stories, was in the shape of a huge oval. This oval, separated into narrow divisions for the purpose of accommodating the shelves with which it was lined, narrowed as it rose above the great Gothic chimney-piece and the five gorgeous windows looking towards the south, till it met and was lost in the tracery of the ceiling, which was of that exquisite and soul-satisfying order which we see in the Henry VII chapel in Westminster Abbey. What break otherwise occurred in the circling round of books reaching thus thirty feet or more above the head was made by the two doors already spoken of and a narrow strip of wall at either end of the space occupied by the windows. No furniture was to be seen there except a couple of stalls taken from some old cathedral, which stood in the two bare places just mentioned.

But within, on the extensive floor-space, several articles were grouped, and Violet, recognizing the possibilities which any one of them afforded for the concealment of so small an object as a folded document, decided to use method in her search, and to that end, mentally divided the space before her into four segments.

The first took in the door, communicating with the suite ending in Mr. Brooks's bedroom. A diagram of this segment will show that the only article of furniture in it was a cabinet.

It was at this cabinet Miss Strange made her first stop.

"You have looked this well through?" she asked as she bent over the glass case on top to examine the row of mediaeval missals displayed within in a manner to show their wonderful illuminations.

"Not the case," explained Hetty. "It is locked you see and no one has as yet succeeded in finding the key. But we searched the drawers underneath with the greatest care. Had we sifted the whole contents through our fingers, I could not be more certain that the paper is not there."

Violet stepped into the next segment.

This was the one dominated by the huge fire-place. A rug lay before the hearth. To this Violet pointed.

Quickly the woman answered: "We not only lifted it, but turned it over."

"And that box at the right?"

"Is full of wood and wood only."

"Did you take out this wood?"

"Every stick."

"And those ashes in the fire-place? Something has been burned there."

"Yes; but not lately. Besides, those ashes are all wood ashes. If the least bit of charred paper had been mixed with them, we should have considered the matter settled. But you can see for yourself that no such particle can be found." While saying this, she had put the poker into Violet's hand. "Rake them about, Miss, and make sure."

Violet did so, with the result that the poker was soon put back into place, and she herself down on her knees looking up the chimney.

"Had she thrust it up there," Hetty made haste to remark, "there would have been some signs of soot on her sleeves. They are white and very long and are always getting in her way when she tries to do anything."

Violet left the fire-place after a glance at the mantel-shelf on which nothing stood but a casket of open fretwork, and two coloured photographs mounted on small easels. The casket was too open to conceal anything and the photographs lifted too high above the shelf for even the smallest paper, let alone a document of any size, to hide behind them.

The chairs, of which there were several in this part of the room, she passed with just an inquiring look. They were all of solid oak, without any attempt at upholstery, and although carved to match the stalls on the other side of the room, offered no place for search.

Her delay in the third segment was brief. Here there was absolutely nothing but the door by which she had entered, and the books. As she flitted on, following the oval of the wall, a small frown appeared on her usually smooth forehead. She felt the oppression of the books—the countless books. If indeed, she should find herself obliged to go through them. What a hopeless outlook!

But she had still a segment to consider, and after that the immense table occupying the centre of the room, a table which in its double capacity (for it was as much desk as table) gave more promise of holding the solution of the mystery than anything to which she had hitherto given her attention.

The quarter in which she now stood was the most beautiful, and, possibly, the most precious of them all. In it blazed the five great windows which were the glory of the room; but there are no hiding-places in windows, and much as she revelled in colour, she dared not waste a moment on them. There was more hope for her in the towering stalls, with their possible drawers for books.

But Hetty was before her in the attempt she made to lift the lids of the two great seats.

"Nothing in either," said she; and Violet, with a sigh, turned towards the table.

This was an immense affair, made to accommodate itself to the shape of the room, but with a hollowed-out space on the window-side large enough to hold a chair for the sitter who would use its top as a desk. On it were various articles suitable to its double use. Without being crowded, it displayed a pile of magazines and pamphlets, boxes for stationery, a writing pad with its accompaniments, a lamp, and some few ornaments, among which was a large box, richly inlaid with pearl and ivory, the lid of which stood wide open.

"Don't touch," admonished Violet, as Hetty stretched out her hand to move some little object aside. "You have already worked here busily in the search you made this morning."

"We handled everything."

"Did you go through these pamphlets?"

"We shook open each one. We were especially particular here, since it was at this table I saw Mrs. Quintard stop."

"With head level or drooped?"

"Drooped."

"Like one looking down, rather than up, or around?"

"Yes. A ray of red light shone on her sleeve. It seemed to me the sleeve moved as though she were reaching out."

"Will you try to stand as she did and as nearly in the same place as possible?"

Hetty glanced down at the table edge, marked where the gules dominated the blue and green, and moved to that spot, and paused with her head sinking slowly towards her breast.

"Very good," exclaimed Violet. "But the moon was probably in a very different position from what the sun is now."

"You are right; it was higher up; I chanced to notice it."

"Let me come," said Violet.

Hetty moved, and Violet took her place but in a spot a step or two farther front. This brought her very near to the centre of the table. Hanging her head, just as Hetty had done, she reached out her right hand.

"Have you looked under this blotter?" she asked, pointing towards the pad she touched. "I mean, between the blotter and the frame which holds it?"

"I certainly did," answered Hetty, with some pride.

Violet remained staring down. "Then you took off everything that was lying on it?"

"Oh, yes."

Violet continued to stare down at the blotter. Then impetuously:

"Put them back in their accustomed places."

Hetty obeyed.

Violet continued to look at them, then slowly stretched out her hand, but soon let it fall again with an air of discouragement. Certainly the missing document was not in the ink-pot or the mucilage bottle. Yet something made her stoop again over the pad and subject it to the closest scrutiny.

"If only nothing had been touched!" she inwardly sighed. But she let no sign of her discontent escape her lips, simply exclaiming as she glanced up at the towering spaces overhead: "The books! the books! Nothing remains but for you to call up all the servants, or get men from the outside and, beginning at one end—I should say the upper one—take down every book standing within reach of a woman of Mrs. Quintard's height."

"Hear first what Mrs. Quintard has to say about that," interrupted the woman as that lady entered in a flutter of emotion springing from more than one cause.

"The young lady thinks that we should remove the books," Hetty observed, as her mistress's eye wandered to hers from Violet's abstracted countenance.

"Useless. If we were to undertake to do that, Carlos would be here before half the job was finished. Besides, Hetty must have told you my extreme aversion to nicely bound books. I will not say that when awake I never place my hand on one, but once in a state of somnambulism, when every natural whim has full control, I am sure that I never would. There is a reason for my prejudice. I was not always rich. I once was very poor. It was when I was first married and long before Clement had begun to make his fortune. I was so poor then that frequently I went hungry, and what was worse saw my little daughter cry for food. And why? Because my husband was a bibliomaniac. He would spend on fine editions what would have kept the family comfortable. It is hard to believe, isn't it? I have seen him bring home a Grolier when the larder was as empty as that box; and it made me hate books so, especially those of extra fine binding, that I have to tear the covers off before I can find courage to read them."

O life! life! how fast Violet was learning it!

"I can understand your idea, Mrs. Quintard, but as everything else has failed, I should make a mistake not to examine these shelves. It is just possible that we may be able to shorten the task very materially; that we may not have to call in help, even. To what extent have they been approached, or the books handled, since you discovered the loss of the paper we are looking for?"

"Not at all. Neither of us went near them." This from Hetty.

"Nor any one else?"

"No one else has been admitted to the room. We locked both doors the moment we felt satisfied that the will had been left here."

"That's a relief. Now I may be able to do something. Hetty, you look like a very strong woman, and I, as you see, am very little. Would you mind lifting me up to these shelves? I want to look at them. Not at the books, but at the shelves themselves."

The wondering woman stooped and raised her to the level of the shelf she had pointed out. Violet peered closely at it and then at the ones just beneath.

"Am I heavy?" she asked; "if not, let me see those on the other side of the door."

Hetty carried her over.

Violet inspected each shelf as high as a woman of Mrs. Quintard's stature could reach, and when on her feet again, knelt to inspect the ones below.

"No one has touched or drawn anything from these shelves in twenty-four hours," she declared. "The small accumulation of dust along their edges has not been disturbed at any point. It was very different with the table-top. That shows very plainly where you had moved things and where you had not."

"Was that what you were looking for? Well, I never!"

Violet paid no heed; she was thinking and thinking very deeply.

Hetty turned towards her mistress, then quickly back to Violet, whom she seized by the arm.

"What's the matter with Mrs. Quintard?" she hurriedly asked. "If it were night, I should think that she was in one of her spells."

Violet started and glanced where Hetty pointed. Mrs. Quintard was within a few feet of them, but as oblivious of their presence as though she stood alone in the room. Possibly, she thought she did. With fixed eyes and mechanical step she began to move straight towards the table, her whole appearance of a nature to make Hetty's blood run cold, but to cause that of Violet's to bound through her veins with renewed hope.

"The one thing I could have wished!" she murmured under her breath. "She has fallen into a trance. She is again under the dominion of her idea. If we watch and do not disturb her she may repeat her action of last night, and herself show where she has put this precious document."

Meanwhile Mrs. Quintard continued to advance. A moment more, and her smooth white locks caught the ruddy glow centred upon the chair standing in the hollow of the table. Words were leaving her lips, and her hand, reaching out over the blotter, groped among the articles scattered there till it settled on a large pair of shears.

"Listen," muttered Violet to the woman pressing close to her side. "You are acquainted with her voice; catch what she says if you can."

Hetty could not; an undistinguishable murmur was all that came to her ears.

Violet took a step nearer. Mrs. Quintard's hand had left the shears and was hovering uncertainly in the air. Her distress was evident. Her head, no longer steady on her shoulders, was turning this way and that, and her tones becoming inarticulate.

"Paper! I want paper" burst from her lips in a shrill unnatural cry.

But when they listened for more and watched to see the uncertain hand settle somewhere, she suddenly came to herself and turned upon them a startled glance, which speedily changed into one of the utmost perplexity.

"What am I doing here?" she asked. "I have a feeling as if I had almost seen—almost touched—oh, it's gone! and all is blank again. Why couldn't I keep it till I knew—" Then she came wholly to herself and, forgetting even the doubts of a moment since, remarked to Violet in her old tremulous fashion:

"You asked us to pull down the books? But you've evidently thought better of it."

"Yes, I have thought better of it." Then, with a last desperate hope of re-arousing the visions lying somewhere back in Mrs. Quintard's troubled brain, Violet ventured to observe: "This is likely to resolve itself into a psychological problem, Mrs. Quintard. Do you suppose that if you fell again into the condition of last night, you would repeat your action and so lead us yourself to where the will lies hidden?"

"Possibly; but it may be weeks before I walk again in my sleep, and meanwhile Carlos will have arrived, and Clement, possibly, died. My nephew is so low that the doctor is coming back at midnight. Miss Strange, Clement is a man in a thousand. He says he wants to see you. Would you be willing to accompany me to his room for a moment? He will not make many more requests and I will take care that the interview is not prolonged."

"I will go willingly. But would it not be better to wait—"

"Then you may never see him at all."

"Very well; but I wish I had some better news to give."

"That will come later. This house was never meant for Carlos. Hetty, you will stay here. Miss Strange, let us go now."

"You need not speak; just let him see you."

Violet nodded and followed Mrs. Quintard into the sick-room.

The sight which met her eyes tried her young emotions deeply. Staring at her from the bed, she saw two piercing eyes over whose brilliance death as yet had gained no control. Clements's soul was in that gaze; Clement halting at the brink of dissolution to sound the depths behind him for the hope which would make departure easy. Would he see in her, a mere slip of a girl dressed in fashionable clothes and bearing about her all the marks of social distinction, the sort of person needed for the task upon the success of which depended his darlings' future? She could hardly expect it. Yet as she continued to meet his gaze with all the seriousness the moment demanded, she beheld those burning orbs lose some of their demand and the fingers, which had lain inert upon the bedspread, flutter gently and move as if to draw attention to his wife and the three beautiful children clustered at the foot-board.

He had not spoken nor could she speak, but the solemnity with which she raised her right hand as to a listening Heaven called forth upon his lips what was possibly his last smile, and with the memory of this faint expression of confidence on his part, she left the room, to make her final attempt to solve the mystery of the missing document.

Facing the elderly lady in the hall, she addressed her with the force and soberness of one leading a forlorn hope:

"I want you to concentrate your mind upon what I have to say to you. Do you think you can do this?"

"I will try," replied the poor woman with a backward glance at the door which had just been closed upon her.

"What we want," said she, "is, as I stated before, an insight into the workings of your brain at the time you took the will from the safe. Try and follow what I have to say, Mrs. Quintard. Dreams are no longer regarded by scientists as prophecies of the future or even as spontaneous and irrelevant conditions of thought, but as reflections of a near past, which can almost without exception be traced back to the occurrences which caused them. Your action with the will had its birth in some previous line of thought afterwards forgotten. Let us try and find that thought. Recall, if you can, just what you did or read yesterday."

Mrs. Quintard looked frightened.

"But, I have no memory," she objected. "I forget quickly, so quickly that in order to fulfill my engagements I have to keep a memorandum of every day's events. Yesterday? yesterday? What did I do yesterday? I went downtown for one thing, but I hardly know where."

"Perhaps your memorandum of yesterday's doings will help you."

"I will get it. But it won't give you the least help. I keep it only for my own eye, and—"

"Never mind; let me see it."

And she waited impatiently for it to be put in her hands.

But when she came to read the record of the last two days, this was all she found:

Saturday: Mauretania nearly due. I must let Mr. Delahunt know today that he's wanted here to-morrow. Hetty will try on my dresses. Says she has to alter them. Mrs. Peabody came to lunch, and we in such trouble! Had to go down street. Errand for Clement. The will, the will! I think of nothing else. Is it safe where it is? No peace of mind till to-morrow. Clement better this afternoon. Says he must live till Carlos gets back; not to triumph over him, but to do what he can to lessen his disappointment. My good Clement!

So nervous, I went to pasting photographs, and was forgetting all my troubles when Hetty brought in another dress to try on.

Quiet in the great house, during which the clock on the staircase sent forth seven musical peals. To Violet waiting alone in the library, they acted as a summons. She was just leaving the room, when the sound of hubbub in the hall below held her motionless in the doorway. An automobile had stopped in front, and several persons were entering the house, in a gay and unseemly fashion. As she stood listening, uncertain of her duty, she perceived the frenzied figure of Mrs. Quintard approaching. As she passed by, she dropped one word: "Carlos!" Then she went staggering on, to disappear a moment later down the stairway.

This vision lost, another came. This time it was that of Clements's wife leaning from the marble balustrade above, the shadow of approaching grief battling with the present terror in her perfect features. Then she too withdrew from view and Violet, left for the moment alone in the great hall, stepped back into the library and began to put on her hat.

The lights had been turned up in the grand salon and it was in this scene of gorgeous colour that Mrs. Quintard came face to face with Carlos Pelacios. Those who were witness to her entrance say that she presented a noble appearance, as with the resolution of extreme desperation she stood waiting for his first angry attack.

He, a short, thick-set, dark man, showing both in features and expression the Spanish blood of his paternal ancestors, started to address her in tones of violence, but changed his note, as he met her eye, to one simply sardonic.

"You here!" he began. "I assure you, madame, that it is a pleasure which is not without its inconveniences. Did you not receive my cablegram requesting this house to be made ready for my occupancy?"

"I did."

"Then why do I find guests here? They do not usually precede the arrival of their host."

"Clement is very ill—"

"So much the greater reason that he should have been removed—"

"You were not expected for two days yet. You cabled that you were coming on the Mauretania."

"Yes, I cabled that. Elisabetta,"—this to his wife standing silently in the background—"we will go to the Plaza for tonight. At three o'clock tomorrow we shall expect to find this house in readiness for our return. Later, if Mrs. Quintard desires to visit us we shall be pleased to receive her. But"—this to Mrs. Quintard herself—"you must come without Clement and the kids."

Mrs. Quintard's rigid hand stole up to her throat.

"Clement is dying. He is failing hourly," she murmured. "He may not live till morning."

Even Carlos was taken aback by this. "Oh, well!" said he, "we will give you two days."

Mrs. Quintard gasped, then she walked straight up to him.

"You will give us all the time his condition requires and more, much more. He is the real owner of this house, not you. My brother left a will bequeathing it to him. You are my nephew's guests, and not he yours. As his representative I entreat you and your wife to remain here until you can find a home to your mind."

The silence seethed. Carlos had a temper of fire and so had his wife. But neither spoke, till he had gained sufficient control over himself to remark without undue rancour:

"I did not think you had the wit to influence your brother to this extent; otherwise, I should have cut my travels short." Then harshly: "Where is this will?"

"It will be produced." But the words faltered.

Carlos glanced at the man standing behind his wife; then back at Mrs. Quintard.

"Wills are not scribbled off on deathbeds; or if they are, it needs something more than a signature to legalize them. I don't believe in this trick of a later will. Mr. Cavanagh"—here he indicated the gentleman accompanying them— "has done my father's business for years, and he assured me that the paper he holds in his pocket is the first, last, and only expression of your brother's wishes. If you are in a position to deny this, show us the document you mention; show us it at once, or inform us where and in whose hands it can be found."

"That, for—for reasons I cannot give, I must refuse to do at present. But I am ready to swear—"

A mocking laugh cut her short. Did it issue from his lips or from those of his highstrung and unfeeling wife? It might have come from either; there was cause enough.

"Oh!" she faltered, "may God have mercy!" and was sinking before their eyes, when she heard her name, called from the threshold, and, looking that way, saw Hetty beaming upon her, backed by a little figure with a face so radiant that instinctively her hand went out to grasp the folded sheet of paper Hetty was seeking to thrust upon her.

"Ah!" she cried, in a great voice, "you will not have to wait, nor Clement either. Here is the will! The children have come into their own." And she fell at their feet in a dead faint.

"Where did you find it? Oh! where did you find it? I have waited a week to know. When, after Carlos's sudden departure, I stood beside Clement's death-bed and saw from the look he gave me that he could still feel and understand, I told him that you had succeeded in your task and that all was well with us. But I was not able to tell him how you had succeeded or in what place the will had been found; and he died, unknowing. But we may know, may we not, now that he is laid away and there is no more talk of our leaving this house?"

Violet smiled, but very tenderly, and in a way not to offend the mourner. They were sitting in the library—the great library which was to remain in

Clement's family after all—and it amused her to follow the dreaming lady's glances as they ran in irrepressible curiosity over the walls. Had Violet wished, she could have kept her secret forever. These eyes would never have discovered it.

But she was of a sympathetic temperament, our Violet, so after a moment's delay, during which she satisfied herself that little, if anything, had been touched in the room since her departure from it a week before, she quietly observed:

"You were right in persisting that you hid it in this room. It was here I found it. Do you notice that photograph on the mantel which does not stand exactly straight on its easel?"

"Yes."

"Supposing you take it down. You can reach it, can you not?"

"Oh, yes. But what—"

"Lift it down, dear Mrs. Quintard; and then turn it round and look at its back."

Agitated and questioning, the lady did as she was bid, and at the first glance gave a cry of surprise, if not of understanding. The square of brown paper, acting as a backing to the picture, was slit across, disclosing a similar one behind it which was still intact.

"Oh! was it hidden in here?" she asked.

"Very completely," assented Violet. "Pasted in out of sight by a lady who amuses herself with mounting and framing photographs. Usually, she is conscious of her work, but this time she performed her task in a dream."

Mrs. Quintard was all amazement.

"I don't remember touching these pictures," she declared. "I never should have remembered. You are a wonderful person, Miss Strange. How came you to think these photographs might have two backings? There was nothing to show that this was so."

"I will tell you, Mrs. Quintard. You helped me."

"I helped you?"

"Yes. You remember the memorandum you gave me? In it you mentioned pasting photographs. But this was not enough in itself to lead me to examine those on the mantel, if you had not given me another suggestion a little while before. We did not tell you this, Mrs. Quintard, at the time, but during the search we were making here that day, you had a lapse into that peculiar state which induces you to walk in your sleep. It was a short one, lasting but a moment, but in a moment one can speak, and, this you did—"

"Spoke? I spoke?"

"Yes, you uttered the word 'paper!' not the paper, but 'paper!' and reached out towards the shears. Though I had not much time to think of it then, afterwards upon reading your memorandum I recalled your words, and asked myself if it was not paper to cut, rather than to hide, you wanted. If it was to cut, and you were but repeating the experience of the night before, then the room should contain some remnants of cut paper. Had we seen any? Yes, in the basket, under the desk we had taken out and thrown back again a strip or so of wrapping paper, which, if my memory did not fail me, showed a clean-cut edge. To pull this strip out again and spread it flat upon the desk was the work of a minute, and what I saw led me to look all over the room, not now for the folded document, but for a square of brown paper, such as had been taken out of this larger sheet. Was I successful? Not for a long while, but when I came to the photographs on the mantel and saw how nearly they corresponded in shape and size to what I was looking for, I recalled again your fancy for mounting photographs and felt that the mystery was solved.

"A glance at the back of one of them brought disappointment, but when I turned about its mate—You know what I found underneath the outer paper. You had laid the will against the original backing and simply pasted another one over it.

"That the discovery came in time to cut short a very painful interview has made me joyful for a week.

"And now may I see the children?"

END OF PROBLEM V

THE HOUSE OF CLOCKS

I

Miss Strange was not in a responsive mood. This her employer had observed on first entering; yet he showed no hesitation in laying on the table behind which she had ensconced herself in the attitude of one besieged, an envelope thick with enclosed papers.

"There," said he. "Telephone me when you have read them."

"I shall not read them."

"No?" he smiled; and, repossessing himself of the envelope, he tore off one end, extracted the sheets with which it was filled, and laid them down still unfolded, in their former place on the table-top.

The suggestiveness of the action caused the corners of Miss Srange's delicate lips to twitch wistfully, before settling into an ironic smile.

Calmly the other watched her.

"I am on a vacation," she loftily explained, as she finally met his studiously non-quizzical glance. "Oh, I know that I am in my own home!" she petulantly acknowledged, as his gaze took in the room; "and that the automobile is at the door; and that I'm dressed for shopping. But for all that I'm on a vacation—a mental one," she emphasized; "and business must wait. I haven't got over the last affair," she protested, as he maintained a discreet silence, "and the season is so gay just now—so many balls, so many—But that isn't the worst. Father is beginning to wake up—and if he ever suspects—" A significant gesture ended this appeal.

The personage knew her father—everyone did—and the wonder had always been that she dared run the risk of displeasing one so implacable. Though she was his favourite child, Peter Strange was known to be quite capable of cutting her off with a shilling, once his close, prejudiced mind conceived it to be his duty. And that he would so interpret the situation, if he ever came to learn the secret of his daughter's fits of abstraction and the sly bank account she was slowly accumulating, the personage holding out this dangerous lure had no doubt at all. Yet he only smiled at her words and remarked in casual suggestion:

"It's out of town this time—'way out. Your health certainly demands a change of air."

"My health is good. Fortunately, or unfortunately, as one may choose to look at it, it furnishes me with no excuse for an outing," she steadily retorted, turning her back on the table.

"Ah, excuse me!" the insidious voice apologized, "your paleness misled me. Surely a night or two's change might be beneficial."

She gave him a quick side look, and began to adjust her boa.

To this hint he paid no attention.

"The affair is quite out of the ordinary," he pursued in the tone of one rehearsing a part. But there he stopped. For some reason, not altogether apparent to the masculine mind, the pin of flashing stones (real stones) which held her hat in place had to be taken out and thrust back again, not once, but twice. It was to watch this performance he had paused. When he was ready to proceed, he took the musing tone of one marshalling facts for another's enlightenment:

"A woman of unknown instincts—"

"Pshaw!" The end of the pin would strike against the comb holding Violet's chestnut-coloured locks.

"Living in a house as mysterious as the secret it contains. But—" here he allowed his patience apparently to forsake him, "I will bore you no longer. Go to your teas and balls; I will struggle with my dark affairs alone."

His hand went to the packet of papers she affected so ostentatiously to despise. He could be as nonchalant as she. But he did not lift them; he let them lie. Yet the young heiress had not made a movement or even turned the slightest glance his way.

"A woman difficult to understand! A mysterious house—possibly a mysterious crime!"

Thus Violet kept repeating in silent self-communion, as flushed with dancing she sat that evening in a highly-scented conservatory, dividing her attention between the compliments of her partner and the splash of a fountain bubbling in the heart of this mass of tropical foliage; and when some hours later she sat down in her chintz-furnished bedroom for a few minutes' thought before retiring, it was to draw from a little oak box at her elbow the half-dozen or so folded sheets of closely written paper which had been left for her perusal by her persistent employer.

Glancing first at the signature and finding it to be one already favourably known at the bar, she read with avidity the statement of events thus vouched for, finding them curious enough in all conscience to keep her awake for another full hour.

We here subscribe it:

I am a lawyer with an office in the Times Square Building. My business is mainly local, but sometimes I am called out of town, as witness the following summons received by me on the fifth of last October.

DEAR SIR,—

I wish to make my will. I am an invalid and cannot leave my room. Will you come to me? The enclosed reference will answer for my respectability. If it satisfies you and you decide to accommodate me, please hasten your visit; I have not many days to live. A carriage will meet you at Highland Station at any hour you designate. Telegraph reply.

A. Postlethwaite,
Gloom Cottage,
——
N. J.

The reference given was a Mr. Weed of Eighty-sixth Street—a well-known man of unimpeachable reputation.

Calling him up at his business office, I asked him what he could tell me about Mr. Postlethwaite of Gloom Cottage, ——, N. J. The answer astonished me:

"There is no Mr. Postlethwaite to be found at that address. He died years ago. There is a Mrs. Postlethwaite—a confirmed paralytic. Do you mean her?"

I glanced at the letter still lying open at the side of the telephone:

"The signature reads A. Postlethwaite."

"Then it's she. Her name is Arabella. She hates the name, being a woman of no sentiment. Uses her initials even on her cheques. What does she want of you?"

"To draw her will."

"Oblige her. It'll be experience for you." And he slammed home the receiver.

I decided to follow the suggestion so forcibly emphasized; and the next day saw me at Highland Station. A superannuated horse and a still more superannuated carriage awaited me—both too old to serve a busy man in these days of swift conveyance. Could this be a sample of the establishment I was about to enter? Then I remembered that the woman who had sent for me was a helpless invalid, and probably had no use for any sort of turnout.

The driver was in keeping with the vehicle, and as noncommittal as the plodding beast he drove. If I ventured upon a remark, he gave me a long and curious look; if I went so far as to attack him with a direct question, he responded with a hitch of the shoulder or a dubious smile which conveyed nothing. Was he deaf or just unpleasant? I soon learned that he was not deaf; for suddenly, after a jog-trot of a mile or so through a wooded road which we had entered from the main highway, he drew in his horse, and, without glancing my way, spoke his first word:

"This is where you get out. The house is back there in the bushes."

As no house was visible and the bushes rose in an unbroken barrier along the road, I stared at him in some doubt of his sanity.

"But—" I began; a protest into which he at once broke, with the sharp direction:

"Take the path. It'll lead you straight to the front door."

"I don't see any path."

For this he had no answer; and confident from his expression that it would be useless to expect anything further from him, I dropped a coin into his hand, and jumped to the ground. He was off before I could turn myself about.

"'Something is rotten in the State of Denmark,'" I quoted in startled comment to myself; and not knowing what else to do, stared down at the turf at my feet.

A bit of flagging met my eye, protruding from a layer of thick moss. Farther on I espied another—the second, probably, of many. This, no doubt, was the path I had been bidden to follow, and without further thought on the subject, I plunged into the bushes which with difficulty I made give way before me.

For a moment all further advance looked hopeless. A more tangled, uninviting approach to a so-called home, I had never seen outside of the tropics; and the complete neglect thus displayed should have prepared me for the appearance of the house I unexpectedly came upon, just as, the way seemed on the point of closing up before me.

But nothing could well prepare one for a first view of Gloom Cottage. Its location in a hollow which had gradually filled itself up with trees and some kind of prickly brush, its deeply stained walls, once picturesque enough in their grouping but too deeply hidden now amid rotting boughs to produce any other effect than that of shrouded desolation, the sough of these same boughs as they rapped a devil's tattoo against each other, and the absence of even the rising column of smoke which bespeaks domestic life wherever seen—all gave to one who remembered the cognomen Cottage and forgot the pre-cognomen of Gloom, a sense of buried life as sepulchral as that which emanates from the mouth of some freshly opened tomb.

But these impressions, natural enough to my youth, were necessarily transient, and soon gave way to others more business-like. Perceiving the curve of an arch rising above the undergrowth still blocking my approach, I pushed my way resolutely through, and presently found myself stumbling upon the steps of an unexpectedly spacious domicile, built not of wood, as its name of Cottage had led me to expect, but of carefully cut stone which, while showing every mark of time, proclaimed itself one of those early, carefully erected Colonial residences which it takes more than a century to destroy, or even to wear to the point of dilapidation.

Somewhat encouraged, though failing to detect any signs of active life in the heavily shuttered windows frowning upon me from either side, I ran up the steps and rang the bell which pulled as hard as if no hand had touched it in years.

Then I waited.

But not to ring again; for just as my hand was approaching the bell a second time, the door fell back and I beheld in the black gap before me the oldest man I had ever come upon in my whole life. He was so old I was astonished when his drawn lips opened and he asked if I was the lawyer from New York. I would as soon have expected a mummy to wag its tongue and utter English, he looked so thin and dried and removed from this life and all worldly concerns.

But when I had answered his question and he had turned to marshal me down the hall towards a door I could dimly see standing open in the twilight of an absolutely sunless interior, I noticed that his step was not without some vigour, despite the feeble bend of his withered body and the incessant swaying of his head, which seemed to be continually saying No!

"I will prepare madam," he admonished me, after drawing a ponderous curtain two inches or less aside from one of the windows. "She is very ill, but she will see you."

The tone was senile, but it was the senility of an educated man, and as the cultivated accents wavered forth, my mind changed in, regard to the position he held in the house. Interested anew, I sought to give him another look, but he had already vanished through the doorway, and so noiselessly, it was more like a shadow's flitting than a man's withdrawal.

The darkness in which I sat was absolute; but gradually, as I continued to look about me, the spaces lightened and certain details came out, which to my astonishment were of a character to show that the plain if substantial exterior of this house with its choked-up approaches and weedy gardens was no sample of what was to be found inside. Though the walls surrounding me were dismal because unlighted, they betrayed a splendour unusual in any country house. The frescoes and paintings were of an ancient order, dating from days when life and not death reigned in this isolated dwelling; but in them high art reigned supreme, an art so high and so finished that only great wealth, combined with the most cultivated taste, could have produced such effects. I was still absorbed in the wonder of it all, when the quiet voice of the old gentleman who had let me in reached me again from the doorway, and I heard:

"Madam is ready for you. May I trouble you to accompany me to her room."

I rose with alacrity. I was anxious to see madam, if only to satisfy myself that she was as interesting as the house in which she was self-immured.

I found her a great deal more so. But before I enter upon our interview, let me mention a fact which had attracted my attention in my passage to her room. During his absence my guide evidently had pulled aside other curtains than those of the room in which he had left me. The hall, no longer a tunnel of darkness, gave me a glimpse as we went by, of various secluded corners, and it seemed as if everywhere I looked I saw—a clock. I counted four before I reached the staircase, all standing on the floor and all of ancient make, though differing much in appearance and value. A fifth one rose grim and tall at the stair foot, and under an impulse I have never understood I stopped, when I reached it, to note the time. But it had paused in its task, and faced me with motionless hands and silent works—a fact which somehow startled me; perhaps, because just then I encountered the old man's eye watching me with an expression as challenging as it was unintelligible.

I had expected to see a woman in bed. I saw instead, a woman sitting up. You felt her influence the moment you entered her presence. She was not young; she was not beautiful;—never had been I should judge,—she had not even the usual marks about her of an ultra strong personality; but that her will was law, had always been, and would continue to be law so long as she lived, was patent to any eye at the first glance. She exacted obedience consciously and unconsciously, and she exacted it with charm. Some few people in the world possess this power. They frown, and the opposing will weakens; they smile, and all hearts succumb. I was hers from the moment I crossed the threshold till—But I will relate the happenings of that instant when it comes.

She was alone, or so I thought, when I made my first bow to her stern but not unpleasing presence. Seated in a great chair, with a silver tray before her containing such little matters as she stood in hourly need of, she confronted me with a piercing gaze startling to behold in eyes so colourless. Then she smiled, and in obedience to that smile I seated myself in a chair placed very near her own. Was she too paralysed to express herself clearly? I waited in some anxiety till she spoke, when this fear vanished. Her voice betrayed the character her features failed to express. It was firm, resonant, and instinct with command. Not loud, but penetrating, and of a quality which made one listen with his heart as well as with his ears. What she said is immaterial. I was there for a certain purpose and we entered immediately upon the business of that purpose. She talked and I listened, mostly without comment. Only once did I interrupt her with a suggestion; and as this led to definite results, I will proceed to relate the occurrence in full.

In the few hours remaining to me before leaving New York, I had learned (no matter how) some additional particulars concerning herself and family; and when after some minor bequests, she proceeded to name the parties to whom she desired to leave the bulk of her fortune, I ventured, with some astonishment at my own temerity, to remark:

"But you have a young relative! Is she not to be included in this partition of your property?"

A hush. Then a smile came to life on her stiff lips, such as is seldom seen, thank God, on the face of any woman, and I heard:

"The young relative of whom you speak, is in the room. She has known for some time that I have no intention of leaving anything to her. There is, in fact, small chance of her ever needing it."

The latter sentence was a muttered one, but that it was loud enough to be heard in all parts of the room I was soon assured. For a quick sigh, which was almost a gasp, followed from a corner I had hitherto ignored, and upon glancing that way, I perceived, peering upon us from the shadows, the white face of a young girl in whose drawn features and wide, staring eyes I beheld such evidences of terror, that in an instant, whatever predilection I had hitherto felt for my client, vanished in distrust, if not positive aversion.

I was still under the sway of this new impression, when Mrs. Postlethwaite's voice rose again, this time addressing the young girl:

"You may go," she said, with such force in the command for all its honeyed modulation, that I expected to see its object fly the room in frightened obedience.

But though the startled girl had lost none of the terror which had made her face like a mask, no power of movement remained to her. A picture of hopeless misery, she stood for one breathless moment, with her eyes fixed in unmistakable appeal on mine; then she began to sway so helplessly that I leaped with bounding heart to catch her. As she fell into my arms I heard her sigh as before. No common anguish spoke in that sigh. I had stumbled unwittingly upon a tragedy, to the meaning of which I held but a doubtful key.

"She seems very ill," I observed with some emphasis, as I turned to lay my helpless burden on a near-by sofa.

"She's doomed."

The words were spoken with gloom and with an attempt at commiseration which no longer rang true in my ears.

"She is as sick a woman as I am myself," continued Mrs. Postlethwaite. "That is why I made the remark I did, never imagining she would hear me at that distance. Do not put her down. My nurse will be here in a moment to relieve you of your burden."

A tinkle accompanied these words. The resolute woman had stretched out a finger, of whose use she was not quite deprived, and touched a little bell standing on the tray before her, an inch or two from her hand.

Pleased to obey her command, I paused at the sofa's edge, and taking advantage of the momentary delay, studied the youthful countenance pressed unconsciously to my breast.

It was one whose appeal lay less in its beauty, though that was of a touching quality, than in the story it told,—a story, which for some unaccountable reason—I did not pause to determine what one—I felt it to be my immediate duty to know. But I asked no questions then; I did not even venture a comment; and yielded her up with seeming readiness when a strong but none too intelligent woman came running in with arms outstretched to carry her off. When the door had closed upon these two, the silence of my client drew my attention back to herself.

"I am waiting," was her quiet observation, and without any further reference to what had just taken place under our eyes, she went on with the business previously occupying us.

I was able to do my part without any too great display of my own disturbance. The clearness of my remarkable client's instructions, the definiteness with which her mind was made up as to the disposal of every dollar of her vast property, made it easy for me to master each detail and make careful note of every wish. But this did not prevent the ebb and flow within me of an undercurrent of thought full of question and uneasiness. What had been the real purport of the scene to which I had just been made a surprised witness? The few, but certainly unusual, facts which had been given me in regard to the extraordinary relations existing between these two closely connected women will explain the intensity of my interest. Those facts shall be yours.

Arabella Merwin, when young, was gifted with a peculiar fascination which, as we have seen, had not altogether vanished with age. Consequently she had many lovers, among them two brothers, Frank and Andrew Postlethwaite. The latter was the older, the handsomer, and the most prosperous (his name is remembered yet in connection with South American schemes of large importance), but it was Frank she married.

That real love, ardent if unreasonable, lay at the bottom of her choice, is evident enough to those who followed the career of the young couple. But it was a jealous love which brooked no rival, and as Frank Postlethwaite was of an impulsive and erratic nature, scenes soon occurred between them which, while revealing the extraordinary force of the young wife's character, led to no serious break till after her son was born, and this, notwithstanding the fact that Frank had long given up making a living, and that they were openly dependent on their wealthy brother, now fast approaching the millionaire status.

This brother—the Peruvian King, as some called him—must have been an extraordinary man. Though cherishing his affection for the spirited Arabella to the point of remaining a bachelor for her sake, he betrayed none of the usual signs of disappointed love; but on the contrary made every effort to advance her happiness, not only by assuring to herself and husband an adequate income, but by doing all he could in other and less open ways to lessen any sense she might entertain of her mistake in preferring for her lifemate his self-centred and unstable brother. She should have adored him; but though she evinced gratitude enough, there is nothing to prove that she ever gave Frank Postlethwaite the least cause to cherish any other sentiment towards his brother than that of honest love and unqualified respect. Perhaps he never did cherish any other. Perhaps the change which everyone saw in the young couple immediately after the birth of their only child was due to another cause. Gossip is silent on this point. All that it insists upon is that from this time evidences of a growing estrangement between them became so obvious that even the indulgent Andrew could not blind himself to it; showing his sense of trouble, not by lessening their income, for that he doubled, but by spending more time in Peru and less in New York where the two were living.

However,—and here we enter upon those details which I have ventured to characterize as uncommon, he was in this country and in the actual company of his brother when the accident occurred which terminated both their lives. It was the old story of a skidding motor, and Mrs. Postlethwaite, having been sent for in great haste to the small inn into which the two injured men had been carried, arrived only in time to witness their last moments. Frank died first and Andrew some few minutes later—an important fact, as was afterwards shown when the latter's will came to be read.

This will was a peculiar one. By its provisions the bulk of the King's great property was left to his brother Frank, but with this especial stipulation that in case his brother failed to survive him, the full legacy as bequeathed to him should be given unconditionally to his widow. Frank's demise, as I have already stated, preceded his brother's by several minutes and consequently Arabella became the chief legatee; and that is how she obtained her millions. But—and here a startling feature comes in—when the will came to be administered, the secret underlying the break between Frank and his wife was brought to light by a revelation of the fact that he had practised a great deception upon her at the time of his marriage. Instead of being a bachelor as was currently believed, he was in reality a widower, and the father of a child. This fact, so long held secret, had become hers when her own child was born; and constituted as she was, she not only never forgave the father, but conceived such a hatred for the innocent object of their quarrel that she refused to admit its claims or even to acknowledge its existence.

But later—after his death, in fact—she showed some sense of obligation towards one who under ordinary conditions would have shared her wealth. When the whole story became heard, and she discovered that this secret had been kept from his brother as well as from herself, and that consequently no provision had been made in any way for the child thus thrown directly upon her mercy, she did the generous thing and took the forsaken girl into her own home. But she never betrayed the least love for her, her whole heart being bound up in her boy, who was, as all agree, a prodigy of talent.

But this boy, for all his promise and seeming strength of constitution, died when barely seven years old, and the desolate mother was left with nothing to fill her heart but the uncongenial daughter of her husband's first wife. The fact that this child, slighted as it had hitherto been, would, in the event of her uncle having passed away before her father, have been the undisputed heiress of a large portion of the wealth now at the disposal of her arrogant step-mother, led many to expect, now that the boy was no more, that Mrs. Postlethwaite would proceed to acknowledge the little Helena as her heir, and give her that place in the household to which her natural claims entitled her.

But no such result followed. The passion of grief into which the mother was thrown by the shipwreck of all her hopes left her hard and implacable, and when, as very soon happened, she fell a victim to the disease which tied her to her chair and made the wealth which had come to her by such a peculiar ordering of circumstances little else than a mockery even in her own eyes, it was upon this child she expended the full fund of her secret bitterness.

And the child? What of her? How did she bear her unhappy fate when she grew old enough to realize it? With a resignation which was the wonder of all who knew her. No murmurs escaped her lips, nor was the devotion she invariably displayed to the exacting invalid who ruled her as well as all the rest of her household with a rod of iron ever disturbed by the least sign of reproach. Though the riches, which in those early days poured into the home in a measure far beyond the needs of its mistress, were expended in making the house beautiful rather than in making the one young life within it happy, she never was heard to utter so much as a wish to leave the walls within which fate had immured her. Content, or seemingly content, with the only home she knew, she never asked for change or demanded friends or amusements. Visitors ceased coming; desolation followed neglect. The garden, once a glory, succumbed to a riot of weeds and undesirable brush, till a towering wall seemed to be drawn about the house cutting it off from the activities of the world as it cut it off from the approach of sunshine by day, and the comfort of a star-lit heaven by night. And yet the young girl continued to smile, though with a pitifulness of late, which some thought betokened secret terror and others the wasting of a body too sensitive for such unwholesome seclusion.

These were the facts, known if not consciously specialized, which gave to the latter part of my interview with Mrs. Postlethwaite a poignancy of interest which had never attended any of my former experiences. The peculiar attitude of Miss Postlethwaite towards her indurate tormentor awakened in my agitated mind something much deeper than curiosity, but when I strove to speak her name with the intent of inquiring more particularly into her condition, such a look confronted me from the steady eye immovably fixed upon my own, that my courage—or was it my natural precaution—bade me subdue the impulse and risk no attempt which might betray the depth of my interest in one so completely outside the scope of the present moment's business. Perhaps Mrs. Postlethwaite appreciated my struggle; perhaps she was wholly blind to it. There was no reading the mind of this woman of sentimental name but inflexible nature, and realizing the fact more fully with every word she uttered I left her at last with no further betrayal of my feelings than might be evinced by the earnestness with which I promised to return for her signature at the earliest possible moment.

This she had herself requested, saying as I rose:

"I can still write my name if the paper is pushed carefully along under my hand. See to it that you come while the power remains to me."

I had hoped that in my passage downstairs I might run upon someone who would give me news of Miss Postlethwaite, but the woman who approached to conduct me downstairs was not of an appearance to invite confidence, and I felt forced to leave the house with my doubts unsatisfied.

Two memories, equally distinct, followed me. One was a picture of Mrs. Postlethwaite's fingers groping among her belongings on the little tray perched upon her lap, and another of the intent and strangely bent figure of the old man who had acted as my usher, listening to the ticking of one of the great clocks. So absorbed was he in this occupation that he not only failed to notice me when I went by, but he did not even lift his head at my cheery greeting. Such mysteries were too much for me, and led me to postpone my departure from town till I had sought out Mrs. Postlethwaite's doctor and propounded to him one or two leading questions. First, would Mrs. Postlethwaite's present condition be likely to hold good till Monday; and secondly, was the young lady living with her as ill as her step-mother said.

He was a mild old man of the easy-going type, and the answers I got from him were far from satisfactory. Yet he showed some surprise when I mentioned the extent of Mrs. Postlethwaite's anxiety about her step-daughter, and paused, in the dubious shaking of his head, to give me a short stare in which I read as much determination as perplexity.

"I will look into Miss Postlethwaite's case more particularly," were his parting words. And with this one gleam of comfort I had to be content.

Monday's interview was a brief one and contained nothing worth repeating. Mrs. Postlethwaite listened with stoical satisfaction to the reading of the will I had drawn up, and upon its completion rang her bell for the two witnesses awaiting her summons, in an adjoining room. They were not of her household, but to all appearance honest villagers with but one noticeable characteristic, an overweening idea of Mrs. Postlethwaite's importance. Perhaps the spell she had so liberally woven for others in other and happier days was felt by them at this hour. It would not be strange; I had almost fallen under it myself, so great was the fascination of her manner even in this wreck of her bodily powers, when triumph assured, she faced us all in a state of complete satisfaction.

But before I was again quit of the place, all my doubts returned and in fuller force than ever. I had lingered in my going as much as decency would permit, hoping to hear a step on the stair or see a face in some doorway which would contradict Mrs. Postlethwaite's cold assurance that Miss Postlethwaite was no better. But no such step did I hear, and no face did I see save the old, old one of the ancient friend or relative, whose bent frame seemed continually to haunt the halls. As before, he stood listening to the monotonous ticking of one of the clocks, muttering to himself and quite oblivious of my presence.

However, this time I decided not to pass him without a more persistent attempt to gain his notice. Pausing at his side, I asked him in the friendly tone I thought best calculated to attract his attention, how Miss Postlethwaite was to-day. He was so intent upon his task, whatever that was, that while he turned my way, it was with a glance as blank as that of a stone image.

"Listen!" he admonished me. "It still says No! No! I don't think it will ever say anything else."

I stared at him in some consternation, then at the clock itself which was the tall one I had found run down at my first visit. There was nothing unusual in its quiet tick, so far as I could hear, and with a compassionate glance at the old man who had turned breathlessly again to listen, proceeded on my way without another word.

The old fellow was daft. A century old, and daft.

I had worked my way out through the vines which still encumbered the porch, and was taking my first steps down the walk, when some impulse made me turn and glance up at one of the windows.

Did I bless the impulse? I thought I had every reason for doing so, when through a network of interlacing branches I beheld the young girl with whom my mind was wholly occupied, standing with her head thrust forward, watching the descent of something small and white which she had just released from her hand.

A note! A note written by her and meant for me! With a grateful look in her direction (which was probably lost upon her as she had already drawn back out of sight), I sprang for it only to meet with disappointment. For it was no billet-doux I received from amid the clustering brush where it had fallen; but a small square of white cloth showing a line of fantastic embroidery. Annoyed beyond measure, I was about to fling it down again, when the thought that it had come from her hand deterred me, and I thrust it into my vest pocket. When I took it out again—which was soon after I had taken my seat in the car—I discovered what a mistake I should have made if I had followed my first impulse. For, upon examining the stitches more carefully, I perceived that what I had considered a mere decorative pattern was in fact a string of letters, and that these letters made words, and that these words were:

I DO NOT WANT TO DIE BUT I SURELY WILL IF

Or, in plain writing:

"I do not want to die, but I surely will if—"

Finish the sentence for me. That is the problem I offer you. It is not a case for the police but one well worth your attention, if you succeed in reaching the heart of this mystery and saving this young girl.

Only, let no delay occur. The doom, if doom it is, is immanent. Remember that the will is signed.

II

"She is too small; I did not ask you to send me a midget."

Thus spoke Mrs. Postlethwaite to her doctor, as he introduced into her presence a little figure in nurse's cap and apron. "You said I needed care,— more care than I was receiving. I answered that my old nurse could give it, and you objected that she or someone else must look after Miss Postlethwaite. I did not see the necessity, but I never contradict a doctor. So I yielded to your wishes, but not without the proviso (you remember that I made a proviso) that whatever sort of young woman you chose to introduce into this room, she should not be fresh from the training schools, and that she should be strong, silent, and capable. And you bring me this mite of a woman—is she a woman? she looks more like a child, of pleasing countenance enough, but who can no more lift me—"

"Pardon me!" Little Miss Strange had advanced. "I think, if you will allow me the privilege, madam, that I can shift you into a much more comfortable position." And with a deftness and ease certainly not to be expected from one of her slight physique, Violet raised the helpless invalid a trifle more upon her pillow.

The act, its manner, and the smile accompanying it, could not fail to please, and undoubtedly did, though no word rewarded her from lips not much given to speech save when the occasion was imperative. But Mrs. Postlethwaite made no further objection to her presence, and, seeing this, the doctor's

81

countenance relaxed and he left the room with a much lighter step than that with which he had entered it.

And thus it was that Violet Strange—an adept in more ways than one—became installed at the bedside of this mysterious woman, whose days, if numbered, still held possibilities of action which those interested in young Helena Postlethwaite's fate would do well to recognize.

Miss Strange had been at her post for two days, and had gathered up the following:

That Mrs. Postlethwaite must be obeyed.

That her step-daughter (who did not wish to die) would die if she knew it to be the wish of this domineering but apparently idolized woman.

That the old man of the clocks, while senile in some regards, was very alert and quite youthful in others. If a century old—which she began greatly to doubt—he had the language and manner of one in his prime, when unaffected by the neighbourhood of the clocks, which seemed in some non-understandable way to exercise an occult influence over him. At table he was an entertaining host; but neither there nor elsewhere would he discuss the family, or dilate in any way upon the peculiarities of a household of which he manifestly regarded himself as the least important member. Yet no one knew them better, and when Violet became quite assured of this, as well as of the futility of looking for explanation of any kind from either of her two patients, she resolved upon an effort to surprise one from him.

She went about it in this way. Noting his custom of making a complete round of the clocks each night after dinner, she took advantage of Mrs. Postlethwaite's inclination to sleep at this hour, to follow him from clock to clock in the hope of overhearing some portion of the monologue with which he bent his head to the swinging pendulum, or put his ear to the hidden works. Soft-footed and discreet, she tripped along at his back, and at each pause he made, paused herself and turned her ear his way. The extreme darkness of the halls, which were more sombre by night than by day, favoured this attempt, and she was able, after a failure or two, to catch the No! no! no! no! which fell from his lips in seeming repetition of what he heard the most of them say.

The satisfaction in his tone proved that the denial to which he listened, chimed in with his hopes and gave ease to his mind. But he looked his oldest when, after pausing at another of the many time-pieces, he echoed in answer to its special refrain, Yes! yes! yes! yes! and fled the spot with shaking body and a distracted air.

The same fear and the same shrinking were observable in him as he returned from listening to the least conspicuous one, standing in a short corridor, where Violet could not follow him. But when, after a hesitation which enabled her to slip behind the curtain hiding the drawing-room door, he approached and laid his ear against the great one standing, as if on guard, at the foot of the stairs, she saw by the renewed vigour he displayed that there was comfort for him in its message, even before she caught the whisper with which he left it and proceeded to mount the stairs:

"It says No! It always says No! I will heed it as the voice of Heaven."

But one conclusion could be the result of such an experiment to a mind like Violet's. This partly touched old man not only held the key to the secret of this house, but was in a mood to divulge it if once he could be induced to hear command instead of dissuasion in the tick of this one large clock. But how could he be induced? Violet returned to Mrs. Postlethwaite's bedside in a mood of extreme thoughtfulness.

Another day passed, and she had not yet seen Miss Postlethwaite. She was hoping each hour to be sent on some errand to that young lady's room, but no such opportunity was granted her. Once she ventured to ask the doctor, whose visits were now very frequent, what he thought of the young lady's condition. But as this question was necessarily put in Mrs. Postlethwaite's presence, the answer was naturally guarded, and possibly not altogether frank.

"Our young lady is weaker," he acknowledged. "Much weaker," he added with marked emphasis and his most professional air, "or she would be here instead of in her own room. It grieves her not to be able to wait upon her generous benefactress."

The word fell heavily. Had it been used as a test? Violet gave him a look, though she had much rather have turned her discriminating eye upon the face staring up at them from the pillow. Had the alarm expressed by others communicated itself at last to the physician? Was the charm which had held him subservient to the mother, dissolving under the pitiable state of the child, and was he trying to aid the little detective-nurse in her effort to sound the mystery of her condition?

His look expressed benevolence, but he took care not to meet the gaze of the woman he had just lauded, possibly because that gaze was fixed upon him in a way to tax his moral courage. The silence which ensued was broken by Mrs. Postlethwaite:

"She will live—this poor Helena—how long?" she asked, with no break in her voice's wonted music.

The doctor hesitated, then with a candour hardly to be expected from him, answered:

"I do not understand Miss Postlethwaite's case. I should like, with your permission, to consult some New York physician."

"Indeed!"

A single word, but as it left this woman's thin lips Violet recoiled, and, perhaps, the doctor did. Rage can speak in one word as well as in a dozen, and the rage which spoke in this one was of no common order, though it was quickly suppressed, as was all other show of feeling when she added, with a touch of her old charm:

"Of course you will do what you think best, as you know I never interfere with a doctor's decisions. But" and here her natural ascendancy of tone and manner returned in all its potency, "it would kill me to know that a stranger was approaching Helena's bedside. It would kill her. She's too sensitive to survive such a shock."

Violet recalled the words worked with so much care by this young girl on a minute piece of linen, I do not want to die, and watched the doctor's face for some sign of resolution. But embarrassment was all she saw there, and all she heard him say was the conventional reply:

"I am doing all I can for her. We will wait another day and note the effect of my latest prescription."

Another day!

The deathly calm which overspread Mrs. Postlethwaite's features as this word left the physician's lips warned Violet not to let another day go by without some action. But she made no remark, and, indeed, betrayed but little interest in anything beyond her own patient's condition. That seemed to occupy her wholly. With consummate art she gave the appearance of being under Mrs. Postlethwaite's complete thrall, and watched with fascinated eyes every movement of the one unstricken finger which could do so much.

This little detective of ours could be an excellent actor when she chose.

III

To make the old man speak! To force this conscience-stricken but rebellious soul to reveal what the clock forbade! How could it be done?

This continued to be Violet's great problem. She pondered it so deeply during all the remainder of the day that a little pucker settled on her brow, which someone (I will not mention who) would have been pained to see. Mrs. Postlethwaite, if she noticed it at all, probably ascribed it to her anxieties as nurse, for never had Violet been more assiduous in her attentions. But Mrs. Postlethwaite was no longer the woman she had been, and possibly never noted it at all.

At five o'clock Violet suddenly left the room. Slipping down into the lower hall, she went the round of the clocks herself, listening to every one. There was no perceptible difference in their tick. Satisfied of this and that it was simply the old man's imagination which had supplied them each with separate speech, she paused before the huge one at the foot of the stairs,—the one whose dictate he had promised himself to follow,—and with an eye upon its broad, staring dial, muttered wistfully:

"Oh! for an idea! For an idea!"

Did this cumbrous relic of old-time precision turn traitor at this ingenuous plea? The dial continued to stare, the works to sing, but Violet's face suddenly lost its perplexity. With a wary look about her and a listening ear turned towards the stair top, she stretched out her hand and pulled open the door guarding the pendulum, and peered in at the works, smiling slyly to herself as she pushed it back into place and retreated upstairs to the sick room.

When the doctor came that night she had a quiet word with him outside Mrs. Postlethwaite's door. Was that why he was on hand when old Mr. Dunbar stole from his room to make his nightly circuit of the halls below? Something quite beyond the ordinary was in the good physician's mind, for the look he cast at the old man was quite unlike any he had ever bestowed upon him before, and when he spoke it was to say with marked urgency:

"Our beautiful young lady will not live a week unless I get at the seat of her malady. Pray that I may be enabled to do so, Mr. Dunbar."

A blow to the aged man's heart which called forth a feeble "Yes, yes," followed by a wild stare which imprinted itself upon the doctor's memory as the look of one hopelessly old, who hears for the first time a distinct call from the grave which has long been awaiting him!

A solitary lamp stood in the lower hall. As the old man picked his slow way down, its small, hesitating flame flared up as in a sudden gust, then sank down flickering and faint as if it, too, had heard a call which summoned it to extinction.

No other sign of life was visible anywhere. Sunk in twilight shadows, the corridors branched away on either side to no place in particular and serving, to all appearance (as many must have thought in days gone by), as a mere hiding-place for clocks.

To listen to their united hum, the old man paused, looking at first a little distraught, but settling at last into his usual self as he started forward upon his course. Did some whisper, hitherto unheard, warn him that it was the last time he would tread that weary round? Who can tell? He was trembling very much when with his task nearly completed, he stepped out again into the main hall and crept rather than walked back to the one great clock to whose dictum he made it a practice to listen last.

Chattering the accustomed words, "They say Yes! They are all saying Yes! now; but this one will say No!" he bent his stiff old back and laid his ear to the unresponsive wood. But the time for no had passed. It was Yes! yes! yes! yes! now, and as his straining ears took in the word, he appeared to shrink where he stood and after a moment of anguished silence, broke forth into a low wail, amid whose lamentations one could hear:

"The time has come! Even the clock she loves best bids me speak. Oh! Arabella, Arabella!"

In his despair he had not noticed that the pendulum hung motionless, or that the hands stood at rest on the dial. If he had, he might have waited long enough to have seen the careful opening of the great clock's tall door and the stepping forth of the little lady who had played so deftly upon his superstition.

He was wandering the corridors like a helpless child, when a gentle hand fell on his arm and a soft voice whispered in his ear:

"You have a story to tell. Will you tell it to me? It may save Miss Postlethwaite's life."

Did he understand? Would he respond if he did; or would the shock of her appeal restore him to a sense of the danger attending disloyalty? For a moment she doubted the wisdom of this startling measure, then she saw that he had passed the point of surprise and that, stranger as she was, she had but to lead the way for him to follow, tell his story, and die.

There was no light in the drawing-room when they entered. But old Mr. Dunbar did not seem to mind that. Indeed, he seemed to have lost all consciousness of present surroundings; he was even oblivious of her. This became quite evident when the lamp, in flaring up again in the hall, gave a momentary glimpse, of his crouching, half-kneeling figure. In the pleading gesture of his trembling, outreaching arms, Violet beheld an appeal, not to herself, but to some phantom of his imagination; and when he spoke, as he presently did, it was with the freedom of one to whom speech is life's last boon, and the ear of the listener quite forgotten in the passion of confession long suppressed.

"She has never loved me," he began, "but I have always loved her. For me no other woman has ever existed, though I was sixty-five years of age when I first saw her, and had long given up the idea that there lived a woman who could sway me from my even life and fixed lines of duty. Sixty-five! and she a youthful bride! Was there ever such folly! Happily I realized it from the first, and piled ashes on my hidden flame. Perhaps that is why I adore her to this day and only give her over to reprobation because Fate is stronger than my age—stronger even than my love.

"She is not a good woman, but I might have been a good man if I had never known the sin which drew a line of isolation about her, and within which I, and only I, have stood with her in silent companionship. What was this sin, and in what did it have its beginning? I think its beginning was in the passion she had for her husband. It was not the every-day passion of her sex in this land of equable affections, but one of foreign fierceness, jealousy, and insatiable demand. Yet he was a very ordinary man. I was once his tutor and I know. She came to know it too, when—but I am rushing on too fast, I have much to tell before I reach that point.

"From the first, I was in their confidence. Not that either he or she put me there, but that I lived with them and was always around, and could not help seeing and hearing what went on between them. Why he continued to want me in the house and at his table, when I could no longer be of service to him, I have never known. Possibly habit explains all. He was accustomed to my presence and so was she; so accustomed they hardly noticed it, as happened one night, when after a little attempt at conversation, he threw down the book he had caught up and, addressing her by name, said without a glance my way, and quite as if he were alone with her:

"'Arabella, there is something I ought to tell you. I have tried to find the courage to do so many times before now but have always failed. Tonight I must.' And then he made his great disclosure,—how, unknown to, his friends and the world, he was a widower when he married her, and the father of a living child.

"With some women this might have passed with a measure of regret, and some possible contempt for his silence, but not so with her. She rose to her feet—I can see her yet—and for a moment stood facing him in the still, overpowering manner of one who feels the icy pang of hate enter where love has been. Never was moment more charged. I could not breathe while it lasted; and when at last she spoke, it was with an impetuosity of concentrated passion, hardly less dreadful than her silence had been.

"'You a father! A father already!' she cried, all her sweetness swallowed up in ungovernable wrath. 'You whom I expected to make so happy with a child? I curse you and your brat. I—'

"He strove to placate her, to explain. But rage has no ears, and before I realized my own position, the scene became openly tempestuous. That her child should be second to another woman's seemed to awaken demon instincts within her. When he ventured to hint that his little girl needed a mother's care, her irony bit like corroding acid. He became speechless before it and had not a protest to raise when she declared that the secret he had kept so long and so successfully he must continue to keep to his dying day. That the child he had failed to own in his first wife's lifetime should remain disowned in hers, and if possible be forgotten. She should never give the girl a thought nor acknowledge her in any way.

"She was Fury embodied; but the fury was of that grand order which allures rather than repels. As I felt myself succumbing to its fascination and beheld how he was weakening under it even more perceptibly than myself, I started from my chair, and sought to glide away before I should hear him utter a fatal acquiescence.

"But the movement I made unfortunately drew their attention to me, and after an instant of silent contemplation of my distracted countenance, Frank said, as though he were the elder by the forty years which separated us:

"'You have listened to Mrs. Postlethwaite's wishes. You will respect them of course.'"

That was all. He knew and she knew that I was to be trusted; but neither of them has ever known why.

A month later her child came, and was welcomed as though it were the first to bear his name. It was a boy, and their satisfaction was so great that I looked to see their old affection revive. But it had been cleft at the root, and nothing could restore it to life. They loved the child; I have never seen evidence of greater parental passion than they both displayed, but there their feelings stopped. Towards each other they were cold. They did not even unite in worship of their treasure. They gloated over him and planned for him, but always apart. He was a child in a thousand, and as he developed, the mother especially, nursed all her energies for the purpose of ensuring for him a future commensurate with his talents. Never a very conscientious woman, and alive to the advantages of wealth as demonstrated by the power wielded by her rich brother-in-law, she associated all the boy's prospects with money, great money, such money as Andrew had accumulated, and now had at his disposal for his natural heirs.

"Hence came her great temptation,—a temptation to which she yielded, to the lasting trouble of us all. Of this I must now make confession though it kills me to do so, and will soon kill her. The deeds of the past do not remain buried, however deep we dig their graves, but rise in an awful resurrection when we are old—old—"

Silence. Then a tremulous renewal of his painful speech.

Violet held her breath to listen. Possibly the doctor, hidden in the darkest corner of the room, did so also.

"I never knew how she became acquainted with the terms of her brother-in-law's will. He certainly never confided them to her, and as certainly the lawyer who drew up the document never did. But that she was well aware of its tenor is as positive a fact as that I am the most wretched man alive tonight. Otherwise, why the darksome deed into which she was betrayed when both the brothers lay dying among strangers, of a dreadful accident?"

"I was witness to that deed. I had accompanied her on her hurried ride and was at her side when she entered the inn where the two Postlethwaites lay. I was always at her side in great joy or in great trouble, though she professed no affection for me and gave me but scanty thanks."

"During our ride she had been silent and I had not disturbed that silence. I had much to think of. Should we find him living, or should we find him dead? If dead, would it sever the relations between us two? Would I ever ride with her again?"

"When I was not dwelling on this theme, I was thinking of the parting look she gave her boy; a look which had some strange promise in it. What had that look meant and why did my flesh creep and my mind hover between dread and a fearsome curiosity when I recalled it? Alas! There was reason for all these sensations as I was soon to learn.

"We found the inn seething with terror and the facts worse than had been represented in the telegram. Her husband was dying. She had come just in time to witness the end. This they told her before she had taken off her veil. If they had waited—if I had been given a full glimpse of her face—But it was hidden, and I could only judge of the nature of her emotions by the stern way in which she held herself.

"'Take me to him,' was the quiet command, with which she met this disclosure. Then, before any of them could move:

"'And his brother, Mr. Andrew Postlethwaite? Is he fatally injured too?'

"The reply was unequivocal. The doctors were uncertain which of the two would pass away first.

"You must remember that at this time I was ignorant of the rich man's will, and consequently of how the fate of a poor child of whom I had heard only one mention, hung in the balance at that awful moment. But in the breathlessness which seized Mrs. Postlethwaite at this sentence of double death, I realized from my knowledge of her that something more than grief was at prey upon her impenetrable heart, and shuddered to the core of my being when she repeated in that voice which was so terrible because so expressionless:

"'Take me to them.'"

They were lying in one room, her husband nearest the door, the other in a small alcove some ten feet away. Both were unconscious; both were surrounded by groups of frightened attendants who fell back as she approached. A doctor stood at the bed-head of her husband, but as her eye met his he stepped aside with a shake of the head and left the place empty for her.

"The action was significant. I saw that she understood what it meant, and with constricted heart watched her as she bent over the dying man and gazed into his wide-open eyes, already sightless and staring. Calculation was in her look and calculation only; and calculation, or something equally unintelligible, sent her next glance in the direction of his brother. What was in her mind? I could understand her indifference to Frank even at the crisis of his fate, but not the interest she showed in Andrew. It was an absorbing one, altering her whole expression. I no longer knew her for my dear young madam, and the jealousy I had never felt towards Frank rose to frantic resentment in my breast as I beheld what very likely might be a tardy recognition of the other's well-known passion, forced into disclosure by the exigencies of the moment.

"Alarmed by the strength of my feelings, and fearing an equal disclosure on my own part, I sought for a refuge from all eyes and found it in a little balcony opening out at my right. On to this balcony I stepped and found myself face to face with a star-lit heaven. Had I only been content with my isolation and the splendour of the spectacle spread out before me! But no, I must look back upon that bed and the solitary woman standing beside it! I must watch the settling of her body into rigidity as a voice rose from beside the other Postlethwaite saying, 'It is a matter of minutes now,' and then—and then—the slow creeping of her hand to her husband's mouth, the outspreading of her palm across the livid lips—its steady clinging there, smothering the feeble gasps of one already moribund, till the quivering form grew still, and Frank Postlethwaite lay dead before my eyes!

"I saw, and made no outcry, but she did, bringing the doctor back to her side with the startled exclamation:

"'Dead? I thought he had an hour's life left in him, and he has passed before his brother.'

"I thought it hate—the murderous impulse of a woman who sees her enemy at her mercy and can no longer restrain the passion of her long-cherished antagonism; and while something within me rebelled at the act, I could not betray her, though silence made a murderer of me too. I could not. Her spell was upon me as in another instant it was upon everyone else in the room. No suspicion of one so self-repressed in her sadness disturbed the universal sympathy; and encouraged by this blindness of the crowd, I vowed within myself never to reveal her secret. The man was dead, or as good as dead, when she touched him; and now that her hate was expended she would grow gentle and good.

"But I knew the worthlessness of this hope as well as my misconception of her motive, when Frank's child by another wife returned to my memory, and Bella's sin stood exposed."

"But only to myself. I alone knew that the fortune now wholly hers, and in consequence her boy's, had been won by a crime. That if her hand had fallen in comfort on her husband's forehead instead of in pressure on his mouth, he would have outlived his brother long enough to have become owner of his millions; in which case a rightful portion would have been insured to his daughter, now left a penniless waif. The thought made my hair rise, as the proceedings over, I faced her and made my first and last effort to rid my conscience of its new and intolerable burden.

"But the woman I had known and loved was no longer before me. The crown had touched her brows, and her charm which had been mainly sexual up to this hour had merged into an intellectual force, with which few men's mentality could cope. Mine yielded at once to it. From the first instant, I knew that a slavery of spirit, as well as of heart, was henceforth to be mine.

"She did not wait for me to speak; she had assumed the dictator's attitude at once.

"'I know of what you are thinking,'" said she, "'and it is a subject you may dismiss at once from your mind. Mr. Postlethwaite's child by his first wife is coming to live with us. I have expressed my wishes in this regard to my lawyer, and there is nothing left to be said. You, with your close mouth and dependable nature, are to remain here as before, and occupy the same position towards my boy that you did towards his father. We shall move soon into a larger house, and the nature of our duties will be changed and their scope greatly increased; but I know that you can be trusted to enlarge with them and meet every requirement I shall see fit to make. Do not try to express your thanks. I see them in your face.'

"Did she, or just the last feeble struggle my conscience was making to break the bonds in which she held me, and win back my own respect? I shall never know, for she left me on completion of this speech, not to resume the subject, then or ever.

"But though I succumbed outwardly to her demands, I had not passed the point where inner conflict ends and peace begins. Her recognition of Helena and her reception into the family calmed me for a while, and gave me hope that all would yet be well. But I had never sounded the full bitterness of madam's morbid heart, well as I thought I knew it. The hatred she had felt from the first for her husband's child ripened into frenzied dislike when she found her a living image of the mother whose picture she had come across among Frank's personal effects. To win a tear from those meek eyes instead of a smile to the sensitive lips was her daily play. She seemed to exult in the joy of impressing upon the girl by how little she had missed a great fortune, and I have often thought, much as I tried to keep my mind free from all extravagant and unnecessary fancies, that half of the money she spent in beautifying this house and maintaining art industries and even great charitable institutions was spent with the base purpose of demonstrating to this child the power of immense wealth, and in what ways she might expect to see her little brother expend the millions in which she had been denied all share.

"I was so sure of this that one night while I was winding up the clocks with which Mrs. Postlethwaite in her fondness for old timepieces has filled the house, I stopped to look at the little figure toiling so wearily upstairs, to bed, without a mother's kiss. There was an appeal in the small wistful face which smote my hard old heart, and possibly a tear welled up in my own eye when I turned back to my duty."

"Was that why I felt the hand of Providence upon me, when in my halt before the one clock to which any superstitious interest was attached—the great one at the foot of the stairs—I saw that it had stopped and at the one minute of all minutes in our wretched lives: Four minutes past two? The hour, the minute in which Frank Postlethwaite had gasped his last under the pressure of his wife's hand! I knew it—the exact minute I mean—because Providence meant that I should know it. There had been a clock on the mantelpiece of the hotel room where he and his brother had died and I had seen her glance steal towards it at the instant she withdrew her palm from her husband's lips. The stare of that dial and the position of its hands had lived still in my mind as I believed it did in hers.

"Four minutes past two! How came our old timepiece here to stop at that exact moment on a day when Duty was making its last demand upon me to remember Frank's unhappy child? There was no one to answer; but as I looked and looked, I felt the impulse of the moment strengthen into purpose to leave those hands undisturbed in their silent accusation. She might see, and, moved by the coincidence, tremble at her treatment of Helena.

"But if this happened—if she saw and trembled—she gave no sign. The works were started up by some other hand, and the incident passed. But it left me with an idea. That clock soon had a way of stopping and always at that one instant of time. She was forced at length to notice it, and I remember, an occasion when she stood stock-still with her eyes on those hands, and failed to find the banister with her hand, though she groped for it in her frantic need for support.

"But no command came from her to remove the worn-out piece, and soon its tricks, and every lesser thing, were forgotten in the crushing calamity which befell us in the sickness and death of little Richard.

"Oh, those days and nights! And oh, the face of the mother when the doctors told her that the case was hopeless! I asked myself then, and I have asked myself a hundred times since, which of all the emotions I saw pictured there bit the deepest, and made the most lasting impression on her guilty heart? Was it remorse? If so, she showed no change in her attitude towards Helena, unless it was by an added bitterness. The sweet looks and gentle ways of Frank's young daughter could not win against a hate sharpened by disappointment. Useless for me to hope for it. Release from the remorse of years was not to come in that way. As I realized this, I grew desperate and resorted again to the old trick of stopping the clock at the fatal hour. This time her guilty heart responded. She acknowledged the stab and let all her miseries appear. But how? In a way to wring my heart almost to madness, and not benefit the child at all. She had her first stroke that night. I had made her a helpless invalid.

"That was eight years ago, and since then what? Stagnation. She lived with her memories, and I with mine. Helena only had a right to hope, and hope perhaps she did, till—Is that the great clock talking? Listen! They all talk, but I heed only the one. What does it say? Tell! tell! tell! Does it think I will be silent now when I come to my own guilt? That I will seek to hide my weakness when I could not hide her sin?"

"Explain!" It was Violet speaking, and her tone was stern in its command. "Of what guilt do you speak? Not of guilt towards Helena; you pitied her too much—"

"But I pitied my dear madam more. It was that which affected me and drew me into crime against my will. Besides, I did not know—not at first—what was in the little bowl of curds and cream I carried to the girl each day. She had eaten them in her step-mother's room, and under her step-mother's eye as long as she had strength to pass from room to room, and how was I to guess that it was not wholesome? Because she failed in health from day to day? Was not my dear madam failing in health also; and was there poison in her cup? Innocent at that time, why am I not innocent now? Because—Oh, I will tell it all; as though at the bar of God. I will tell all the secrets of that day.

"She was sitting with her hand trembling on the tray from which I had just lifted the bowl she had bid me carry to Helena. I had seen her so a hundred times before, but not with just that look in her eyes, or just that air of desolation in her stony figure. Something made me speak; something made me ask if she were not quite so well as usual, and something made her reply with the dreadful truth that the doctor had given her just two months more to live. My fright and mad anguish stupefied me; for I was not prepared for this, no, not at all;—and unconsciously I stared down at the bowl I held, unable to breathe or move or even to meet her look."

As usual she misinterpreted my emotion.

"'Why do you stand like that?' I heard her say in a tone of great irritation. 'And why do you stare into that bowl? Do you think I mean to leave that child to walk these halls after I am carried out of them forever? Do you measure my hate by such a petty yard-stick as that? I tell you that I would rot above ground rather than enter it before she did?'

"I had believed I knew this woman; but what soul ever knows another's? What soul ever knows itself?

"'Bella!' I cried; the first time I had ever presumed to address her so intimately. 'Would you poison the girl?' And from sheer weakness my fingers lost their clutch, and the bowl fell to the floor, breaking into a dozen pieces.

"For a minute she stared down at these from over her tray, and then she remarked very low and very quietly:

"'Another bowl, Humphrey, and fresh curds from the kitchen. I will do the seasoning. The doses are too small to be skipped. You won't?'—I had shaken my head—'But you will! It will not be the first time you have gone down the hall with this mixture.'

"'But that was before I knew—' I began.

"'And now that you do, you will go just the same.' Then as I stood hesitating, a thousand memories overwhelming me in an instant, she added in a voice to tear the heart, 'Do not make me hate the only being left in this world who understands and loves me.'

"She was a helpless invalid, and I a broken man, but when that word 'love' fell from her lips, I felt the blood start burning in my veins, and all the crust of habit and years of self-control loosen about my heart, and make me young again. What if her thoughts were dark and her wishes murderous! She was born to rule and sway men to her will even to their own undoing."

"'I wish I might kiss your hand,' was what I murmured, gazing at her white fingers groping over her tray.

"'You may,' she answered, and hell became heaven to me for a brief instant. Then I lifted myself and went obediently about my task.

"But puppet though I was, I was not utterly without sympathy. When I entered Helena's room and saw how her startled eyes fell shrinkingly on the bowl I set down before her, my conscience leaped to life and I could not help saying:

"'Don't you like the curds, Helena? Your brother used to love them very much.'

"'His were—'

"'What, Helena?'

"'What these are not,' she murmured.

"I stared at her, terror-stricken. So she knew, and yet did not seize the bowl and empty it out of the window! Instead, her hand moved slowly towards it and drew it into place before her.

"'Yet I must eat,' she said, lifting her eyes to mine in a sort of patient despair, which yet was without accusation.

"But my hand had instinctively gone to hers and grasped it.

"'Why must you eat it?' I asked. 'If—if you do not find it wholesome, why do you touch it?'

"'Because my step-mother expects me to,' she cried, 'and I have no other will than hers. When I was a little, little child, my father made me promise that if I ever came to live with her I would obey her simplest wish. And I always have. I will not disappoint the trust he put in me.'

"'Even if you die of it?'

"I do not know whether I whispered these words or only thought them. She answered as though I had spoken.

"'I am not afraid to die. I am more afraid to live. She may ask me some day to do something I feel to be wrong.'

"When I fled down the hall that night, I heard one of the small clocks speak to me. Tell! it cried, tell! tell! tell! tell! I rushed away from it with beaded forehead and rising hair.

"Then another's note piped up. No it droned. No! no! no! no! I stopped and took heart. Disgrace the woman I loved, on the brink of the grave? I—, who asked no other boon from heaven than to see her happy, gracious, and good? Impossible. I would obey the great clock's voice; the others were mere chatterboxes.

"But it has at last changed its tune, for some reason, quite changed its tune. Now, it is Yes! Yes! instead of No! and in obeying it I save Helena. But what of Bella? and O God, what of myself?"

A sigh, a groan, then a long and heavy silence, into which there finally broke the pealing of the various clocks striking the hour. When all were still again and Violet had drawn aside the portiere, it was to see the old man on his knees, and between her and the thin streak of light entering from the hall, the figure of the doctor hastening to Helena's bedside.

When with inducements needless to name, they finally persuaded the young girl to leave her unholy habitation, it was in the arms which had upheld her once before, and to a life which promised to compensate her for her twenty years of loneliness and unsatisfied longing.

But a black shadow yet remained which she must cross before reaching the sunshine!

It lay at her step-mother's door.

In the plans made for Helena's release, Mrs. Postlethwaite's consent had not been obtained nor was she supposed to be acquainted with the doctor's intentions towards the child whose death she was hourly awaiting.

It was therefore with an astonishment, bordering on awe, that on their way downstairs, they saw the door of her room open and herself standing alone and upright on the threshold—she who had not been seen to take a step in years. In the wonder of this miracle of suddenly restored power, the little procession stopped,—the doctor with his hand upon the rail, the lover with his burden clasped yet more protectingly to his breast. That a little speech awaited them could be seen from the force and fury of the gaze which the indomitable woman bent upon the lax and half-unconscious figure she beheld thus sheltered and conveyed. Having but one arrow left in her exhausted quiver, she launched it straight at the innocent breast which had never harboured against her a defiant thought.

"Ingrate!" was the word she hurled in a voice from which all its seductive music had gone forever. "Where are you going? Are they carrying you alive to your grave?"

A moan from Helena's pale lips, then silence. She had fainted at that barbed attack. But there was one there who dared to answer for her and he spoke relentlessly. It was the man who loved her.

"No, madam. We are carrying her to safety. You must know what I mean by that. Let her go quietly and you may die in peace. Otherwise—"

She interrupted him with a loud call, startling into life the echoes of that haunted hall:

"Humphrey! Come to me, Humphrey!"

But no Humphrey appeared.

Another call, louder and more peremptory than before:

"Humphrey! I say, Humphrey!"

But the answer was the same—silence, and only silence. As the horror of this grew, the doctor spoke:

"Mr. Humphrey Dunbar's ears are closed to all earthly summons. He died last night at the very hour he said he would—four minutes after two."

"Four minutes after two!" It came from her lips in a whisper, but with a revelation of her broken heart and life. "Four minutes after two!" And defiant to the last, her head rose, and for an instant, for a mere breath of time, they saw her as she had looked in her prime, regal in form, attitude, and expression; then the will which had sustained her through so much, faltered and succumbed, and with a final reiteration of the words "Four minutes after two!" she broke into a rattling laugh, and fell back into the arms of her old nurse.

And below, one clock struck the hour and then another. But not the big one at the foot of the stairs. That still stood silent, with its hands pointing to the hour and minute of Frank Postlethwaite's hastened death.

END OF PROBLEM VI

I

THE DOCTOR, HIS WIFE, AND THE CLOCK

Violet had gone to her room. She had a task before her. That afternoon, a packet had been left at the door, which, from a certain letter scribbled in one corner, she knew to be from her employer. The contents of that packet must be read, and she had made herself comfortable with the intention of setting to work at once. But ten o'clock struck and then eleven before she could bring herself to give any attention to the manuscript awaiting her perusal. In her present mood, a quiet sitting by the fire, with her eyes upon the changeful flame, was preferable to the study of any affair her employer might send her. Yet, because she was conscious of the duty she thus openly neglected, she sat crouched over her desk with her hand on the mysterious packet, the string of which, however, she made no effort to loosen.

What was she thinking of?

We are not alone in our curiosity on this subject. Her brother Arthur, coming unperceived into the room, gives tokens of a similar interest. Never before had he seen her oblivious to an approaching step; and after a momentary contemplation of her absorbed figure, so girlishly sweet and yet so deeply intent, he advances to her side, and peering earnestly into her face, observes with a seriousness quite unusual to him:

"Puss, you are looking worried,—not like yourself at all. I've noticed it for some time. What's up. Getting tired of the business?"

"No—not altogether—that is, it's not that, if it's anything. I'm not sure that it's anything. I—"

She had turned back to her desk and was pushing about the various articles with which it was plentifully bespread; but this did not hide the flush which had crept into her cheeks and even dyed the snowy whiteness of her neck. Arthur's astonishment at this evidence of emotion was very great; but he said nothing, only watched her still more closely, as with a light laugh she regained her self-possession, and with the practical air of a philosopher uttered this trite remark:

"Everyone has his sober moments. I was only thinking—"

"Of some new case?"

"Not exactly." The words came softly but with a touch of mingled humour and gravity which made Arthur stare again.

"See here, Puss!" he cried. His tone had changed. "I've just come up from the den. Father and I have had a row—a beastly row."

"A row? You and father? Oh, Arthur, I don't like that. Don't quarrel with father. Don't, don't. Some day he and I may have a serious difference about what I am doing. Don't let him feel that he has lost us all."

"That's all right, Puss; but I've got to think of you a bit. I can't see you spoil all your good times with these police horrors and not do something to help. To-morrow I begin life as a salesman in Clarke & Stebbin's. The salary is not great, but every little helps and I don't dislike the business. But father does. He had rather see me loafing about town setting the fashions for fellows as idle as myself than soil my hands with handling merchandise. That's why we quarreled. But don't worry. Your name didn't come up, or—or—you know whose. He hasn't an idea of why I want to work—There, Violet there!"

Two soft arms were around his neck and Violet was letting her heart out in a succession of sisterly kisses.

"O, Arthur, you good, good boy! Together we'll soon make up the amount, and then—"

"Then what?"

A sweet soft look robbed her face of its piquancy, but gave it an aspect of indescribable beauty quite new to Arthur's eyes.

Tapping his lips with a thoughtful forefinger, he asked:

"Who was that sombre-looking chap I saw bowing to you as we came out of church last Sunday?"

She awoke from her dreamy state with an astonishing quickness.

"He? Surely you remember him. Have you forgotten that evening in Massachusetts—the grotto—and—"

"Oh, it's Upjohn, is it? Yes, I remember him. He's fond of church, isn't he? That is, when he's in New York."

Her lips took a roguish curve then a very serious one; but she made no answer.

"I have noticed that he's always in his seat and always looking your way."

"That's very odd of him," she declared, her dimples coming and going in a most bewildering fashion. "I can't imagine why he should do that."

"Nor I,—" retorted Arthur with a smile. "But he's human, I suppose. Only do be careful, Violet. A man so melancholy will need a deal of cheering."

He was gone before he had fully finished this daring remark, and Violet, left again with her thoughts, lost her glowing colour but not her preoccupation. The hand which lay upon the packet already alluded to did not move for many minutes, and when she roused at last to the demands of her employer, it was with a start and a guilty look at the small gold clock ticking out its inexorable reminder.

"He will want an answer the first thing in the morning," she complained to herself. And opening the packet, she took out first a letter, and then a mass of typewritten manuscript.

She began with the letter which was as characteristic of the writer as all the others she had had from his hand; as witness:

You probably remember the Hasbrouck murder,—or, perhaps, you don't; it being one of a time previous to your interest in such matters. But whether you remember it or not, I beg you to read the accompanying summary with due care and attention to business. When you have well mastered it with all its details, please communicate with me in any manner most convenient to yourself, for I shall have a word to say to you then, which you may be glad to hear, if as you have lately intimated you need to earn but one or two more substantial rewards in order to cry halt to the pursuit for which you have proved yourself so well qualified.

The story, in deference to yourself as a young and much preoccupied woman, has been written in a way to interest. Though the work of an everyday police detective, you will find in it no lack of mystery or romance; and if at the end you perceive that it runs, as such cases frequently do, up against a perfectly blank wall, you must remember that openings can be made in walls, and that the loosening of one weak stone from its appointed place, sometimes leads to the downfall of all.

So much for the letter.

Laying it aside, with a shrug of her expressive shoulders, Violet took up the manuscript.

Let us take it up too. It runs thus:

On the 17th of July, 19—, a tragedy of no little interest occurred in one of the residences of the Colonnade in Lafayette Place.

Mr. Hasbrouck, a well known and highly respected citizen, was attacked in his room by an unknown assailant, and shot dead before assistance could reach him. His murderer escaped, and the problem offered to the police was how to identify this person who, by some happy chance or by the exercise of the most remarkable forethought, had left no traces behind him, or any clue by which he could be followed.

The details of the investigation which ended so unsatisfactorily are here given by the man sent from headquarters at the first alarm.

When, some time after midnight on the date above mentioned, I reached Lafayette Place, I found the block lighted from end to end. Groups of excited men and women peered from the open doorways, and mingled their shadows with those of the huge pillars which adorn the front of this picturesque block of dwellings.

The house in which the crime had been committed was near the centre of the row, and, long before I reached it, I had learned from more than one source that the alarm was first given to the street by a woman's shriek, and secondly by the shouts of an old man-servant who had appeared, in a half-dressed condition, at the window of Mr. Hasbrouck's room, crying "Murder! murder!"

But when I had crossed the threshold, I was astonished at the paucity of facts to be gleaned from the inmates themselves. The old servant, who was the first to talk, had only this account of the crime to give:

The family, which consisted of Mr. Hasbrouck, his wife, and three servants, had retired for the night at the usual hour and under the usual auspices. At eleven o'clock the lights were all extinguished, and the whole household asleep, with the possible exception of Mr. Hasbrouck himself, who, being a man of large business responsibilities, was frequently troubled with insomnia.

Suddenly Mrs. Hasbrouck woke with a start. Had she dreamed the words that were ringing in her ears, or had they been actually uttered in her hearing? They were short, sharp words, full of terror and menace, and she had nearly satisfied herself that she had imagined them, when there came, from somewhere near the door, a sound she neither understood nor could interpret, but which filled her with inexplicable terror, and made her afraid to breathe, or even to stretch forth her hand towards her husband, whom she supposed to be sleeping at her side. At length another strange sound, which she was sure was not due to her imagination, drove her to make an attempt to rouse him, when she was horrified to find that she was alone in bed, and her husband nowhere within reach.

Filled now with something more than nervous apprehension, she flung herself to the floor, and tried to penetrate with frenzied glances, the surrounding darkness. But the blinds and shutters both having been carefully closed by Mr. Hasbrouck before retiring, she found this impossible, and she was about to sink in terror to the floor, when she heard a low gasp on the other side of the room followed by a suppressed cry.

"God! what have I done!"

The voice was a strange one, but before the fear aroused by this fact could culminate in a shriek of dismay, she caught the sound of retreating footsteps, and, eagerly listening, she heard them descend the stairs and depart by the front door.

Had she known what had occurred—had there been no doubt in her mind as to what lay in the darkness on the other side of the room—it is likely that, at the noise caused by the closing front door, she would have made at once for the balcony that opened out from the window before which she was standing, and taken one look at the flying figure below. But her uncertainty as to what lay hidden from her by the darkness chained her feet to the floor, and there is no knowing when she would have moved, if a carriage had not at that moment passed down Astor Place, bringing with it a sense of companionship which broke the spell holding her, and gave her strength to light the gas which was in ready reach of her hand.

As the sudden blaze illuminated the room, revealing in a burst the old familiar walls and well-known pieces of furniture, she felt for a moment as if released from some heavy nightmare and restored to the common experiences of life. But in another instant her former dread returned, and she found herself quaking at the prospect of passing around the foot of the bed into that part of the room which was as yet hidden from her eyes.

But the desperation which comes with great crises finally drove her from her retreat; and, creeping slowly forward, she cast one glance at the floor before her, when she found her worst fears realized by the sight of the dead body of her husband lying prone before the open doorway, with a bullet-hole in his forehead.

Her first impulse was to shriek, but, by a powerful exercise of will, she checked herself, and ringing frantically for the servants who slept on the top floor of the house, flew to the nearest window and endeavoured to open it. But the shutters had been bolted so securely by Mr. Hasbrouck, in his endeavour to shut out all light and sound, that by the time she had succeeded in unfastening them, all trace of the flying murderer had vanished from the street.

Sick with grief and terror, she stepped back into the room just as the three frightened servants descended the stairs. As they appeared in the open doorway, she pointed at her husband's inanimate form, and then, as if suddenly realizing in its full force the calamity which had befallen her, she threw up her arms, and sank forward to the floor in a dead faint.

The two women rushed to her assistance, but the old butler, bounding over the bed, sprang to the window, and shrieked his alarm to the street.

In the interim that followed, Mrs. Hasbrouck was revived, and the master's body laid decently on the bed; but no pursuit was made, nor any inquiries started likely to assist me in establishing the identity of the assailant.

Indeed, everyone both in the house and out, seemed dazed by the unexpected catastrophe, and as no one had any suspicions to offer as to the probable murderer, I had a difficult task before me.

I began in the usual way, by inspecting the scene of the murder. I found nothing in the room, or in the condition of the body itself, which added an iota to the knowledge already obtained. That Mr. Hasbrouck had been in bed; that he had risen upon hearing a noise; and that he had been shot before reaching the door, were self-evident facts. But there was nothing to guide me further. The very simplicity of the circumstances caused a dearth of clues, which made the difficulty of procedure as great as any I had ever encountered.

My search through the hall and down the stairs elicited nothing; and an investigation of the bolts and bars by which the house was secured, assured me that the assassin had either entered by the front door, or had already been secreted in the house when it was locked up for the night.

"I shall have to trouble Mrs. Hasbrouck for a short interview," I hereupon announced to the trembling old servant, who had followed me like a dog about the house.

He made no demur, and in a few minutes I was ushered into the presence of the newly made widow, who sat quite alone, in a large chamber in the rear. As I crossed the threshold she looked up, and I encountered a good, plain face, without the shadow of guile in it.

"Madam," said I, "I have not come to disturb you. I will ask two or three questions only, and then leave you to your grief. I am told that some words came from the assassin before he delivered his fatal shot. Did you hear these distinctly enough to tell me what they were?"

"I was sound asleep," said she, "and dreamt, as I thought, that a fierce, strange voice cried somewhere to some one: 'Ah! you did not expect me!' But I dare not say that these words were really uttered to my husband, for he was not the man to call forth hate, and only a man in the extremity of passion could address such an exclamation in such a tone as rings in my memory in connection with the fatal shot which woke me."

"But that shot was not the work of a friend," I argued. "If, as these words seem to prove, the assassin had some other motive than plunder in his assault, then your husband had an enemy, though you never suspected it."

"Impossible!" was her steady reply, uttered in the most convincing tone. "The man who shot him was a common burglar, and frightened at having been betrayed into murder, fled without looking for booty. I am sure I heard him cry out in terror and remorse: 'God! what have I done!'"

"Was that before you left the side of the bed?"

"Yes; I did not move from my place till I heard the front door close. I was paralysed by fear and dread."

"Are you in the habit of trusting to the security of a latch-lock only in the fastening of your front door at night? I am told that the big key was not in the lock, and that the bolt at the bottom of the door was not drawn."

"The bolt at the bottom of the door is never drawn. Mr. Hasbrouck was so good a man that he never mistrusted any one. That is why the big lock was not fastened. The key, not working well, he took it some days ago to the locksmith, and when the latter failed to return it, he laughed, and said he thought no one would ever think of meddling with his front door."

"Is there more than one night-key to your house?" I now asked.

She shook her head.

"And when did Mr. Hasbrouck last use his?"

"To-night, when he came home from prayer meeting," she answered, and burst into tears.

Her grief was so real and her loss so recent that I hesitated to afflict her by further questions. So returning to the scene of the tragedy, I stepped out upon the balcony which ran in front. Soft voices instantly struck my ears. The neighbours on either side were grouped in front of their own windows, and were exchanging the remarks natural under the circumstances. I paused, as in duty bound, and listened. But I heard nothing worth recording, and would have instantly reentered the house, if I had not been impressed by the appearance of a very graceful woman who stood at my right. She was clinging to her husband, who was gazing at one of the pillars before him in a strange fixed way which astonished me till he attempted to move, and then I saw that he was blind. I remembered that there lived in this row a blind doctor, equally celebrated for his skill and for his uncommon personal attractions, and greatly interested not only by his affliction, but in the sympathy evinced by his young and affectionate wife, I stood still, till I heard her say in the soft and appealing tones of love:

"Come in, Constant; you have heavy duties for to-morrow, and you should get a few hours' rest if possible."

He came from the shadow of the pillar, and for one minute I saw his face with the lamplight shining full upon it. It was as regular of feature as a sculptured Adonis, and it was as white.

"Sleep!" he repeated, in the measured tones of deep but suppressed feeling. "Sleep! with murder on the other side of the wall!" And he stretched out his arms in a dazed way that insensibly accentuated the horror I myself felt of the crime which had so lately taken place in the room behind me.

She, noting the movement, took one of the groping hands in her own and drew him gently towards her.

"This way," she urged; and, guiding him into the house, she closed the window and drew down the shades.

I have no excuse to offer for my curiosity, but the interest excited in me by this totally irrelevant episode was so great that I did not leave the neighbourhood till I had learned something of this remarkable couple.

The story told me was very simple. Dr. Zabriskie had not been born blind, but had become so after a grievous illness which had stricken him down soon after he received his diploma. Instead of succumbing to an affliction which would have daunted most men, he expressed his intention of practising his profession, and soon became so successful in it that he found no difficulty in establishing himself in one of the best paying quarters of the city. Indeed, his intuition seemed to have developed in a remarkable degree after the loss of his sight, and he seldom, if ever, made a mistake in diagnosis. Considering this fact, and the personal attractions which gave him distinction, it was no wonder that he soon became a popular physician whose presence was a benefaction and whose word law.

He had been engaged to be married at the time of his illness, and when he learned what was likely to be its result, had offered to release the young lady from all obligation to him. But she would not be released, and they were married. This had taken place some five years previous to Mr. Hasbrouck's death, three of which had been spent by them in Lafayette Place.

So much for the beautiful woman next door.

There being absolutely no clue to the assailant of Mr. Hasbrouck, I naturally looked forward to the inquest for some evidence upon which to work. But there seemed to be no underlying facts to this tragedy. The most careful study into the habits and conduct of the deceased brought nothing to light save his general beneficence and rectitude, nor was there in his history or in that of his wife, any secret or hidden obligation calculated to provoke any such act of revenge as murder. Mrs. Hasbrouck's surmise that the intruder was simply a burglar, and that she had rather imagined than heard the words which pointed to the shooting as a deed of vengeance, soon gained general credence.

But though the police worked long and arduously in this new direction their efforts were without fruit and the case bids fair to remain an unsolvable mystery.

That was all. As Violet dropped the last page from her hand, she recalled a certain phrase in her employer's letter. "If at the end you come upon a perfectly blank wall—" Well, she had come upon this wall. Did he expect her to make an opening in it? Or had he already done so himself, and was merely testing her much vaunted discernment.

Piqued by the thought, she carefully reread the manuscript, and when she had again reached its uncompromising end, she gave herself up to a few minutes of concentrated thought, then, taking a sheet of paper from the rack before her, she wrote upon it a single sentence, and folding the sheet, put it in an envelope which she left unaddressed. This done, she went to bed and slept like the child she really was.

At an early hour the next morning she entered her employer's office. Acknowledging with a nod his somewhat ceremonious bow, she handed him the envelope in which she had enclosed that one mysterious sentence.

He took it with a smile, opened it offhand, glanced at what she had written, and flushed a vivid red.

"You are a—brick," he was going to say, but changed the last word to one more in keeping with her character and appearance. "Look here. I expected this from you and so prepared myself." Taking out a similar piece of paper from his own pocket-book, he laid it down beside hers on the desk before him. It also held a single sentence and, barring a slight difference of expression, the one was the counterpart of the other. "The one loose stone," he murmured.

"Seen and noted by both."

"Why not?" he asked. Then as she glanced expectantly his way, he earnestly added: "Together we may be able to do something. The reward offered by Mrs. Hasbrouck for the detection of the murderer was a very large one. She is a woman of means. I have never heard of its being withdrawn."

"Then it never has been," was Violet's emphatic conclusion, her dimples enforcing the statement as only such dimples can. "But—what do you want of me in an affair of this kind? Something more than to help you locate the one possible clue to further enlightenment. You would not have mentioned the big reward just for that."

"Perhaps not. There is a sequel to the story I sent you. I have written it out, with my own hand. Take it home and read it at your leisure. When you see into what an unhappy maze my own inquiries have led me, possibly you will be glad to assist me in clearing up a situation which is inflicting great suffering on one whom you will be the first to pity. If so, a line mentioning the fact will be much appreciated by me." And disregarding her startled look and the impetuous shaking of her head, he bowed her out with something more than his accustomed suavity but also with a seriousness which affected her in spite of herself and effectually held back the protest it was in her heart to make. She was glad of this when she read his story; but later on—

However, it is not for me to intrude Violet, or Violet's feelings into an affair which she is so anxious to forget. I shall therefore from this moment on, leave her as completely out of this tale of crime and retribution as is possible and keep a full record of her work. When she is necessary to the story, you will see her again. Meanwhile, read with her, this relation of her employer's unhappy attempt to pursue an investigation so openly dropped by the police. You will perceive, from its general style and the accentuation put upon the human side of this sombre story, a likeness to the former manuscript which may prove to you, as it certainly did to Violet, to whose consideration she was indebted for the readableness of the policeman's report, which in all probability had been a simple statement of facts.

But there, I am speaking of Violet again. To prevent a further mischance of this nature, I will introduce at once the above mentioned account.

II

No man in all New York was ever more interested than myself in the Hasbrouck affair, when it was the one and only topic of interest at a period when news was unusually scarce. But, together with many such inexplicable mysteries, it had passed almost completely from my mind, when it was forcibly brought back, one day, by a walk I took through Lafayette Place.

At sight of the long row of uniform buildings, with their pillared fronts and connecting balconies every detail of the crime which had filled the papers at the time with innumerable conjectures returned to me with extraordinary clearness, and, before I knew it, I found myself standing stockstill in the middle of the block with my eye raised to the Hasbrouck house and my ears— or rather my inner consciousness, for no one spoke I am sure—ringing with a question which, whether the echo of some old thought or the expression of a new one, so affected me by the promise it held of some hitherto unsuspected clue, that I hesitated whether to push this new inquiry then or there by an attempted interview with Mrs. Hasbrouck, or to wait till I had given it the thought which such a stirring of dead bones rightfully demanded.

You know what that question was. I shall have communicated it to you, if you have not already guessed it, before perusing these lines:

"Who uttered the scream which gave the first alarm of Mr. Hasbrouck's violent death?"

I was in a state of such excitement as I walked away—for I listened to my better judgment as to the inadvisability of my disturbing Mrs. Hasbrouck with these new inquiries—that the perspiration stood out on my forehead. The testimony she had given at the inquest recurred to me, and I remembered as distinctly as if she were then speaking, that she had expressly stated that she did not scream when confronted by the sight of her husband's dead body. But someone had screamed and that very loudly. Who was it, then? One of the maids, startled by the sudden summons from below, or someone else—some involuntary witness of the crime, whose testimony had been suppressed at the inquest, by fear or influence?

The possibility of having come upon a clue even at this late day so fired my ambition that I took the first opportunity of revisiting Lafayette Place. Choosing such persons as I thought most open to my questions, I learned that there were many who could testify to having heard a woman's shrill scream on that memorable night, just prior to the alarm given by old Cyrus, but no one who could tell from whose lips it had come. One fact, however, was immediately settled. It had not been the result of the servant-women's fears. Both of the girls were positive that they had uttered no sound, nor had they themselves heard any till Cyrus rushed to the window with his wild cries. As the scream, by whomever given, was uttered before they descended the stairs, I was convinced by these assurances that it had issued from one of the front windows, and not from the rear of the house, where their own rooms lay. Could it be that it had sprung from the adjoining dwelling, and that—

I remembered who had lived there and was for ringing the bell at once. But, missing the doctor's sign, I made inquiries and found that he had moved from the block. However, a doctor is soon found, and in less than fifteen, minutes I was at the door of his new home, where I asked, not for him, but for Mrs. Zabriskie.

It required some courage to do this, for I had taken particular notice of the doctor's wife at the inquest, and her beauty, at that time, had worn such an aspect of mingled sweetness and dignity that I hesitated to encounter it under any circumstances likely to disturb its pure serenity. But a clue once grasped cannot be lightly set aside by a true detective, and it would have taken more than a woman's frowns to stop me at this point.

However, it was not with frowns she received me, but with a display of emotion for which I was even less prepared. I had sent up my card and I saw it trembling in her hand as she entered the room. As she neared me, she glanced at it, and with a show of gentle indifference which did not in the least disguise her extreme anxiety, she courteously remarked:

"Your name is an unfamiliar one to me. But you told my maid that your business was one of extreme importance, and so I have consented to see you. What can an agent from a private detective office have to say to me?"

Startled by this evidence of the existence of some hidden skeleton in her own closet, I made an immediate attempt to reassure her.

"Nothing which concerns you personally," said I. "I simply wish to ask you a question in regard to a small matter connected with Mr. Hasbrouck's violent death in Lafayette Place, a couple of years ago. You were living in the adjoining house at the time I believe, and it has occurred to me that you might on that account be able to settle a point which has never been fully cleared up."

Instead of showing the relief I expected, her pallor increased and her fine eyes, which had been fixed curiously upon me, sank in confusion to the floor.

"Great heaven!" thought I. "She looks as if at one more word from me, she would fall at my feet in a faint. What is this I have stumbled upon!"

"I do not see how you can have any question to ask me on that subject," she began with an effort at composure which for some reason disturbed me more than her previous open display of fear. "Yet if you have," she continued, with a rapid change of manner that touched my heart in spite of myself, "I shall, of course, do my best to answer you."

There are women whose sweetest tones and most charming smiles only serve to awaken distrust in men of my calling; but Mrs. Zabriskie was not of this number. Her face was beautiful, but it was also candid in its expression, and beneath the agitation which palpably disturbed her, I was sure there lurked nothing either wicked or false. Yet I held fast by the clue which I had grasped as it were in the dark, and without knowing whither I was tending, much less whither I was leading her, I proceeded to say:

"The question which I presume to put to you as the next door neighbour of Mr. Hasbrouck is this: Who was the woman who on the night of that gentleman's assassination screamed out so loudly that the whole neighbourhood heard her?"

The gasp she gave answered my question in a way she little realized, and struck as I was by the impalpable links that had led me to the threshold of this hitherto unsolvable mystery, I was about to press my advantage and ask another question, when she quickly started forward and laid her hand on my lips.

Astonished, I looked at her inquiringly, but her head was turned aside, and her eyes, fixed upon the door, showed the greatest anxiety. Instantly I realized what she feared. Her husband was entering the house, and she dreaded lest his ears should catch a word of our conversation.

Not knowing what was in her mind, and unable to realize the importance of the moment to her, I yet listened to the advance of her blind husband with an almost painful interest. Would he enter the room where we were, or would he pass immediately to his office in the rear? She seemed to wonder too, and almost held her breath as he neared the door, paused, and stood in the open doorway, with his ear turned towards us.

As for myself, I remained perfectly still, gazing at his face in mingled surprise and apprehension. For besides its beauty, which was of a marked order, as I have already observed, it had a touching expression which irresistibly aroused both pity and interest in the spectator. This may have been the result of his affliction, or it may have sprung from some deeper cause; but, whatever its source, this look in his face produced a strong impression upon me and interested me at once in his personality. Would he enter; or would he pass on? Her look of silent appeal showed me in which direction her wishes lay, but while I answered her glance by complete silence, I was conscious in some indistinct way that the business I had undertaken would be better furthered by his entrance.

The blind have often been said to possess a sixth sense in place of the one they have lost. Though I am sure we made no noise, I soon perceived that he was aware of our presence. Stepping hastily forward he said, in the high and vibrating tone of restrained passion:

"Zulma, are you there?"

For a moment I thought she did not mean to answer, but knowing doubtless from experience the impossibility of deceiving him, she answered with a cheerful assent, dropping her hand as she did so from before my lips.

He heard the slight rustle which accompanied the movement, and a look I found it hard to comprehend flashed over his features, altering his expression so completely that he seemed another man.

"You have someone with you," he declared, advancing another step, but with none of the uncertainty which usually accompanies the movements of the blind. "Some dear friend," he went on, with an almost sarcastic emphasis and a forced smile that had little of gaiety in it.

The agitated and distressed blush which answered him could have but one interpretation. He suspected that her hand had been clasped in mine, and she perceived his thought and knew that I perceived it also.

Drawing herself up, she moved towards him, saying in a sweet womanly tone:

"It is no friend, Constant, not even an acquaintance. The person whom I now present to you is a representative from some detective agency. He is here upon a trivial errand which will soon be finished, when I will join you in the office."

I knew she was but taking a choice between two evils, that she would have saved her husband the knowledge of my calling as well as of my presence in the house, if her self-respect would have allowed it; but neither she nor I anticipated the effect which this introduction of myself in my business capacity would produce upon him.

"A detective," he repeated, staring with his sightless eyes, as if, in his eagerness to see, he half hoped his lost sense would return. "He can have no trivial errand here; he has been sent by God Himself to—"

"Let me speak for you," hastily interposed his wife, springing to his side and clasping his arm with a fervour that was equally expressive of appeal and command. Then turning to me, she explained: "Since Mr. Hasbrouck's unaccountable death, my husband has been labouring under an hallucination which I have only to mention, for you to recognize its perfect absurdity. He thinks—oh! do not look like that, Constant; you know it is an hallucination which must vanish the moment we drag it into broad daylight—that he—he, the best man in all the world, was himself the assailant of Mr. Hasbrouck."

"Good God!"

"I say nothing of the impossibility of this being so," she went on in a fever of expostulation. "He is blind, and could not have delivered such a shot even if he had desired to; besides, he had no weapon. But the inconsistency of the thing speaks for itself, and should assure him that his mind is unbalanced and that he is merely suffering from a shock that was greater than we realized. He is a physician and has had many such instances in his own practice. Why, he was very much attached to Mr. Hasbrouck! They were the best of friends, and though he insists that he killed him, he cannot give any reason for the deed."

At these words the doctor's face grew stern, and he spoke like an automaton repeating some fearful lesson:

"I killed him. I went to his room and deliberately shot him. I had nothing against him, and my remorse is extreme. Arrest me and let me pay the penalty of my crime. It is the only way in which I can obtain peace."

Shocked beyond all power of self-control by this repetition of what she evidently considered the unhappy ravings of a madman, she let go his arm and turned upon me in frenzy.

"Convince him!" she cried. "Convince him by your questions that he never could have done this fearful thing."

I was labouring under great excitement myself, for as a private agent with no official authority such as he evidently attributed to me in the blindness of his passion, I felt the incongruity of my position in the face of a matter of such tragic consequence. Besides, I agreed with her that he was in a distempered state of mind, and I hardly knew how to deal with one so fixed in his hallucination and with so much intelligence to support it. But the emergency was great, for he was holding out his wrists in the evident expectation of my taking him into instant custody; and the sight was killing his wife, who had sunk on the floor between us, in terror and anguish.

"You say you killed Mr. Hasbrouck," I began. "Where did you get your pistol, and what did you do with it after you left his house?"

"My husband had no pistol; never had any pistol," put in Mrs. Zabriskie, with vehement assertion. "If I had seen him with such a weapon—"

"I threw it away. When I left the house, I cast it as far from me as possible, for I was frightened at what I had done, horribly frightened."

"No pistol was ever found," I answered with a smile, forgetting for the moment that he could not see. "If such an instrument had been found in the street after a murder of such consequence, it certainly would have been brought to the police."

"You forget that a good pistol is valuable property," he went on stolidly. "Someone came along before the general alarm was given; and seeing such a treasure lying on the sidewalk, picked it up and carried it off. Not being an honest man, he preferred to keep it to drawing the attention of the police upon himself."

"Hum, perhaps," said I; "but where did you get it. Surely you can tell where you procured such a weapon, if, as your wife intimates, you did not own one."

"I bought it that selfsame night of a friend; a friend whom I will not name, since he resides no longer in this country. I—" He paused; intense passion was in his face; he turned towards his wife, and a low cry escaped him, which made her look up in fear.

"I do not wish to go into any particulars," said he. "God forsook me and I committed a horrible crime. When I am punished, perhaps peace will return to me and happiness to her. I would not wish her to suffer too long or too bitterly for my sin."

"Constant!" What love was in the cry! It seemed to move him and turn his thoughts for a moment into a different channel.

"Poor child!" he murmured, stretching out his hands by an irresistible impulse towards her. But the change was but momentary, and he was soon again the stern and determined self-accuser. "Are you going to take me before a magistrate?" he asked. "If so, I have a few duties to perform which you are welcome to witness."

This was too much; I felt that the time had come for me to disabuse his mind of the impression he had unwittingly formed of me. I therefore said as considerately as I could:

"You mistake my position, Dr. Zabriskie. Though a detective of some experience, I have no connection with the police and no right to intrude myself in a matter of such tragic importance. If, however, you are as anxious as you say to subject yourself to police examination, I will mention the same to the proper authorities, and leave them to take such action as they think best."

"That will be still more satisfactory to me," said he; "for though I have many times contemplated giving myself up, I have still much to do before I can leave my home and practice without injury to others. Good-day; when you want me you will find me here."

He was gone, and the poor young wife was left crouching on the floor alone. Pitying her shame and terror, I ventured to remark that it was not an uncommon thing for a man to confess to a crime he had never committed, and assured her that the matter would be inquired into very carefully before any attempt was made upon his liberty.

She thanked me, and slowly rising, tried to regain her equanimity; but the manner as well as the matter of her husband's self-condemnation was too overwhelming in its nature for her to recover readily from her emotions.

"I have long dreaded this," she acknowledged. "For months I have foreseen that he would make some rash communication or insane avowal. If I had dared, I would have consulted some physician about this hallucination of his; but he was so sane on other points that I hesitated to give my dreadful secret to the world. I kept hoping that time and his daily pursuits would have their effect and restore him to himself. But his illusion grows, and now I fear that nothing will ever convince him that he did not commit the deed of which he accuses himself. If he were not blind I would have more hope, but the blind have so much time for brooding."

"I think he had better be indulged in his fancies for the present," I ventured. "If he is labouring under an illusion it might be dangerous to cross him."

"If?" she echoed in an indescribable tone of amazement and dread. "Can you for a moment harbour the idea that he has spoken the truth?"

"Madam," I returned, with something of the cynicism of my calling, "what caused you to give such an unearthly scream just before this murder was made known to the neighbourhood?"

She stared, paled, and finally began to tremble, not, as I now believe, at the insinuation latent in my words, but at the doubts which my question aroused in her own breast.

"Did I?" she asked; then with a burst of candour which seemed inseparable from her nature, she continued: "Why do I try to mislead you or deceive myself? I did give a shriek just before the alarm was raised next door; but it was not from any knowledge I had of a crime having been committed, but because I unexpectedly saw before me my husband whom I supposed to be on his way to Poughkeepsie. He was looking very pale and strange, and for a moment I thought I stood face to face with his ghost. But he soon explained his appearance by saying that he had fallen from the train and had only been saved by a miracle from being dismembered; and I was just bemoaning his mishap and trying to calm him and myself, when that terrible shout was heard next door of 'Murder! murder!' Coming so soon after the shock he had himself experienced, it quite unnerved him, and I think we can date his mental disturbance from that moment. For he began immediately to take a morbid interest in the affair next door, though it was weeks, if not months, before he let a word fall of the nature of those you have just heard. Indeed it was not till I repeated to him some of the expressions he was continually letting fall in his sleep, that he commenced to accuse himself of crime and talk of retribution."

"You say that your husband frightened you on that night by appearing suddenly at the door when you thought him on his way to Poughkeepsie. Is Dr. Zabriskie in the habit of thus going and coming alone at an hour so late as this must have been?"

"You forget that to the blind, night is less full of perils than the day. Often and often has my husband found his way to his patients' houses alone after midnight; but on this especial evening he had Leonard with him. Leonard was his chauffeur, and always accompanied him when he went any distance."

"Well, then," said I, "all we have to do is to summon Leonard and hear what he has to say concerning this affair. He will surely know whether or not his master went into the house next door."

"Leonard has left us," she said. "Dr. Zabriskie has another chauffeur now. Besides (I have nothing to conceal from you), Leonard was not with him when he returned to the house that evening or the doctor would not have been without his portmanteau till the next day. Something—I have never known what—caused them to separate, and that is why I have no answer to give the doctor when he accuses himself of committing a deed that night so wholly out of keeping with every other act of his life."

"And have you never asked Leonard why they separated and why he allowed his master to come home alone after the shock he had received at the station?"

"I did not know there was any reason for my doing so till long after he had left us."

"And when did he leave?"

"That I do not remember. A few weeks or possibly a few days after that dreadful night."

"And where is he now?"

"Ah, that I have not the least means of knowing. But," she objected, in sudden distrust, "what do you want of Leonard? If he did not follow Dr. Zabriskie to his own door, he could tell us nothing that would convince my husband that he is labouring under an illusion."

"But he might tell us something which would convince us that Dr. Zabriskie was not himself after the accident; that he—"

"Hush!" came from her lips in imperious tones. "I will not believe that he shot Mr. Hasbrouck even if you prove him to have been insane at the time. How could he? My husband is blind. It would take a man of very keen sight to force himself into a house closed for the night, and kill a man in the dark at one shot."

"On the contrary, it is only a blind man who could do this," cried a voice from the doorway. "Those who trust to eyesight must be able to catch a glimpse of the mark they aim at, and this room, as I have been told, was

108

without a glimmer of light. But the blind trust to sound, and as Mr. Hasbrouck spoke—"

"Oh!" burst from the horrified wife, "is there no one to stop him when he speaks like that?"

<h1 style="text-align:center">III</h1>

As you will see, this matter, so recklessly entered into, had proved to be of too serious a nature for me to pursue it farther without the cognizance of the police. Having a friend on the force in whose discretion I could rely, I took him into my confidence and asked for his advice. He pooh-poohed the doctor's statements, but said that he would bring the matter to the attention of the superintendent and let me know the result. I agreed to this, and we parted with the mutual understanding that mum was the word till some official decision had been arrived at. I had not long to wait. At an early day he came in with the information that there had been, as might be expected, a division of opinion among his superiors as to the importance of Dr. Zabriskie's so-called confession, but in one point they had been unanimous and that was the desirability of his appearing before them at Headquarters for a personal examination. As, however, in the mind of two out of three of them his condition was attributed entirely to acute mania, it had been thought best to employ as their emissary one in whom he had already confided and submitted his case to,—in other words, myself. The time was set for the next afternoon at the close of his usual office hours.

He went without reluctance, his wife accompanying him. In the short time which elapsed between their leaving home and entering Headquarters, I embraced the opportunity of observing them, and I found the study equally exciting and interesting. His face was calm but hopeless, and his eye, dark and unfathomable, but neither frenzied nor uncertain. He spoke but once and listened to nothing, though now and then his wife moved as if to attract his attention, and once even stole her hand towards his, in the tender hope that he would feel its approach and accept her sympathy. But he was deaf as well as blind; and sat wrapped up in thoughts which she, I know, would have given worlds to penetrate.

Her countenance was not without its mystery also. She showed in every lineament passionate concern and misery, and a deep tenderness from which the element of fear was not absent. But she, as well as he, betrayed that some misunderstanding deeper than any I had previously suspected drew its intangible veil between them and made the near proximity in which they sat at once a heart-piercing delight and an unspeakable pain. What was the misunderstanding; and what was the character of the fear that modified her every look of love in his direction? Her perfect indifference to my presence proved that it was not connected with the position in which he had placed himself towards the police by his voluntary confession of crime, nor could I thus interpret the expression, of frantic question which now and then contracted her features, as she raised her eyes towards his sightless orbs, and

109

strove to read in his firm set lips the meaning of those assertions she could only ascribe to loss of reason.

The stopping of the carriage seemed to awaken both from thoughts that separated rather than united them. He turned his face in her direction, and she stretching forth her hand, prepared to lead him from the carriage, without any of that display of timidity which had previously been evident in her manner.

As his guide she seemed to fear nothing; as his lover, everything.

"There is another and a deeper tragedy underlying the outward and obvious one," was my inward conclusion, as I followed them into the presence of the gentlemen awaiting them.

Dr. Zabriskie's quiet appearance was in itself a shock to those who had anticipated the feverish unrest of a madman; so was his speech, which was calm, straightforward, and quietly determined.

"I shot Mr. Hasbrouck," was his steady affirmation, given without any show of frenzy or desperation. "If you ask me why I did it, I cannot answer; if you ask me how, I am ready to state all that I know concerning the matter."

"But, Dr. Zabriskie," interposed one of the inspectors, "the why is the most important thing for us to consider just now. If you really desire to convince us that you committed this dreadful crime of killing a totally inoffensive man, you should give us some reason for an act so opposed to all your instincts and general conduct."

But the doctor continued unmoved:

"I had no reason for murdering Mr. Hasbrouck. A hundred questions can elicit no other reply; you had better keep to the how."

A deep-drawn breath from the wife answered the looks of the three gentlemen to whom this suggestion was offered. "You see," that breath seemed to protest, "that he is not in his right mind."

I began to waver in my own opinion, and yet the intuition which has served me in cases seemingly as impenetrable as this bade me beware of following the general judgment.

"Ask him to inform you how he got into the house," I whispered to Inspector D—, who sat nearest me.

Immediately the inspector put the question which I had suggested:

"By what means did you enter Mr. Hasbrouck's house at so late an hour as this murder occurred?"

The blind doctor's head fell forward on his breast, and he hesitated for the first and only time.

"You will not believe me," said he; "but the door was ajar when I came to it. Such things make crime easy; it is the only excuse I have to offer for this dreadful deed."

The front door of a respectable citizen's house ajar at half-past eleven at night! It was a statement that fixed in all minds the conviction of the speaker's irresponsibility. Mrs. Zabriskie's brow cleared, and her beauty became for a moment dazzling as she held out her hands in irrepressible relief towards those who were interrogating her husband. I alone kept my impassibility. A possible explanation of this crime had flashed like lightning across my mind; an explanation from which I inwardly recoiled, even while I felt forced to consider it.

"Dr. Zabriskie," remarked the inspector formerly mentioned as friendly to him, "such old servants as those kept by Mr. Hasbrouck do not leave the front door ajar at twelve o'clock at night."

"Yet ajar it was," repeated the blind doctor, with quiet emphasis; "and finding it so, I went in. When I came out again, I closed it. Do you wish me to swear to what I say? If so, I am ready."

What reply could they give? To see this splendid-looking man, hallowed by an affliction so great that in itself it called forth the compassion of the most indifferent, accusing himself of a cold-blooded crime, in tones which sounded dispassionate because of the will forcing their utterance, was too painful in itself for any one to indulge in unnecessary words. Compassion took the place of curiosity, and each and all of us turned involuntary looks of pity upon the young wife pressing so eagerly to his side.

"For a blind man," ventured one, "the assault was both deft and certain. Are you accustomed to Mr. Hasbrouck's house, that you found your way with so little difficulty to his bedroom?"

"I am accustomed—" he began.

But here his wife broke in with irrepressible passion:

"He is not accustomed to that house. He has never been beyond the first floor. Why, why do you question him? Do you not see—"

His hand was on her lips.

"Hush!" he commanded. "You know my skill in moving about a house; how I sometimes deceive those who do not know me into believing that I can see, by the readiness with which I avoid obstacles and find my way even in strange and untried scenes. Do not try to make them think I am not in my right mind, or you will drive me into the very condition you attribute to me."

His face, rigid, cold, and set, looked like that of a mask. Hers, drawn with horror and filled with question that was fast taking the form of doubt, bespoke an awful tragedy from which more than one of us recoiled.

"Can you shoot a man dead without seeing him?" asked the Superintendent, with painful effort.

"Give me a pistol and I will show you," was the quick reply.

A low cry came from the wife. In a drawer near to every one of us there lay a pistol, but no one moved to take it out. There was a look in the doctor's eye which made us fear to trust him with a pistol just then.

"We will accept your assurance that you possess a skill beyond that of most men," returned the Superintendent. And beckoning me forward, he whispered: "This is a case for the doctors and not for the police. Remove him quietly, and notify Dr. Southyard of what I say."

But Dr. Zabriskie, who seemed to have an almost supernatural acuteness of hearing, gave a violent start at this, and spoke up for the first time with real passion in his voice:

"No, no, I pray you. I can bear anything but that. Remember, gentlemen, that I am blind; that I cannot see who is about me; that my life would be a torture if I felt myself surrounded by spies watching to catch some evidence of madness in me. Rather conviction at once, death, dishonour, and obloquy. These I have incurred. These I have brought upon myself by crime, but not this worse fate—oh! not this worse fate."

His passion was so intense and yet so confined within the bounds of decorum, that we felt strangely impressed by it. Only the wife stood transfixed, with the dread growing in her heart, till her white, waxen visage seemed even more terrible to contemplate than his passion-distorted one.

"It is not strange that my wife thinks me demented," the doctor continued, as if afraid of the silence that answered him. "But it is your business to discriminate, and you should know a sane man when you see him."

Inspector D—— no longer hesitated.

"Very well," said he, "give me the least proof that your assertions are true, and we will lay your case before the prosecuting attorney."

"Proof? Is not a man's word—"

"No man's confession is worth much without some evidence to support it. In your case there is none. You cannot even produce the pistol with which you assert yourself to have committed the deed."

"True, true. I was frightened by what I had done, and the instinct of self-preservation led me to rid myself of the weapon in any way I could. But someone found this pistol; someone picked it up from the sidewalk of Lafayette Place on that fatal night. Advertise for it. Offer a reward. I will give you the money." Suddenly he appeared to realize how all this sounded. "Alas!" cried he, "I know the story seems improbable; but it is not the probable things that happen in this life, as, you should know, who every day dig deep into the heart of human affairs."

Were these the ravings of insanity? I began to understand the wife's terror.

"I bought the pistol," he went on, "of—alas! I cannot tell you his name. Everything is against me. I cannot adduce one proof; yet even she is beginning to fear that my story is true. I know it by her silence, a silence that yawns between us like a deep and unfathomable gulf."

But at these words her voice rang out with passionate vehemence.

"No, no, it is false! I will never believe that your hands have been plunged in blood. You are my own pure-hearted Constant, cold, perhaps, and stern, but with no guilt upon your conscience save in your own wild imagination."

"Zulma, you are no friend to me," he declared, pushing her gently aside. "Believe me innocent, but say nothing to lead these others to doubt my word."

And she said no more, but her looks spoke volumes.

The result was that he was not detained, though he prayed for instant commitment. He seemed to dread his own home, and the surveillance to which he instinctively knew he would henceforth be subjected. To see him shrink from his wife's hand as she strove to lead him from the room was sufficiently painful; but the feeling thus aroused was nothing to that with which we observed the keen and agonized expectancy of his look as he turned and listened for the steps of the officer who followed him.

"From this time on I shall never know whether or not I am alone," was his final observation as he left the building.

Here is where the matter rests and here, Miss Strange, is where you come in. The police were for sending an expert alienist into the house; but agreeing with me, and, in fact, with the doctor himself, that if he were not already out of his mind, this would certainly make them so, they, at my earnest intercession, have left the next move to me.

That move as you must by this time understand involves you. You have advantages for making Mrs. Zabriskie's acquaintance of which I beg you to

avail yourself. As friend or patient, you must win your way into that home?
You must sound to its depths one or both of these two wretched hearts. Not so
much now for any possible reward which may follow the elucidation of this
mystery which has come so near being shelved, but for pity's sake and the
possible settlement of a question which is fast driving a lovely member of your
sex distracted.

May I rely on you? If so—

Various instructions followed, over which Violet mused with a deprecatory
shaking of her head till the little clock struck two. Why should she, already in
a state of secret despondency, intrude herself into an affair at once so painful
and so hopeless?

IV

But by morning her mood changed. The pathos of the situation had seized
upon her in her dreams, and before the day was over, she was to be seen, as a
prospective patient, in Dr. Zabriskie's office. She had a slight complaint as her
excuse, and she made the most of it. That is, at first, but as the personality of
this extraordinary man began to make its usual impression, she found herself
forgetting her own condition in the intensity of interest she felt in his. Indeed,
she had to pull herself together more than once lest he should suspect the
double nature of her errand, and she actually caught herself at times rejoicing
in his affliction since it left her with only her voice to think of, in her hated but
necessary task of deception.

That she succeeded in this effort, even with one of his nice ear, was evident
from the interested way in which he dilated upon her malady, and the minute
instructions he was careful to give her—the physician being always uppermost
in his strange dual nature, when he was in his office or at the bedside of the
sick;—and had she not been a deep reader of the human soul she would have
left his presence in simple wonder at his skill and entire absorption in an
exacting profession.

But as it was, she carried with her an image of subdued suffering, which
drove her, from that moment on, to ask herself what she could do to aid him
in his fight against his own illusion; for to associate such a man with a
senseless and cruel murder was preposterous.

What this wish, helped by no common determination, led her into, it was
not in her mind to conceive. She was making her one great mistake, but as yet
she was in happy ignorance of it, and pursued the course laid out for her
without a doubt of the ultimate result.

Having seen and made up her mind about the husband, she next sought to
see and gauge the wife. That she succeeded in doing this by means of one of
her sly little tricks is not to the point; but what followed in natural
consequence is very much so. A mutual interest sprang up between them
which led very speedily to actual friendship. Mrs. Zabriskie's hungry heart
opened to the sympathetic little being who clung to her in such evident
admiration; while Violet, brought face to face with a real woman, succumbed

to feelings which made it no imposition on her part to spend much of her leisure in Zulma Zabriskie's company.

The result were the following naive reports which drifted into her employer's office from day to day, as this intimacy deepened.

The doctor is settling into a deep melancholy, from which he tries to rise at times, but with only indifferent success. Yesterday he rode around to all his patients for the purpose of withdrawing his services on the plea of illness. But he still keeps his office open, and today I had the opportunity of witnessing his reception and treatment of the many sufferers who came to him for aid. I think he was conscious of my presence, though an attempt had been made to conceal it. For the listening look never left his face from the moment he entered the room, and once he rose and passed quickly from wall to wall, groping with out-stretched hands into every nook and corner, and barely escaping contact with the curtain behind which I was hidden. But if he suspected my presence, he showed no displeasure at it, wishing perhaps for a witness to his skill in the treatment of disease.

And truly I never beheld a finer manifestation of practical insight in cases of a more or less baffling nature. He is certainly a most wonderful physician, and I feel bound to record that his mind is as clear for business as if no shadow had fallen upon it.

Dr. Zabriskie loves his wife, but in a way torturing to himself and to her. If she is gone from the house he is wretched, and yet when she returns he often forbears to speak to her, or if he does speak it is with a constraint that hurts her more than his silence. I was present when she came in today. Her step, which had been eager on the stairway, flagged as she approached the room, and he naturally noted the change and gave his own interpretation to it. His face, which had been very pale, flushed suddenly, and a nervous trembling seized him which he sought in vain to hide. But by the time her tall and beautiful figure stood in the doorway, he was his usual self again in all but the expression of his eyes, which stared straight before him in an agony of longing only to be observed in those who have once seen.

"Where have you been, Zulma?" he asked, as contrary to his wont, he moved to meet her.

"To my mother's, to Arnold & Constable's, and to the hospital, as you requested," was her quick answer, made without faltering or embarrassment.

He stepped still nearer and took her hand, and as he did so my eye fell on his and I noted that his finger lay over her pulse in seeming unconsciousness.

"Nowhere else?" he queried.

She smiled the saddest kind of smile and shook her head; then, remembering that he could not see this movement, she cried in a wistful tone:

"Nowhere else, Constant; I was too anxious to get back."

I expected him to drop her hand at this, but he did not; and his finger still rested on her pulse.

"And whom did you see while you were gone?" he continued.

She told him, naming over several names.

"You must have enjoyed yourself," was his cold comment, as he let go her hand and turned away. But his manner showed relief, and I could not but sympathize with the pitiable situation of a man who found himself forced into means like this for probing the heart of his young wife.

Yet when I turned towards her, I realized that her position was but little happier than his. Tears are no strangers to her eyes, but those which welled up at this moment seemed to possess a bitterness that promised but little peace for her future. Yet she quickly dried them and busied herself with ministrations for his comfort.

If I am any judge of woman, Zulma Zabriskie is superior to most of her sex. That her husband mistrusts her is evident, but whether this is the result of the stand she has taken in his regard, or only a manifestation of dementia, I have as yet been unable to determine. I dread to leave them alone together, and yet when I presume to suggest that she should be on her guard in her interviews with him, she smiles very placidly and tells me that nothing would give her greater joy than to see him lift his hand against her, for that would argue that he is not accountable for his deeds or assertions.

Yet it would be a grief to see her injured by this passionate and unhappy man.

You have said that you wanted all the details I could give; so I feel bound to say that Dr. Zabriskie tries to be considerate of his wife, though he often fails in the attempt. When she offers herself as his guide, or assists him with his mail or performs any of the many acts of kindness by which she continually manifests her sense of his affliction, he thanks her with courtesy and often with kindness, yet I know she would willingly exchange all his set phrases for one fond embrace or impulsive smile of affection. It would be too much to say that he is not in the full possession of his faculties, and yet upon what other hypothesis can we account for the inconsistencies of his conduct?

I have before me two visions of mental suffering. At noon I passed the office door, and looking within, saw the figure of Dr. Zabriskie seated in his great chair, lost in thought or deep in those memories which make an abyss in one's consciousness. His hands, which were clenched, rested upon the arms of his chair, and in one of them I detected a woman's glove, which I had no difficulty in recognizing as one of the pair worn by his wife this morning. He held it as a tiger might hold his prey or a miser his gold, but his set features and sightless eyes betrayed that a conflict of emotions was being waged within him, among which tenderness had but little share.

Though alive as he usually is to every sound, he was too absorbed at this moment to notice my presence, though I had taken no pains to approach quietly. I therefore stood for a full minute watching him, till an irresistible sense of the shame at thus spying upon a blind man in his moments of secret anguish compelled me to withdraw. But not before I saw his features relax in a storm of passionate feeling, as he rained kisses after kisses on the senseless kid he had so long held in his motionless grasp. Yet when an hour later he entered the dining-room on his wife's arm, there was nothing in his manner to show that he had in any way changed in his attitude towards her.

The other picture was more tragic still. I was seeking Mrs. Zabriskie in her own room, when I caught a fleeting vision of her tall form, with her arms thrown up over her head in a paroxysm of feeling which made her as oblivious to my presence as her husband had been several hours before. Were the words that escaped her lips "Thank God we have no children!" or was this exclamation suggested to me by the passion and unrestrained impulse of her action?

So much up to date. Interesting enough, or so her employer seemed to think, as he went hurriedly through the whole story, one special afternoon in his office, tapping each sheet as he laid it aside with his sagacious forefinger, as though he would say, "Enough! My theory still holds good; nothing contradictory here; on the contrary complete and undisputable confirmation of the one and only explanation of this astounding crime."

What was that theory; and in what way and through whose efforts had he been enabled to form one? The following notes may enlighten us. Though written in his own hand, and undoubtedly a memorandum of his own activities, he evidently thinks it worth while to reperuse them in connection with those he had just laid aside.

We can do no better than read them also.

We omit dates.

Watched the Zabriskie mansion for five hours this morning, from the second story window of an adjoining hotel. Saw the doctor when he drove away on his round of visits, and saw him when he returned. A coloured man accompanied him.

Today I followed Mrs. Zabriskie. She went first to a house in Washington Place where I am told her mother lives. Here she stayed some time, after which she drove down to Canal Street, where she did some shopping, and later stopped at the hospital, into which I took the liberty of following her. She seemed to know many there, and passed from cot to cot with a smile in which I alone discerned the sadness of a broken heart. When she left, I left also, without having learned anything beyond the fact that Mrs. Zabriskie is one who does her duty in sorrow as in joy. A rare, and trustworthy woman I should say, and yet her husband does not trust her. Why?

I have spent this day in accumulating details in regard to Dr. and Mrs. Zabriskie's life previous to the death of Mr. Hasbrouck. I learned from sources it would be unwise to quote just here, that Mrs. Zabriskie had not lacked enemies to charge her with coquetry; that while she had never sacrificed her dignity in public, more than one person had been heard to declare that Dr. Zabriskie was fortunate in being blind, since the sight of his wife's beauty would have but poorly compensated him for the pain he would have suffered in seeing how that beauty was admired.

That all gossip is more or less tinged with exaggeration I have no doubt, yet when a name is mentioned in connection with such stories, there is usually some truth at the bottom of them. And a name is mentioned in this case, though I do not think it worth my while to repeat it here; and loth as I am to recognize the fact, it is a name that carries with it doubts that might easily account for the husband's jealousy. True, I have found no one who dares hint that she still continues to attract attention or to bestow smiles in any direction save where they legally belong. For since a certain memorable night which we all know, neither Dr. Zabriskie nor his wife have been seen save in their own domestic circle, and it is not into such scenes that this serpent, to whom I have just alluded, ever intrudes, nor is it in places of sorrow or suffering that his smile shines, or his fascinations flourish.

And so one portion of my theory is proved to be sound. Dr. Zabriskie is jealous of his wife; whether with good cause or bad I am not prepared to decide; since her present attitude, clouded as it is by the tragedy in which she and her husband are both involved, must differ very much from that which she held when her life was unshadowed by doubt, and her admirers could be counted by the score.

I have just found out where Leonard is. As he is in service some miles up the river, I shall have to be absent from my post for several hours, but I consider the game well worth the candle.

Light at last. I have not only seen Leonard, but succeeded in making him talk. His story is substantially this: That on the night so often mentioned, he packed his master's portmanteau at eight o'clock and at ten called a taxi and rode with the doctor to the Central station. He was told to buy tickets to Poughkeepsie where his master had been called in consultation, and having done this, hurried back to join Dr. Zabriskie on the platform. They had walked together as far as the cars, and Dr. Zabriskie was just stepping on to the train, when a man pushed himself hurriedly between them and whispered something into his master's ear, which caused him to fall back and lose his footing. Dr. Zabriskie's body slid half under the car, but he was withdrawn before any harm was done, though the cars gave a lurch at that moment which must have frightened him exceedingly, for his face was white when he rose to his feet, and when Leonard offered to assist him again on the train, he refused to go and said he would return home and not attempt to ride to Poughkeepsie that night.

The gentleman, whom Leonard now saw to be Mr. Stanton, an intimate friend of Dr. Zabriskie, smiled very queerly at this, and taking the doctor's arm led him back to his own auto. Leonard naturally followed them, but the doctor, hearing his steps, turned and bade him, in a very peremptory tone, to take the cars home, and then, as if on second thought, told him to go to Poughkeepsie in his stead and explain to the people there that he was too shaken up by his misstep to do his duty, and that he would be with them next morning. This seemed strange to Leonard, but he had no reasons for disobeying his master's orders, and so rode to Poughkeepsie. But the doctor did not follow him the next day; on the contrary he telegraphed for him to return, and when he got back dismissed him with a month's wages. This ended Leonard's connection with the Zabriskie family.

A simple story bearing out what the wife has already told us; but it furnishes a link which may prove invaluable. Mr. Stanton, whose first name is Theodore, knows the real reason why Dr. Zabriskie returned home on the night of the seventeenth of July, 19—. Mr. Stanton, consequently, is the man to see, and this shall be my business tomorrow.

Checkmate! Theodore Stanton is not in this country. Though this points him out as the man from whom Dr. Zabriskie bought the pistol, it does not facilitate my work, which is becoming more and more difficult.

Mr. Stanton's whereabouts are not even known to his most intimate friends. He sailed from this country most unexpectedly on the eighteenth of July a year ago, which was the day after the murder of Mr. Hasbrouck. It looks like a flight, especially as he has failed to maintain open communication even with his relatives. Was he the man who shot Mr. Hasbrouck? No; but he was the man who put the pistol in Dr. Zabriskie's hand that night, and whether he did this with purpose or not, was evidently so alarmed at the catastrophe which followed that he took the first outgoing steamer to Europe. So far, all is clear, but there are mysteries yet to be solved, which will require my utmost tact. What if I should seek out the gentleman with whose name that of Mrs. Zabriskie has been linked, and see if I can in any way connect him with Mr. Stanton or the events of that night.

Eureka! I have discovered that Mr. Stanton cherished a mortal hatred for the gentleman above mentioned. It was a covert feeling, but no less deadly on that account; and while it never led him into any extravagances, it was of force sufficient to account for many a secret misfortune occurring to that gentleman. Now if I can prove that he is the Mephistopheles who whispered insinuations into the ear of our blind Faust, I may strike a fact that will lead me out of this maze.

But how can I approach secrets so delicate without compromising the woman I feel bound to respect if only for the devoted love she manifests for her unhappy husband!

I shall have to appeal to Joe Smithers. This is something which I always hate to do, but as long as he will take money, and as long as he is fertile in resources for obtaining the truth from people I am myself unable to reach, I must make use of his cupidity and his genius. He is an honourable fellow in one way, and never retails as gossip what he acquires for our use. How will he proceed in this case, and by what tactics will he gain the very delicate information which we need? I own that I am curious to see.

I shall really have to put down at length the incidents of this night. I always knew that Joe Smithers was invaluable not only to myself but to the police, but I really did not know he possessed talents of so high an order. He wrote me this morning that he had succeeded in getting Mr. T—'s promise to spend the evening with him, and advised me that if I desired to be present as well, his own servant would not be at home, and that an opener of bottles would be required.

As I was very anxious to see Mr. T—— with my own eyes, I accepted this invitation to play the spy, and went at the proper hour to Mr. Smithers's rooms. I found them picturesque in the extreme. Piles of books stacked here and there to the ceiling made nooks and corners which could be quite shut off by a couple of old pictures set into movable frames capable of swinging out or in at the whim or convenience of the owner.

As I had use for the dark shadows cast by these pictures, I pulled them both out, and made such other arrangements as appeared likely to facilitate the purpose I had in view; then I sat down and waited for the two gentlemen who were expected to come in together.

They arrived almost immediately, whereupon I rose and played my part with all necessary discretion. While ridding Mr. T—— of his overcoat, I stole a look at his face. It is not a handsome one, but it boasts of a gay, devil-may-care expression which doubtless makes it dangerous to many women, while his manners are especially attractive, and his voice the richest and most persuasive that I ever heard. I contrasted him, almost against my will, with Dr. Zabriskie, and decided that with most women the former's undoubted fascinations of speech and bearing would outweigh the latter's great beauty and mental endowments; but I doubted if they would with her.

The conversation which immediately began was brilliant but desultory, for Mr. Smithers, with an airy lightness for which he is remarkable, introduced topic after topic, perhaps for the purpose of showing off Mr. T-'s versatility, and perhaps for the deeper and more sinister purpose of shaking the kaleidoscope of talk so thoroughly, that the real topic which we were met to discuss should not make an undue impression on the mind of his guest.

Meanwhile one, two, three bottles passed, and I had the pleasure of seeing Joe Smithers's eye grow calmer and that of Mr. T—— more brilliant and more uncertain. As the last bottle was being passed, Joe cast me a meaning glance, and the real business of the evening began.

I shall not attempt to relate the half dozen failures which Joe made in endeavouring to elicit the facts we were in search of, without arousing the suspicion of his visitor. I am only going to relate the successful attempt. They had been talking now for some hours, and I, who had long before been waved aside from their immediate presence, was hiding my curiosity and growing excitement behind one of the pictures, when I suddenly heard Joe say:

"He has the most remarkable memory I ever met. He can tell to a day when any notable event occurred."

"Pshaw!" answered his companion, who, by the way, was known to pride himself upon his own memory for dates, "I can state where I went and what I did on every day in the year. That may not embrace what you call 'notable events,' but the memory required is all the more remarkable, is it not?"

"Pooh!" was his friend's provoking reply, "you are bluffing, Ben; I will never believe that."

Mr. T-, who had passed by this time into that stage of intoxication which makes persistence in an assertion a duty as well as a pleasure, threw back his head, and as the wreaths of smoke rose in airy spirals from his lips, reiterated his statement, and offered to submit to any test of his vaunted powers which the other might dictate.

"You keep a diary—" began Joe.

"Which at the present moment is at home," completed the other.

"Will you allow me to refer to it tomorrow, if I am suspicious of the accuracy of your recollections?"

"Undoubtedly," returned the other.

"Very well, then, I will wager you a cool fifty that you cannot tell where you were between the hours of ten and eleven on a certain night which I will name."

"Done!" cried the other, bringing out his pocket-book and laying it on the table before him.

Joe followed his example and then summoned me.

"Write a date down here," he commanded, pushing a piece of paper towards me, with a look keen as the flash of a blade. "Any date, man," he added, as I appeared to hesitate in the embarrassment I thought natural under the circumstances. "Put down day, month, and year, only don't go too far back; not farther than two years."

Smiling with the air of a flunkey admitted to the sports of his superiors, I wrote a line and laid it before Mr. Smithers, who at once pushed it with a careless gesture towards his companion. You can of course guess the date I made use of: July 17, 19—. Mr. T—, who had evidently looked upon this matter as mere play, flushed scarlet as he read these words, and for one instant looked as if he had rather fly the house than answer Joe Smithers's nonchalant glance of inquiry.

"I have given my word and will keep it," he said at last, but with a look in my direction that sent me reluctantly back to my retreat. "I don't suppose you want names," he went on; "that is, if anything I have to tell is of a delicate nature?"

"Oh, no," answered the other, "only facts and places."

"I don't think places are necessary either," he returned. "I will tell you what I did and that must serve you. I did not promise to give number and street."

"Well, well," Joe exclaimed; "earn your fifty, that is all. Show that you remember where you were on the night of"—and with an admirable show of indifference he pretended to consult the paper between them—"the seventeenth of July, two years ago, and I shall be satisfied."

"I was at the club for one thing," said Mr. T-; "then I went to see a lady friend, where I stayed until eleven. She wore a blue muslin—What is that?"

I had betrayed myself by a quick movement which sent a glass tumbler crashing to the floor. Zulma Zabriskie had worn a blue muslin on that same night. You will find it noted in the report given me by the policeman who saw her on their balcony.

"That noise?" It was Joe who was speaking. "You don't know Reuben as well as I do or you wouldn't ask. It is his practice, I am sorry to say, to accentuate his pleasure in draining my bottles by dropping a glass at every third one."

Mr. T—— went on.

"She was a married woman and I thought she loved me; but—and this is the greatest proof I can offer you that I am giving you a true account of that night—she had not the slightest idea of the extent of my passion, and only consented to see me at all because she thought, poor thing, that a word from her would set me straight, and rid her of attentions she evidently failed to appreciate. A sorry figure for a fellow like me to cut; but you caught me on the most detestable date in my calendar and—"

There he ceased being interesting and I anxious. The secret of a crime for which there seemed to be no reasonable explanation is no longer a mystery to me. I have but to warn Miss Strange—

He had got thus far when a sound in the room behind him led him to look up. A lady had entered; a lady heavily veiled and trembling with what appeared to be an intense excitement.

He thought he knew the figure, but the person, whoever it was, stood so still and remained so silent, he hesitated to address her; which seeing, she pushed up her veil and all doubt vanished.

It was Violet herself. In disregard of her usual practice she had come alone to the office. This meant urgency of some kind. Had she too sounded this mystery? No, or her aspect would not have worn this look of triumph. What had happened then? He made an instant endeavour to find out.

"You have news," he quietly remarked. "Good news, I should judge, by your very cheery smile."

"Yes; I think I have found the way of bringing Dr. Zabriskie to himself."

Astonished beyond measure, so little did these words harmonize with the impressions and conclusions at which he had just arrived, something very like doubt spoke in his voice as he answered with the simple exclamation:

"You do!"

"Yes. He is obsessed by a fixed idea, and must be given an opportunity to test the truth of that idea. The shock of finding it a false one may restore him to his normal condition. He believes that he shot Mr. Hasbrouck with no other guidance than his sense of hearing. Now if it can be proved that his hearing is an insufficient guide for such an act (as of course it is) the shock of the discovery may clear his brain of its cobwebs. Mrs. Zabriskie thinks so, and the police—"

"What's that? The police?"

"Yes, Dr. Zabriskie would be taken before them again this morning. No entreaties on the part of his wife would prevail; he insisted upon his guilt and asked her to accompany him there; and the poor woman found herself forced to go. Of course he encountered again the same division of opinion among the men he talked with. Three out of the four judged him insane, which observing, he betrayed great agitation and reiterated his former wish to be allowed an opportunity to prove his sanity by showing his skill in shooting. This made an impression; and a disposition was shown to grant his request then and there. But Mrs. Zabriskie would not listen to this. She approved of the experiment but begged that it might be deferred till another day and then take place in some spot remote from the city. For some reason they heeded her, and she has just telephoned me that this attempt of his is to take place tomorrow in the New Jersey woods. I am sorry that this should have been put through without you; and when I tell you that the idea originated with me—that from some word I purposely let fall one day, they both conceived this plan of ending the uncertainty that was devouring their lives, you will understand my excitement and the need I have of your support. Tell me that I have done well. Do not show me such a face—you frighten me—"

"I do not wish to frighten you. I merely wish to know just who are going on this expedition."

"Some members of the police, Dr. Zabriskie, his wife, and—and myself. She begged—"

"You must not go."

"Why? The affair is to be kept secret. The doctor will shoot, fail—Oh!" she suddenly broke in, alarmed by his expression, "you think he will not fail—"

"I think that you had better heed my advice and stay out of it. The affair is now in the hands of the police, and your place is anywhere but where they are."

"But I go as her particular friend. They have given her the privilege of taking with her one of her own sex and she has chosen me. I shall not fail her. Father is away, and if the awful disappointment you suggest awaits her, there is all the more reason why she should have some sympathetic support?"

This was so true, that the fresh protest he was about to utter died on his lips. Instead, he simply remarked as he bowed her out:

"I foresee that we shall not work much longer together. You are nearing the end of your endurance."

He never forgot the smile she threw back at him.

V

There are some events which impress the human mind so deeply that their memory mingles with all after-experiences. Though Violet had made it a rule to forget as soon as possible the tragic episodes incident to the strange career upon which she had so mysteriously embarked, there was destined to be one scene, if not more, which she has never been able to dismiss at will.

This was the sight which met her eyes from the bow of the small boat in which Dr. Zabriskie and his wife were rowed over to Jersey on the afternoon which saw the end of this most sombre drama.

Though it was by no means late in the day, the sun was already sinking, and the bright red glare which filled the west and shone full upon the faces of the half dozen people before her added much to the tragic nature of the scene, though she was far from comprehending its full significance.

The doctor sat with his wife in the stern and it was upon their faces Violet's glance was fixed. The glare shone luridly on his sightless eyeballs, and as she noticed his unwinking lids, she realized as never before what it was to be blind in the midst of sunshine. His wife's eyes, on the contrary, were lowered, but there was a look of hopeless misery in her colourless face which made her appearance infinitely pathetic, and Violet felt confident that if he could only have seen her, he would not have maintained the cold and unresponsive manner which chilled the words on his poor wife's lips and made all advance on her part impossible.

On the seat in front of them sat an inspector and from some quarter, possibly from under the inspector's coat, there came the monotonous ticking of the small clock, which was to serve as a target for the blind man's aim.

This ticking was all Violet heard, though the river was alive with traffic and large and small boats were steaming by them on every side. And I am sure it was all that Mrs. Zabriskie heard also, as with hand pressed to her heart, and eyes fixed on the opposite shore, she waited for the event which was to determine whether the man she loved was a criminal or only a being afflicted of God and worthy of her unceasing care and devotion.

As the sun cast its last scarlet gleam over the water, the boat grounded, and Violet was enabled to have one passing word with Mrs. Zabriskie. She hardly knew what she said but the look she received in return was like that of a frightened child.

But there was always to be seen in Mrs. Zabriskie's countenance this characteristic blending of the severe and the childlike, and beyond an added pang of pity for this beautiful but afflicted woman, Violet let the moment pass without giving it the weight it perhaps demanded.

"The doctor and his wife had a long talk last night," was whispered in her ear as she wound her way with the rest into the heart of the woods. With a start she turned and perceived her employer following close behind her. He had come by another boat.

"But it did not seem to heal whatever breach lies between them," he proceeded. Then, in a quick, anxious tone, he whispered: "Whatever happens, do not lift your veil. I thought I saw a reporter skulking in the rear."

"I will be careful," Violet assured him, and could say no more, as they had

122

already reached the ground which had been selected for this trial at arms, and the various members of the party were being placed in their several positions.

The doctor, to whom light and darkness were alike, stood with his face towards the western glow, and at his side were grouped the inspector and the two physicians. On the arm of one of the latter hung Dr. Zabriskie's overcoat, which he had taken off as soon as he reached the field.

Mrs. Zabriskie stood at the other end of the opening near a tall stump, upon which it had been decided that the clock should be placed when the moment came for the doctor to show his skill. She had been accorded the privilege of setting the clock on this stump, and Violet saw it shining in her hand as she paused for a moment to glance back at the circle of gentlemen who were awaiting her movements. The hands of the clock stood at five minutes to five, though Violet scarcely noted it at the time, for Mrs. Zabriskie was passing her and had stopped to say:

"If he is not himself, he cannot be trusted. Watch him carefully and see that he does no mischief to himself or others. Ask one of the inspectors to stand at his right hand, and stop him if he does not handle his pistol properly."

Violet promised, and she passed on, setting the clock upon the stump and immediately drawing back to a suitable distance at the right, where she stood, wrapped in her long dark cloak. Her face shone ghastly white, even in its environment of snow-covered boughs, and noting this, Violet wished the minutes fewer between the present moment and the hour of five, at which time he was to draw the trigger.

"Dr. Zabriskie," quoth the inspector, "we have endeavoured to make this trial a perfectly fair one. You are to have a shot at a small clock which has been placed within a suitable distance, and which you are expected to hit, guided only by the sound which it will make in striking the hour of five. Are you satisfied with the arrangement?"

"Perfectly. Where is my wife?"

"On the other side of the field some ten paces from the stump upon which the clock is fixed." He bowed, and his face showed satisfaction.

"May I expect the clock to strike soon?"

"In less than five minutes," was the answer.

"Then let me have the pistol; I wish to become acquainted with its size and weight."

We glanced at each other, then across at her.

She made a gesture; it was one of acquiescence.

Immediately the inspector placed the weapon in the blind man's hand. It was at once apparent that he understood the instrument, and Violet's hopes which had been strong up to this moment, sank at his air of confidence.

"Thank God I am blind this hour and cannot see her," fell from his lips, then, before the echo of these words had died away, he raised his voice and observed calmly enough, considering that he was about to prove himself a criminal in order to save himself from being thought a madman:

"Let no one move. I must have my ears free for catching the first stroke of the clock." And he raised the pistol before him.

There was a moment of torturing suspense and deep, unbroken silence. Violet's eyes were on him so she did not watch the clock, but she was suddenly moved by some irresistible impulse to note how Mrs. Zabriskie was bearing herself at this critical moment, and casting a hurried glance in her direction she perceived her tall figure swaying from side to side, as if under an intolerable strain of feeling. Her eyes were on the clock, the hands of which seemed to creep with snail-like pace along the dial, when unexpectedly, and a full minute before the minute hand had reached the stroke of five, Violet caught a movement on her part, saw the flash of something round and white show for an instant against the darkness of her cloak, and was about to shriek warning to the doctor, when the shrill, quick stroke of a clock rang out on the frosty air, followed by the ping and flash of a pistol.

A sound of shattered glass, followed by a suppressed cry, told the bystanders that the bullet had struck the mark, but before any one could move, or they could rid their eyes of the smoke which the wind had blown into their faces, there came another sound which made their hair stand on end and sent the blood back in terror to their hearts. Another clock was striking, which they now perceived was still standing upright on the stump where Mrs. Zabriskie had placed it.

Whence came the clock, then, which had struck before the time and been shattered for its pains? One quick look told them. On the ground, ten paces to the right, lay Zulma Zabriskie, a broken clock at her side, and in her breast a bullet which was fast sapping the life from her sweet eyes.

They had to tell him, there was such pleading in her looks; and never will any of the hearers forget the scream which rang from his lips as he realized the truth. Breaking from their midst, he rushed forward, and fell at her feet as if guided by some supernatural instinct.

"Zulma," he shrieked, "what is this? Were not my hands dyed deep enough in blood that you should make me answerable for your life also?"

Her eyes were closed but she opened them. Looking long and steadily at his agonized face, she faltered forth:

"It is not you who have killed me; it is your crime. Had you been innocent of Mr. Hasbrouck's death your bullet would never have found my heart. Did you think I could survive the proof that you had killed that good man?"

"I did it unwittingly. I—"

"Hush!" she commanded, with an awful look, which happily he could not see. "I had another motive. I wished to prove to you, even at the cost of my life, that I loved you, had always loved you, and not—"

It was now his turn to silence her. His hand crept to her lips, and his despairing face turned itself blindly towards those about them.

"Go!" he cried; "leave us! Let me take a last farewell of my dying wife, without listeners or spectators."

Consulting the eye of her employer who stood close beside her, and seeing no hope in it, Violet fell slowly back. The others, followed, and the doctor was left alone with his wife. From the distant position they took, they saw her arms creep round his neck, saw her head fall confidingly on his breast, then silence settled upon them, and upon all nature, the gathering twilight deepening, till the last glow disappeared from the heavens above and from the circle of leafless trees which enclosed this tragedy from the outside world.

But at last there came a stir, and Dr. Zabriskie, rising up before them with the dead body of his wife held closely to his breast, confronted them with a countenance so rapturous that he looked like a man transfigured.

"I will carry her to the boat," said he. "Not another hand shall touch her. She was my true wife, my true wife!" And he towered into an attitude of such dignity and passion that for a moment he took on heroic proportions and they forgot that he had just proved himself to have committed a cold-blooded and ghastly crime.

The stars were shining when the party again took their seats in the boat; and if the scene of their crossing to Jersey was impressive, what shall be said of the return?

The doctor, as before, sat in the stern, an awesome figure, upon which the moon shone with a white radiance that seemed to lift his face out of the surrounding darkness and set it like an image of frozen horror before their eyes. Against his breast he held the form of his dead wife, and now and then Violet saw him stoop as if he were listening for some token of life from her set lips. Then he would lift himself again with hopelessness stamped upon his features, only to lean forward in renewed hope that was again destined to disappointment.

Violet had been so overcome by this tragic end to all her hopes, that her employer had been allowed to enter the boat with her. Seated at her side in the seat directly in front of the doctor, he watched with her these simple tokens of a breaking heart, saying nothing till they reached midstream, when true to his instincts for all his awe and compassion, he suddenly bent towards him and said:

"Dr. Zabriskie, the mystery of your crime is no longer a mystery to me. Listen and see if I do not understand your temptation, and how you, a conscientious and God-fearing man, came to slay your innocent neighbour.

"A friend of yours, or so he called himself, had for a long time filled your ears with tales tending to make you suspicious of your wife and jealous of a certain man whom I will not name. You knew that your friend had a grudge against this man, and so for many months turned a deaf ear to his insinuations. But finally some change which you detected in your wife's bearing or conversation roused your own suspicions, and you began to doubt her truth and to curse your blindness, which in a measure rendered you helpless. The jealous fever grew and had risen to a high point when one night—a memorable night—this friend met you just as you were leaving town, and with cruel craft whispered in your ear that the man you hated was even then with your wife and that if you would return at once to your home you would find him in her company.

"The demon that lurks at the heart of all men, good or bad, thereupon took complete possession of you, and you answered this false friend by saying that you would not return without a pistol. Whereupon he offered to take you to his house and give you his. You consented, and getting rid of your servant by sending him to Poughkeepsie with your excuses, you entered your friend's automobile.

"You say you bought the pistol, and perhaps you did, but, however that may be, you left his house with it in your pocket, and declining companionship, walked home, arriving at the Colonnade a little before midnight.

"Ordinarily you have no difficulty in recognizing your own doorstep. But, being in a heated frame of mind, you walked faster than usual and so passed your own house and stopped at that of Mr. Hasbrouck, one door beyond. As the entrances of these houses are all alike, there was but one way by which you could have made yourself sure that you had reached your own dwelling, and that was by feeling for the doctor's sign at the side of the door. But you never thought of that. Absorbed in dreams of vengeance, your sole impulse was to enter by the quickest means possible. Taking out your night key, you thrust it into the lock. It fitted, but it took strength to turn it, so much strength that the key was twisted and bent by the effort. But this incident, which would have attracted your attention at another time, was lost upon you at this moment. An entrance had been effected, and you were in too excited a frame of mind to notice at what cost, or to detect the small differences apparent in the atmosphere and furnishings of the two houses, trifles which would have arrested your attention under other circumstances, and made you pause before the upper floor had been reached.

"It was while going up the stairs that you took out your pistol, so that by the time you arrived at the front room door you held it already drawn and cocked in your hand. For, being blind, you feared escape on the part of your victim, and so waited for nothing but the sound of a man's voice before firing. When, therefore, the unfortunate Mr. Hasbrouck, roused by this sudden intrusion, advanced with an exclamation of astonishment, you pulled the trigger, and killed him on the spot. It must have been immediately upon his fall that you recognized from some word he uttered, or from some contact you may have had with your surroundings, that you were in the wrong house and had killed the wrong man; for you cried out, in evident remorse, 'God! what have I done!' and fled without approaching your victim.

"Descending the stairs, you rushed from the house, closing the front door behind you and regaining your own without being seen. But here you found yourself baffled in your attempted escape, by two things. First, by the pistol you still held in your hand, and secondly, by the fact that the key upon which you depended for entering your own door was so twisted out of shape that you knew it would be useless for you to attempt to use it. What did you do in this emergency? You have already told us, though the story seemed so improbable at the time, you found nobody to believe it but myself. The pistol you flung far away from you down the pavement, from which, by one of those rare chances which sometimes happen in this world, it was presently picked up by some late passer-by of more or less doubtful character. The door offered less of an obstacle than you had anticipated; for when you turned again you found it, if I am not greatly mistaken, ajar, left so, as we have reason to believe, by one who had gone out of it but a few minutes before in a state which left him but little master of his actions. It was this fact which provided you with an answer when you were asked how you succeeded in getting into Mr. Hasbrouck's house after the family had retired for the night.

"Astonished at the coincidence, but hailing with gladness the deliverance which it offered, you went in and ascended at once into your wife's presence; and it was from her lips, and not from those of Mrs. Hasbrouck, that the cry arose which startled the neighbourhood and prepared men's minds for the tragic words which were shouted a moment later from the next house.

"But she who uttered the scream knew of no tragedy save that which was taking place in her own breast. She had just repulsed a dastardly suitor, and seeing you enter so unexpectedly in a state of unaccountable horror and agitation, was naturally stricken with dismay, and thought she saw your ghost, or what was worse, a possible avenger; while you, having failed to kill the man you sought, and having killed a man you esteemed, let no surprise on her part lure you into any dangerous self-betrayal. You strove instead to soothe her, and even attempted to explain the excitement under which you laboured, by an account of your narrow escape at the station, till the sudden alarm from next door distracted her attention, and sent both your thoughts and hers in a different direction. Not till conscience had fully awakened and the horror of your act had had time to tell upon your sensitive nature, did you breathe forth those vague confessions, which, not being supported by the only explanations which would have made them credible, led her, as well as the police, to consider you affected in your mind. Your pride as a man and your consideration for her as a woman kept you silent, but did not keep the worm from preying upon your heart.

"Am I not correct in my surmises, Dr. Zabriskie, and is not this the true explanation of your crime?"

With a strange look, he lifted up his face.

"Hush!" said he; "you will waken her. See how peacefully she sleeps! I should not like to have her wakened now, she is so tired, and I—I have not watched over her as I should."

Appalled at his gesture, his look, his tone, Violet drew back, and for a few minutes no sound was to be heard but the steady dip-dip of the oars and the lap-lap of the waters against the boat. Then there came a quick uprising, the swaying before her of something dark and tall and threatening, and before she could speak or move, or even stretch forth her hands to stay him, the seat before her was empty and darkness had filled the place where but an instant previous he had sat, a fearsome figure, erect and rigid as a sphinx.

What little moonlight there was, only served to show a few rising bubbles, marking the spot where the unfortunate man had sunk with his much-loved burden. As the widening circles fled farther and farther out, the tide drifted the boat away, and the spot was lost which had seen the termination of one of earth's saddest tragedies.

END OF PROBLEM VII

MISSING: PAGE THIRTEEN

I

"One more! just one more well paying affair, and I promise to stop; really and truly to stop."

"But, Puss, why one more? You have earned the amount you set for yourself,—or very nearly,—and though my help is not great, in three months I can add enough—"

"No, you cannot, Arthur. You are doing well; I appreciate it; in fact, I am just delighted to have you work for me in the way you do, but you cannot, in your present position, make enough in three months, or in six, to meet the situation as I see it. Enough does not satisfy me. The measure must be full, heaped up, and running over. Possible failure following promise must be provided for. Never must I feel myself called upon to do this kind of thing again. Besides, I have never got over the Zabriskie tragedy. It haunts me continually. Something new may help to put it out of my head. I feel guilty. I was responsible—"

"No, Puss. I will not have it that you were responsible. Some such end was bound to follow a complication like that. Sooner or later he would have been driven to shoot himself—"

"But not her."

"No, not her. But do you think she would have given those few minutes of perfect understanding with her blind husband for a few years more of miserable life?"

Violet made no answer; she was too absorbed in her surprise. Was this Arthur? Had a few weeks' work and a close connection with the really serious things of life made this change in him? Her face beamed at the thought, which seeing, but not understanding what underlay this evidence of joy, he bent and kissed her, saying with some of his old nonchalance:

"Forget it, Violet; only don't let any one or anything lead you to interest yourself in another affair of the kind. If you do, I shall have to consult a certain friend of yours as to the best way of stopping this folly. I mention no names. Oh! you need not look so frightened. Only behave; that's all."

"He's right," she acknowledged to herself, as he sauntered away; "altogether right."

Yet because she wanted the extra money—

The scene invited alarm,—that is, for so young a girl as Violet, surveying it from an automobile some time after the stroke of midnight. An unknown house at the end of a heavily shaded walk, in the open doorway of which could be seen the silhouette of a woman's form leaning eagerly forward with arms outstretched in an appeal for help! It vanished while she looked, but the effect remained, holding her to her seat for one startled moment. This seemed strange, for she had anticipated adventure. One is not summoned from a private ball to ride a dozen miles into the country on an errand of investigation, without some expectation of encountering the mysterious and the tragic. But Violet Strange, for all her many experiences, was of a most susceptible nature, and for the instant in which that door stood open, with only the memory of that expectant figure to disturb the faintly lit vista of the hall beyond, she felt that grip upon the throat which comes from an indefinable fear which no words can explain and no plummet sound.

But this soon passed. With the setting of her foot to ground, conditions changed and her emotions took on a more normal character. The figure of a man now stood in the place held by the vanished woman; and it was not only that of one she knew but that of one whom she trusted—a friend whose very presence gave her courage. With this recognition came a better understanding of the situation, and it was with a beaming eye and unclouded features that she tripped up the walk to meet the expectant figure and outstretched hand of Roger Upjohn.

"You here!" she exclaimed, amid smiles and blushes, as he drew her into the hall.

He at once launched forth into explanations mingled with apologies for the presumption he had shown in putting her to this inconvenience. There was trouble in the house—great trouble. Something had occurred for which an explanation must be found before morning, or the happiness and honour of more than one person now under this unhappy roof would be wrecked. He knew it was late—that she had been obliged to take a long and dreary ride alone, but her success with the problem which had once come near wrecking his own life had emboldened him to telephone to the office and—"But you are in ball-dress," he cried in amazement. "Did you think—"

"I came from a ball. Word reached me between the dances. I did not go home. I had been bidden to hurry."

He looked his appreciation, but when he spoke it was to say:

"This is the situation. Miss Digby—"

"The lady who is to be married tomorrow?"

"Who hopes to be married tomorrow."

"How, hopes?"

"Who will be married tomorrow, if a certain article lost in this house tonight can be found before any of the persons who have been dining here leave for their homes."

Violet uttered an exclamation.

"Then, Mr. Cornell," she began—

"Mr. Cornell has our utmost confidence," Roger hastened to interpose. "But the article missing is one which he might reasonably desire to possess and which he alone of all present had the opportunity of securing. You can therefore see why he, with his pride—the pride off a man not rich, engaged to marry a woman who is—should declare that unless his innocence is established before daybreak, the doors of St. Bartholomew will remain shut to-morrow."

"But the article lost—what is it?"

"Miss Digby will give you the particulars. She is waiting to receive you," he added with a gesture towards a half-open door at their right.

Violet glanced that way, then cast her looks up and down the hall in which they stood.

"Do you know that you have not told me in whose house I am? Not hers, I know. She lives in the city."

"And you are twelve miles from Harlem. Miss Strange, you are in the Van Broecklyn mansion, famous enough you will acknowledge. Have you never been here before?"

"I have been by here, but I recognized nothing in the dark. What an exciting place for an investigation!"

"And Mr. Van Broecklyn? Have you never met him?"

"Once, when a child. He frightened me then."

"And may frighten you now; though I doubt it. Time has mellowed him. Besides, I have prepared him for what might otherwise occasion him some astonishment. Naturally he would not look for just the sort of lady investigator I am about to introduce to him."

She smiled. Violet Strange was a very charming young woman, as well as a keen prober of odd mysteries.

The meeting between herself and Miss Digby was a sympathetic one. After the first inevitable shock which the latter felt at sight of the beauty and fashionable appearance of the mysterious little being who was to solve her difficulties, her glance, which, under other circumstances, might have lingered unduly upon the piquant features and exquisite dressing of the fairy-like figure before her, passed at once to Violet's eyes, in whose steady depths beamed an intelligence quite at odds with the coquettish dimples which so often misled the casual observer in his estimation of a character singularly subtle and well-poised.

As for the impression she herself made upon Violet, it was the same she made upon everyone. No one could look long at Florence Digby and not recognize the loftiness of her spirit and the generous nature of her impulses. In person she was tall and as she leaned to take Violet's hand, the difference between them brought out the salient points in each, to the great admiration of the one onlooker.

Meantime, for all her interest in the case in hand, Violet could not help casting a hurried look about her, in gratification of the curiosity incited by her entrance into a house signalized from its foundation by such a series of tragic events. The result was disappointing. The walls were plain, the furniture simple. Nothing suggestive in either, unless it was the fact that nothing was new, nothing modern. As it looked in the days of Burr and Hamilton so it looked to-day, even to the rather startling detail of candles which did duty on every side in place of gas.

As Violet recalled the reason for this, the fascination of the past seized upon her imagination. There was no knowing where this might have carried her, had not the feverish gleam in Miss Digby's eyes warned her that the present held its own excitement. Instantly, she was all attention and listening with undivided mind to that lady's disclosures.

They were brief and to the following effect:

The dinner which had brought some half-dozen people together in this house had been given in celebration of her impending marriage. But it was also in a way meant as a compliment to one of the other guests, a Mr.

Spielhagen, who, during the week, had succeeded in demonstrating to a few experts the value of a discovery he had made which would transform a great industry.

In speaking of this discovery, Miss Digby did not go into particulars, the whole matter being far beyond her understanding; but in stating its value she openly acknowledged that it was in the line of Mr. Cornell's own work, and one which involved calculations and a formula which, if prematurely disclosed, would invalidate the contract Mr. Spielhagen hoped to make, and thus destroy his present hopes.

Of this formula but two copies existed. One was locked up in a safe deposit vault in Boston, the other he had brought into the house on his person, and it was the latter which was now missing, having been abstracted during the evening from a manuscript of sixteen or more sheets, under circumstances which she would now endeavour to relate.

Mr. Van Broecklyn, their host, had in his melancholy life but one interest which could be at all absorbing. This was for explosives. As consequence, much of the talk at the dinner-table had been on Mr. Spielhagen's discovery, and possible changes it might introduce into this especial industry. As these, worked out from a formula kept secret from the trade, could not but affect greatly Mr. Cornell's interests, she found herself listening intently, when Mr. Van Broecklyn, with an apology for his interference, ventured to remark that if Mr. Spielhagen had made a valuable discovery in this line, so had he, and one which he had substantiated by many experiments. It was not a marketable one, such as Mr. Spielhagen's was, but in his work upon the same, and in the tests which he had been led to make, he had discovered certain instances he would gladly name, which demanded exceptional procedure to be successful. If Mr. Spielhagen's method did not allow for these exceptions, nor make suitable provision for them, then Mr. Spielhagen's method would fail more times than it would succeed. Did it so allow and so provide? It would relieve him greatly to learn that it did.

The answer came quickly. Yes, it did. But later and after some further conversation, Mr. Spielhagen's confidence seemed to wane, and before they left the dinner-table, he openly declared his intention of looking over his manuscript again that very night, in order to be sure that the formula therein contained duly covered all the exceptions mentioned by Mr. Van Broecklyn.

If Mr. Cornell's countenance showed any change at this moment, she for one had not noticed it; but the bitterness with which he remarked upon the other's good fortune in having discovered this formula of whose entire success he had no doubt, was apparent to everybody, and naturally gave point to the circumstances which a short time afterward associated him with the disappearance of the same.

The ladies (there were two others besides herself) having withdrawn in a body to the music-room, the gentlemen all proceeded to the library to smoke. Here, conversation loosed from the one topic which had hitherto engrossed it, was proceeding briskly, when Mr. Spielhagen, with nervous gesture, impulsively looked about him and said:

"I cannot rest till I have run through my thesis again. Where can I find a quiet spot? I won't be long; I read very rapidly."

It was for Mr. Van Broecklyn to answer, but no word coming from him, every eye turned his way, only to find him sunk in one of those fits of abstraction so well known to his friends, and from which no one who has this strange man's peace of mind at heart ever presumes to rouse him.

What was to be done? These moods of their singular host sometimes lasted half an hour, and Mr. Spielhagen had not the appearance of a man of patience. Indeed he presently gave proof of the great uneasiness he was labouring under, for noticing a door standing ajar on the other side of the room, he remarked to those around him:

"A den! and lighted! Do you see any objection to my shutting myself in there for a few minutes?"

No one venturing to reply, he rose, and giving a slight push to the door, disclosed a small room exquisitely panelled and brightly lighted, but without one article of furniture in it, not even a chair.

"The very place," quoth Mr. Spielhagen, and lifting a light cane-bottomed chair from the many standing about, he carried it inside and shut the door behind him.

Several minutes passed during which the man who had served at table entered with a tray on which were several small glasses evidently containing some choice liqueur. Finding his master fixed in one of his strange moods, he set the tray down and, pointing to one of the glasses, said:

"That is for Mr. Van Broecklyn. It contains his usual quieting powder." And urging the gentlemen to help themselves, he quietly left the room. Mr. Upjohn lifted the glass nearest him, and Mr. Cornell seemed about to do the same when he suddenly reached forward and catching up one farther off started for the room in which Mr. Spielhagen had so deliberately secluded himself.

Why he did all this—why, above all things, he should reach across the tray for a glass instead of taking the one under his hand, he can no more explain than why he has followed many another unhappy impulse. Nor did he understand the nervous start given by Mr. Spielhagen at his entrance, or the stare with which that gentleman took the glass from his hand and mechanically drank its contents, till he saw how his hand had stretched itself across the sheet of paper he was reading, in an open attempt to hide the lines visible between his fingers. Then indeed the intruder flushed and withdrew in great embarrassment, fully conscious of his indiscretion but not deeply disturbed till Mr. Van Broecklyn, suddenly arousing and glancing down at the tray placed very near his hand remarked in some surprise: "Dobbs seems to have forgotten me." Then indeed, the unfortunate Mr. Cornell realized what he had done. It was the glass intended for his host which he had caught up and carried into the other room—the glass which he had been told contained a drug. Of what folly he had been guilty, and how tame would be any effort at excuse!

Attempting none, he rose and with a hurried glance at Mr. Upjohn who flushed in sympathy at his distress, he crossed to the door he had lately closed upon Mr. Spielhagen. But feeling his shoulder touched as his hand pressed the knob, he turned to meet the eye of Mr. Van Broecklyn fixed upon him with an expression which utterly confounded him.

"Where are you going?" that gentleman asked.

The questioning tone, the severe look, expressive at once of displeasure and

132

astonishment, were most disconcerting, but Mr. Cornell managed to stammer forth:

"Mr. Spielhagen is in here consulting his thesis. When your man brought in the cordial, I was awkward enough to catch up your glass and carry it in to. Mr. Spielhagen. He drank it and I—I am anxious to see if it did him any harm."

As he uttered the last word he felt Mr. Van Broecklyn's hand slip from his shoulder, but no word accompanied the action, nor did his host make the least move to follow him into the room.

This was a matter of great regret to him later, as it left him for a moment out of the range of every eye, during which he says he simply stood in a state of shock at seeing Mr. Spielhagen still sitting there, manuscript in hand, but with head fallen forward and eyes closed; dead, asleep or—he hardly knew what; the sight so paralysed him.

Whether or not this was the exact truth and the whole truth, Mr. Cornell certainly looked very unlike himself as he stepped back into Mr. Van Broecklyn's presence; and he was only partially reassured when that gentleman protested that there was no real harm in the drug, and that Mr. Spielhagen would be all right if left to wake naturally and without shock. However, as his present attitude was one of great discomfort, they decided to carry him back and lay him on the library lounge. But before doing this, Mr. Upjohn drew from his flaccid grasp, the precious manuscript, and carrying it into the larger room placed it on a remote table, where it remained undisturbed till Mr. Spielhagen, suddenly coming to himself at the end of some fifteen minutes, missed the sheets from his hand, and bounding up, crossed the room to repossess himself of them.

His face, as he lifted them up and rapidly ran through them with ever-accumulating anxiety, told them what they had to expect.

The page containing the formula was gone!

Violet now saw her problem.

II

There was no doubt about the loss I have mentioned; all could see that page 13 was not there. In vain a second handling of every sheet, the one so numbered was not to be found. Page 14 met the eye on the top of the pile, and page 12 finished it off at the bottom, but no page 13 in between, or anywhere else.

Where had it vanished, and through whose agency had this misadventure occurred? No one could say, or, at least, no one there made any attempt to do so, though everybody started to look for it.

But where look? The adjoining small room offered no facilities for hiding a cigar-end, much less a square of shining white paper. Bare walls, a bare floor, and a single chair for furniture, comprised all that was to be seen in this direction. Nor could the room in which they then stood be thought to hold it, unless it was on the person of some one of them. Could this be the explanation of the mystery? No man looked his doubts; but Mr. Cornell, possibly divining the general feeling, stepped up to Mr. Van Broecklyn and in a cool voice, but with the red burning hotly on either cheek, said, so as to be heard by everyone present:

"I demand to be searched—at once and thoroughly."

A moment's silence, then the common cry:

"We will all be searched."

"Is Mr. Spielhagen sure that the missing page was with the others when he sat down in the adjoining room to read his thesis?" asked their perturbed host.

"Very sure," came the emphatic reply. "Indeed, I was just going through the formula itself when I fell asleep."

"You are ready to assert this?"

"I am ready to swear it."

Mr. Cornell repeated his request.

"I demand that you make a thorough search of my person. I must be cleared, and instantly, of every suspicion," he gravely asserted, "or how can I marry Miss Digby to-morrow."

After that there was no further hesitation. One and all subjected themselves to the ordeal suggested; even Mr. Spielhagen. But this effort was as futile as the rest. The lost page was not found.

What were they to think? What were they to do?

There seemed to be nothing left to do, and yet some further attempt must be made towards the recovery of this important formula. Mr. Cornell's marriage and Mr. Spielhagen's business success both depended upon its being in the latter's hands before six in the morning, when he was engaged to hand it over to a certain manufacturer sailing for Europe on an early steamer.

Five hours!

Had Mr. Van Broecklyn a suggestion to offer? No, he was as much at sea as the rest.

Simultaneously look crossed look. Blankness was on every face.

"Let us call the ladies," suggested one.

It was done, and however great the tension had been before, it was even greater when Miss Digby stepped upon the scene. But she was not a woman to be shaken from her poise even by a crisis of this importance. When the dilemma had been presented to her and the full situation grasped, she looked first at Mr. Cornell and then at Mr. Spielhagen, and quietly said:

"There is but one explanation possible of this matter. Mr. Spielhagen will excuse me, but he is evidently mistaken in thinking that he saw the lost page among the rest. The condition into which he was thrown by the unaccustomed drug he had drank, made him liable to hallucinations. I have not the least doubt he thought he had been studying the formula at the time he dropped off to sleep. I have every confidence in the gentleman's candour. But so have I in that of Mr. Cornell," she supplemented, with a smile.

An exclamation from Mr. Van Broecklyn and a subdued murmur from all but Mr. Spielhagen testified to the effect of this suggestion, and there is no saying what might have been the result if Mr. Cornell had not hurriedly put in this extraordinary and most unexpected protest:

"Miss Digby has my gratitude," said he, "for a confidence which I hope to prove to be deserved. But I must say this for Mr. Spielhagen. He was correct in stating that he was engaged in looking over his formula when I stepped into his presence with the glass of cordial. If you were not in a position to see the hurried way in which his hand instinctively spread itself over the page he was reading, I was; and if that does not seem conclusive to you, then I feel bound to state that in unconsciously following this movement of his, I plainly saw the number written on the top of the page, and that number was—13."

A loud exclamation, this time from Spielhagen himself, announced his gratitude and corresponding change of attitude toward the speaker.

"Wherever that damned page has gone," he protested, advancing towards Cornell with outstretched hand, "you have nothing to do with its disappearance."

Instantly all constraint fled, and every countenance took on a relieved expression. But the problem remained.

Suddenly those very words passed some one's lips, and with their utterance Mr. Upjohn remembered how at an extraordinary crisis in his own life he had been helped and an equally difficult problem settled, by a little lady secretly attached to a private detective agency. If she could only be found and hurried here before morning, all might yet be well. He would make the effort. Such wild schemes sometimes work. He telephoned to the office and—

Was there anything else Miss Strange would like to know?

III

Miss Strange, thus appealed to, asked where the gentlemen were now.

She was told that they were still all together in the library; the ladies had been sent home.

"Then let us go to them," said Violet, hiding under a smile her great fear that here was an affair which might very easily spell for her that dismal word, failure.

So great was that fear that under all ordinary circumstances she would have had no thought for anything else in the short interim between this stating of the problem and her speedy entrance among the persons involved. But the circumstances of this case were so far from ordinary, or rather let me put it in this way, the setting of the case was so very extraordinary, that she scarcely thought of the problem before her, in her great interest in the house through whose rambling halls she was being so carefully guided. So much that was tragic and heartrending had occurred here. The Van Broecklyn name, the Van Broecklyn history, above all the Van Broecklyn tradition, which made the house unique in the country's annals (of which more hereafter), all made an appeal to her imagination, and centred her thoughts on what she saw about her. There was door which no man ever opened—had never opened since Revolutionary times—should she see it? Should she know it if she did see it? Then Mr. Van Broecklyn himself! just to meet him, under any conditions and in any place, was an event. But to meet him here, under the pall of his own mystery! No wonder she had no words for her companions, or that her thoughts clung to this anticipation in wonder and almost fearsome delight.

His story was a well-known one. A bachelor and a misanthrope, he lived absolutely alone save for a large entourage of servants, all men and elderly ones at that. He never visited. Though he now and then, as on this occasion, entertained certain persons under his roof, he declined every invitation for himself, avoiding even, with equal strictness, all evening amusements of whatever kind, which would detain him in the city after ten at night. Perhaps this was to ensure no break in his rule of life never to sleep out of his own bed. Though he was a man well over fifty he had not spent, according to his own statement, but two nights out of his own bed since his return from Europe in early boyhood, and those were in obedience to a judicial summons which took him to Boston.

This was his main eccentricity, but he had another which is apparent enough from what has already been said. He avoided women. If thrown in with them during his short visits into town, he was invariably polite and at times companionable, but he never sought them out, nor had gossip, contrary to its usual habit, ever linked his name with one of the sex.

Yet he was a man of more than ordinary attraction. His features were fine and his figure impressive. He might have been the cynosure of all eyes had he chosen to enter crowded drawing-rooms, or even to frequent public assemblages, but having turned his back upon everything of the kind in his youth, he had found it impossible to alter his habits with advancing years; nor was he now expected to. The position he had taken was respected. Leonard Van Broecklyn was no longer criticized.

Was there any explanation for this strangely self-centred life? Those who knew him best seemed to think so. In the first place he had sprung from an unfortunate stock. Events of unusual and tragic nature had marked the family of both parents. Nor had his parents themselves been exempt from this seeming fatality. Antagonistic in tastes and temperament, they had dragged on an unhappy existence in the old home, till both natures rebelled, and a separation ensued which not only disunited their lives but sent them to opposite sides of the globe never to return again. At least, that was the inference drawn from the peculiar circumstances attending the event. On the morning of one never-to-be-forgotten day, John Van Broecklyn, the grandfather of the present representative of the family, found the following note from his son lying on the library table:

"FATHER:

"Life in this house, or any house, with her is no longer endurable. One of us must go. The mother should not be separated from her child. Therefore it is I whom you will never see again. Forget me, but be considerate of her and the boy.

"WILLIAM"

Six hours later another note was found, this time from the wife:

"FATHER:

"Tied to a rotting corpse what does one do? Lop off one's arm if
136

necessary to rid one of the contact. As all love between your son and myself is dead, I can no longer live within the sound of his voice. As this is his home, he is the one to remain in it. May our child reap the benefit of his mother's loss and his father's affection.

"RHODA"

Both were gone, and gone forever. Simultaneous in their departure, they preserved each his own silence and sent no word back. If the one went east and the other west, they may have met on the other side of the globe, but never again in the home which sheltered their boy. For him and for his grandfather they had sunk from sight in the great sea of humanity, leaving them stranded on an isolated and mournful shore. The grand-father steeled himself to the double loss, for the child's sake; but the boy of eleven succumbed. Few of the world's great sufferers, of whatever age or condition, have mourned as this child mourned, or shown the effects of his grief so deeply or so long. Not till he had passed his majority did the line, carved in one day in his baby forehead, lose any of its intensity; and there are those who declare that even later than that, the midnight stillness of the house was disturbed from time to time by his muffled shriek of "Mother! Mother!", sending the servants from the house, and adding one more horror to the many which clung about this accursed mansion.

Of this cry Violet had heard, and it was that and the door—But I have already told you about the door which she was still looking for, when her two companions suddenly halted, and she found herself on the threshold of the library, in full view of Mr. Van Broecklyn and his two guests.

Slight and fairy-like in figure, with an air of modest reserve more in keeping with her youth and dainty dimpling beauty than with her errand, her appearance produced an astonishment none of which the gentlemen were able to disguise. This the clever detective, with a genius for social problems and odd elusive cases! This darling of the ball-room in satin and pearls! Mr. Spielhagen glanced at Mr. Cornell, and Mr. Cornell at Mr. Spielhagen, and both at Mr. Upjohn, in very evident distrust. As for Violet, she had eyes only for Mr. Van Broecklyn who stood before her in a surprise equal to that of the others but with more restraint in its expression.

She was not disappointed in him. She had expected to see a man, reserved almost to the point of austerity. And she found his first look even more awe-compelling than her imagination had pictured; so much so indeed, that her resolution faltered, and she took a quick step backward; which seeing, he smiled and her heart and hopes grew warm again. That he could smile, and smile with absolute sweetness, was her great comfort when later—But I am introducing you too hurriedly to the catastrophe. There is much to be told first.

I pass over the preliminaries, and come at once to the moment when Violet, having listened to a repetition of the full facts, stood with downcast eyes before these gentlemen, complaining in some alarm to herself: "They expect me to tell them now and without further search or parley just where this missing page is. I shall have to balk that expectation without losing their confidence. But how?"

Summoning up her courage and meeting each inquiring eye with a look which seemed to carry a different message to each, she remarked very quietly:

"This is not a matter to guess at. I must have time and I must look a little deeper into the facts just given me. I presume that the table I see over there is the one upon which Mr. Upjohn laid the manuscript during Mr. Spielhagen's unconsciousness."

All nodded.

"Is it—I mean the table—in the same condition it was then? Has nothing been taken from it except the manuscript?"

"Nothing."

"Then the missing page is not there," she smiled, pointing to its bare top. A pause, during which she stood with her gaze fixed on the floor before her. She was thinking and thinking hard.

Suddenly she came to a decision. Addressing Mr. Upjohn she asked if he were quite sure that in taking the manuscript from Mr. Spielhagen's hand he had neither disarranged nor dropped one of its pages.

The answer was unequivocal.

"Then," she declared, with quiet assurance and a steady meeting with her own of every eye, "as the thirteenth page was not found among the others when they were taken from this table, nor on the persons of either Mr. Cornell or Mr. Spielhagen, it is still in that inner room."

"Impossible!" came from every lip, each in a different tone. "That room is absolutely empty."

"May I have a look at its emptiness?" she asked, with a naive glance at Mr. Van Broecklyn.

"There is positively nothing in the room but the chair Mr. Spielhagen sat on," objected that gentleman with a noticeable air of reluctance.

"Still, may I not have a look at it?" she persisted, with that disarming smile she kept for great occasions.

Mr. Van Broecklyn bowed. He could not refuse a request so urged, but his step was slow and his manner next to ungracious as he led the way to the door of the adjoining room and threw it open.

Just what she had been told to expect! Bare walls and floors and an empty chair! Yet she did not instantly withdraw, but stood silently contemplating the panelled wainscoting surrounding her, as though she suspected it of containing some secret hiding-place not apparent to the eye.

Mr. Van Broecklyn, noting this, hastened to say:

"The walls are sound, Miss Strange. They contain no hidden cupboards."

"And that door?" she asked, pointing to a portion of the wainscoting so exactly like the rest that only the most experienced eye could detect the line of deeper colour which marked an opening.

For an instant Mr. Van Broecklyn stood rigid, then the immovable pallor, which was one of his chief characteristics, gave way to a deep flush as he explained:

"There was a door there once; but it has been permanently closed. With cement," he forced himself to add, his countenance losing its evanescent colour till it shone ghastly again in the strong light.

With difficulty Violet preserved her show of composure. "The door!" she murmured to herself. "I have found it. The great historic door!" But her tone was light as she ventured to say:

"Then it can no longer be opened by your hand or any other?"

"It could not be opened with an axe."

Violet sighed in the midst of her triumph. Her curiosity had been satisfied, but the problem she had been set to solve looked inexplicable. But she was not one to yield easily to discouragement. Marking the disappointment approaching to disdain in every eye but Mr. Upjohn's, she drew herself up— (she had not far to draw) and made this final proposal.

"A sheet of paper," she remarked, "of the size of this one cannot be spirited away, or dissolved into thin air. It exists; it is here; and all we want is some happy thought in order to find it. I acknowledge that that happy thought has not come to me yet, but sometimes I get it in what may seem to you a very odd way. Forgetting myself, I try to assume the individuality of the person who has worked the mystery. If I can think with his thoughts, I possibly may follow him in his actions. In this case I should like to make believe for a few moments that I am Mr. Spielhagen" (with what a delicious smile she said this) "I should like to hold his thesis in my hand and be interrupted in my reading by Mr. Cornell offering his glass of cordial; then I should like to nod and slip off mentally into a deep sleep. Possibly in that sleep the dream may come which will clarify the whole situation. Will you humour me so far?"

A ridiculous concession, but finally she had her way; the farce was enacted and they left her as she had requested them to do, alone with her dreams in the small room.

Suddenly they heard her cry out, and in another moment she appeared before them, the picture of excitement.

"Is this chair standing exactly as it did when Mr. Spielhagen occupied it?" she asked.

"No," said Mr. Upjohn, "it faced the other way."

She stepped back and twirled the chair about with her disengaged hand. "So?"

Mr. Upjohn and Mr. Spielhagen both nodded, so did the others when she glanced at them.

With a sign of ill-concealed satisfaction, she drew their attention to herself; then eagerly cried:

"Gentlemen, look here!"

Seating herself, she allowed her whole body to relax till she presented the picture of one calmly asleep. Then, as they continued to gaze at with fascinated eyes, not knowing what to expect, they saw something white escape from her lap and slide across the floor till it touched and was stayed by the wainscot. It was the top page of the manuscript she held, and as some inkling of the truth reached their astonished minds, she sprang impetuously to her feet and, pointing to the fallen sheet, cried:

"Do you understand now? Look where it lies and then look here!"

She had bounded towards the wall and was now on her knees pointing to the bottom of the wainscot, just a few inches to the left of the fallen page.

"A crack!" she cried, "under what was once the door. It's a very thin one, hardly perceptible to the eye. But see!" Here she laid her finger on the fallen paper and drawing it towards her, pushed it carefully against the lower edge of the wainscot. Half of it at once disappeared.

"I could easily slip it all through," she assured them, withdrawing the sheet and leaping to her feet in triumph. "You know now where the missing page lies, Mr. Spielhagen. All that remains is for Mr. Van Broecklyn to get it for you."

IV

The cries of mingled astonishment and relief which greeted this simple elucidation of the mystery were broken by a curiously choked, almost unintelligible, cry. It came from the man thus appealed to, who, unnoticed by them all, had started at her first word and gradually, as action followed action, withdrawn himself till he now stood alone and in an attitude almost of defiance behind the large table in the centre of the library.

"I am sorry," he began, with a brusqueness which gradually toned down into a forced urbanity as he beheld every eye fixed upon him in amazement, "that circumstances forbid my being of assistance to you in this unfortunate matter. If the paper lies where you say, and I see no other explanation of its loss, I am afraid it will have to remain there for this night at least. The cement in which that door is embedded is thick as any wall; it would take men with pickaxes, possibly with dynamite, to make a breach there wide enough for any one to reach in. And we are far from any such help."

In the midst of the consternation caused by these words, the clock on the mantel behind his back rang out the hour. It was but a double stroke, but that meant two hours after midnight and had the effect of a knell in the hearts of those most interested.

"But I am expected to give that formula into the hands of our manager before six o'clock in the morning. The steamer sails at a quarter after."

"Can't you reproduce a copy of it from memory?" some one asked; "and insert it in its proper place among the pages you hold there?"

"The paper would not be the same. That would lead to questions and the truth would come out. As the chief value of the process contained in that formula lies in its secrecy, no explanation I could give would relieve me from the suspicions which an acknowledgment of the existence of a third copy, however well hidden, would entail. I should lose my great opportunity."

Mr. Cornell's state of mind can be imagined. In an access of mingled regret and despair, he cast a glance at Violet, who, with a nod of understanding, left the little room in which they still stood, and approached Mr. Van Broecklyn.

Lifting up her head,—for he was very tall,—and instinctively rising on her toes the nearer to reach his ear, she asked in a cautious whisper:

"Is there no other way of reaching that place?"

She acknowledged afterwards, that for one moment her heart stood still from fear, such a change took place in his face, though she says he did not move a muscle. Then, just when she was expecting from him some harsh or forbidding word, he wheeled abruptly away from her and crossing to a window at his side, lifted the shade and looked out. When he returned, he was his usual self so far as she could see.

"There is a way," he now confided to her in a tone as low as her own, "but it can only be taken by a child."

"Not by me?" she asked, smiling down at her own childish proportions.

For an instant he seemed taken aback, then she saw his hand begin to tremble and his lips twitch. Somehow—she knew not why—she began to pity him, and asked herself as she felt rather than saw the struggle in his mind, that here was a trouble which if once understood would greatly dwarf that of the two men in the room behind them.

"I am discreet," she whisperingly declared. "I have heard the history of that door—how it was against the tradition of the family to have it opened. There must have been some very dreadful reason. But old superstitions do not affect me, and if you will allow me to take the way you mention, I will follow your bidding exactly, and will not trouble myself about anything but the recovery of this paper, which must lie only a little way inside that blocked-up door."

Was his look one of rebuke at her presumption, or just the constrained expression of a perturbed mind? Probably, the latter, for while she watched him for some understanding of his mood, he reached out his hand and touched one of the satin folds crossing her shoulder.

"You would soil this irretrievably," said he.

"There is stuff in the stores for another," she smiled. Slowly his touch deepened into pressure. Watching him she saw the crust of some old fear or dominant superstition melt under her eyes, and was quite prepared, when he remarked, with what for him was a lightsome air:

"I will buy the stuff, if you will dare the darkness and intricacies of our old cellar. I can give you no light. You will have to feel your way according to my direction."

"I am ready to dare anything."

He left her abruptly.

"I will warn Miss Digby," he called back. "She shall go with you as far as the cellar."

<h1 style="text-align:center">V</h1>

Violet in her short career as an investigator of mysteries had been in many a situation calling for more than womanly nerve and courage. But never—or so it seemed to her at the time—had she experienced a greater depression of spirit than when she stood with Miss Digby before a small door at the extreme end of the cellar, and understood that here was her road—a road which once entered, she must take alone.

First, it was such a small door! No child older than eleven could possibly squeeze through it. But she was of the size of a child of eleven and might possibly manage that difficulty.

Secondly: there are always some unforeseen possibilities in every situation, and though she had listened carefully to Mr. Van Broecklyn's directions and

141

was sure that she knew them by heart, she wished she had kissed her father more tenderly in leaving him that night for the ball, and that she had not pouted so undutifully at some harsh stricture he had made. Did this mean fear? She despised the feeling if it did.

Thirdly: She hated darkness. She knew this when she offered herself for this undertaking; but she was in a bright room at the moment and only imagined what she must now face as a reality. But one jet had been lit in the cellar and that near the entrance. Mr. Van Broecklyn seemed not to need light, even in his unfastening of the small door which Violet was sure had been protected by more than one lock.

Doubt, shadow, and a solitary climb between unknown walls, with only a streak of light for her goal, and the clinging pressure of Florence Digby's hand on her own for solace—surely the prospect was one to tax the courage of her young heart to its limit. But she had promised, and she would fulfill. So with a brave smile she stooped to the little door, and in another moment had started her journey.

For journey the shortest distance may seem when every inch means a heart-throb and one grows old in traversing a foot. At first the way was easy; she had but to crawl up a slight incline with the comforting consciousness that two people were within reach of her voice, almost within sound of her beating heart. But presently she came to a turn, beyond which her fingers failed to reach any wall on her left. Then came a step up which she stumbled, and farther on a short flight, each tread of which she had been told to test before she ventured to climb it, lest the decay of innumerable years should have weakened the wood too much to bear her weight. One, two, three, four, five steps! Then a landing with an open space beyond. Half of her journey was done. Here she felt she could give a minute to drawing her breath naturally, if the air, unchanged in years, would allow her to do so. Besides, here she had been enjoined to do a certain thing and to do it according to instructions. Three matches had been given her and a little night candle. Denied all light up to now, it was at this point she was to light her candle and place it on the floor, so that in returning she should not miss the staircase and get a fall. She had promised to do this, and was only too happy to see a spark of light scintillate into life in the immeasurable darkness.

She was now in a great room long closed to the world, where once officers in Colonial wars had feasted, and more than one council had been held. A room, too, which had seen more than one tragic happening, as its almost unparalleled isolation proclaimed. So much Mr. Van Broecklyn had told her; but she was warned to be careful in traversing it and not upon any pretext to swerve aside from the right-hand wall till she came to a huge mantelpiece. This passed, and a sharp corner turned, she ought to see somewhere in the dim spaces before her a streak of vivid light shining through the crack at the bottom of the blocked-up door. The paper should be somewhere near this streak.

All simple, all easy of accomplishment, if only that streak of light were all she was likely to see or think of. If the horror which was gripping her throat should not take shape! If things would remain shrouded in impenetrable darkness, and not force themselves in shadowy suggestion upon her excited fancy! But the blackness of the passage-way through which she had just struggled was not to be found here. Whether it was the effect of that small flame flickering at the top of the staircase behind her, or of some change in her own powers of seeing, surely there was a difference in her present outlook. Tall shapes were becoming visible—the air was no longer blank—she could see—Then suddenly she saw why. In the wall high up on her right was a window. It was small and all but invisible, being covered on the outside with vines, and on the inside with the cobwebs of a century. But some small gleams from the star-light night came through, making phantasms out of ordinary things, which unseen were horrible enough, and half seen choked her heart with terror.

"I cannot bear it," she whispered to herself even while creeping forward, her hand upon the wall. "I will close my eyes" was her next thought. "I will make my own darkness," and with a spasmodic forcing of her lids together, she continued to creep on, passing the mantelpiece, where she knocked against something which fell with an awful clatter.

This sound, followed as it was by that of smothered voices from the excited group awaiting the result of her experiment from behind the impenetrable wall she should be nearing now if she had followed her instructions aright, freed her instantly from her fancies; and opening her eyes once more, she cast a look ahead, and to her delight, saw but a few steps away, the thin streak of bright light which marked the end of her journey.

It took her but a moment after that to find the missing page, and picking it up in haste from the dusty floor, she turned herself quickly about and joyfully began to retrace her steps. Why then, was it that in the course of a few minutes more her voice suddenly broke into a wild, unearthly shriek, which ringing with terror burst the bounds of that dungeon-like room, and sank, a barbed shaft, into the breasts of those awaiting the result of her doubtful adventure, at either end of this dread no-thoroughfare.

What had happened?

If they had thought to look out, they would have seen that the moon—held in check by a bank of cloud occupying half the heavens—had suddenly burst its bounds and was sending long bars of revealing light into every uncurtained window.

VI

Florence Digby, in her short and sheltered life, had possibly never known any very great or deep emotion. But she touched the bottom of extreme terror at that moment, as with her ears still thrilling with Violet's piercing cry, she turned to look at Mr. Van Broecklyn, and beheld the instantaneous wreck it had made of this seemingly strong man. Not till he came to lie in his coffin would he show a more ghastly countenance; and trembling herself almost to the point of falling, caught him by the arm and sought to read his face what had happened. Something disastrous she was sure; something which he had feared and was partially prepared for, yet which in happening had crushed him. Was it a pitfall into which the poor little lady had fallen? If so—But he is speaking—mumbling low words to himself. Some of them she can hear. He is reproaching himself—repeating over and over that he should never have taken such a chance; that he should have remembered her youth—the weakness of a young girl's nerve. He had been mad, and now—and now—

With the repetition of this word his murmuring ceased. All his energies were now absorbed in listening at the low door separating him from what he was agonizing to know—a door impossible to enter, impossible to enlarge—a barrier to all help—an opening whereby sound might pass but nothing else, save her own small body, now lying—where?

"Is she hurt?" faltered Florence, stooping, herself, to listen. "Can you hear anything—anything?"

For an instant he did not answer; every faculty was absorbed in the one sense; then slowly and in gasps he began to mutter:

"I think—I hear—something. Her step—no, no, no step. All is as quiet as death; not a sound, not a breath—she has fainted. O God! O God! Why this calamity on top of all!"

He had sprung to his feet at the utterance this invocation, but next moment was down on knees again, listening—listening.

Never was silence more profound; they were hearkening for murmurs from a tomb. Florence began to sense the full horror of it all, and was swaying helplessly when Mr. Van Broecklyn impulsively lifted his hand in an admonitory Hush! and through the daze of her faculties a small far sound began to make itself heard, growing louder as she waited, then becoming faint again, then altogether ceasing only to renew itself once more, till it resolved into an approaching step, faltering in its course, but coming ever nearer and nearer.

"She's safe! She's not hurt!" sprang from Florence's lips in inexpressible relief; and expecting Mr. Van Broecklyn to show an equal joy, she turned towards him, with the cheerful cry,

"Now if she has been so fortunate as to that missing page, we shall all be repaid for our fright."

A movement on his part, a shifting of position which brought him finally to his feet, but he gave no other proof of having heard her, nor did his countenance mirror her relief. "It is as if he dreaded, instead of hailed, her return," was Florence's inward comment as she watched him involuntarily recoil at each fresh token of Violet's advance.

Yet because this seemed so very unnatural, she persisted in her efforts to lighten the situation, and when he made no attempt to encourage Violet in her approach, she herself stooped and called out a cheerful welcome which must have rung sweetly in the poor little detective's ears.

A sorry sight was Violet, when, helped by Florence, she finally crawled into view through the narrow opening and stood once again on the cellar floor. Pale, trembling, and soiled with the dust of years, she presented a helpless figure enough, till the joy in Florence's face recalled some of her spirit, and, glancing down at her hand in which a sheet of paper was visible, she asked for Mr. Spielhagen.

"I've got the formula," she said. "If you will bring him, I will hand it over to him here."

Not a word of her adventure; nor so much as one glance at Mr. Van Broecklyn, standing far back in the shadows.

Nor was she more communicative, when, the formula restored and everything made right with Mr. Spielhagen, they all came together again in the library for a final word. "I was frightened by the silence and the darkness, and so cried out," she explained in answer to their questions. "Any one would have done so who found himself alone in so musty a place," she added, with an attempt at lightsomeness which deepened the pallor on Mr. Van Broecklyn's cheek, already sufficiently noticeable to have been remarked upon by more than one.

"No ghosts?" laughed Mr. Cornell, too happy in the return of his hopes to be fully sensible of the feelings of those about him. "No whispers from impalpable lips or touches from spectre hands? Nothing to explain the mystery of that room long shut up that even Mr. Van Broecklyn declares himself ignorant of its secret?"

"Nothing," returned Violet, showing her dimples in full force now.

"If Miss Strange had any such experiences—if she has anything to tell worthy of so marked a curiosity, she will tell it now," came from the gentleman just alluded to, in tones so stern and strange that all show of frivolity ceased on the instant. "Have you anything to tell, Miss Strange?"

Greatly startled, she regarded him with widening eyes for a moment, then with a move towards the door, remarked, with a general look about her:

"Mr. Van Broecklyn knows his own house, and doubtless can relate its histories if he will. I am a busy little body who having finished my work am now ready to return home, there to wait for the next problem which an indulgent fate may offer me."

She was near the threshold—she was about to take her leave, when suddenly she felt two hands fall on her shoulder, and turning, met the eyes of Mr. Van Broecklyn burning into her own.

"You saw!" dropped in an almost inaudible whisper from his lips.

The shiver which shook her answered him better than any word.

With an exclamation of despair, he withdrew his hands, and facing the others now standing together in a startled group, he said, as soon as he could recover some of his self-possession:

"I must ask for another hour of your company. I can no longer keep my sorrow to myself. A dividing line has just been drawn across my life, and I must have the sympathy of someone who knows my past, or I shall go mad in my self-imposed solitude. Come back, Miss Strange. You of all others have the prior right to hear."

VII

"I shall have to begin," said he, when they were all seated and ready to listen, "by giving you some idea, not so much of the family tradition, as of the effect of this tradition upon all who bore the name of Van Broecklyn. This is not the only house, even in America, which contains a room shut away from intrusion. In England there are many. But there is this difference between most of them and ours. No bars or locks forcibly held shut the door we were forbidden to open. The command was enough; that and the superstitious fear which such a command, attended by a long and unquestioning obedience, was likely to engender.

"I know no more than you do why some early ancestor laid his ban upon this room. But from my earliest years I was given to understand that there was one latch in the house which was never to be lifted; that any fault would be forgiven sooner than that; that the honour of the whole family stood in the way of disobedience, and that I was to preserve that honour to my dying day. You will say that all this is fantastic, and wonder that sane people in these modern times should subject themselves to such a ridiculous restriction, especially when no good reason was alleged, and the very source of the tradition from which it sprung forgotten. You are right; but if you look long into human nature, you will see that the bonds which hold the firmest are not material ones—that an idea will make a man and mould a character—that it lies at the source of all heroisms and is to be courted or feared as the case may be.

"For me it possessed a power proportionate to my loneliness. I don't think there was ever a more lonely child. My father and mother were so unhappy in each other's companionship that one or other of them was almost always away. But I saw little of either even when they were at home. The constraint in their attitude towards each other affected their conduct towards me. I have asked myself more than once if either of them had any real affection for me. To my father I spoke of her; to her of him; and never pleasurably. This I am forced to say, or you cannot understand my story. Would to God I could tell another tale! Would to God I had such memories as other men have of a father's clasp, a mother's kiss—but no! my grief, already profound, might have become abysmal. Perhaps it is best as it is; only, I might have been a different child, and made for myself a different fate—who knows.

"As it was, I was thrown almost entirely upon my own resources for any amusement. This led me to a discovery I made one day. In a far part of the cellar behind some heavy casks, I found a little door. It was so low—so exactly fitted to my small body, that I had the greatest desire to enter it. But I could not get around the casks. At last an expedient occurred to me. We had an old servant who came nearer loving me than any one else. One day when I chanced to be alone in the cellar, I took out my ball and began throwing it about. Finally it landed behind the casks, and I ran with a beseeching cry to Michael, to move them.

"It was a task requiring no little strength and address, but he managed, after a few herculean efforts, to shift them aside and I saw with delight, my way opened to that mysterious little door. But I did not approach it then; some instinct deterred me. But when the opportunity came for me to venture there alone, I did so, in the most adventurous spirit, and began my operations by sliding behind the casks and testing the handle of the little door. It turned, and after a pull or two the door yielded. With my heart in my mouth, I stooped and peered in. I could see nothing—a black hole and nothing more. This caused me a moment's hesitation. I was afraid of the dark—had always been. But curiosity and the spirit of adventure triumphed. Saying to myself that I was Robinson Crusoe exploring the cave, I crawled in, only to find that I had gained nothing. It was as dark inside as it had looked to be from without.

"There was no fun in this, so I crawled back, and when I tried the experiment again, it was with a bit of candle in my hand, and a surreptitious match or two. What I saw, when with a very trembling little hand I had lighted one of the matches, would have been disappointing to most boys, but not to me. The litter and old boards I saw in odd corners about me were full of possibilities, while in the dimness beyond I seemed to perceive a sort of staircase which might lead—I do not think I made any attempt to answer that question even in my own mind, but when, after some hesitation and a sense of great daring, I finally crept up those steps, I remember very well my sensation at finding myself in front of a narrow closed door. It suggested too vividly the one in Grandfather's little room—the door in the wainscot which we were never to open. I had my first real trembling fit here, and at once fascinated and repelled by this obstruction I stumbled and lost my candle, which, going out in the fall, left me in total darkness and a very frightened state of mind. For my imagination which had been greatly stirred by my own vague thoughts of the forbidden room, immediately began to people the space about me with ghoulish figures. How should I escape them, how ever reach my own little room again undetected and in safety?

"But these terrors, deep as they were, were nothing to the real fright which seized me when, the darkness finally braved, and the way found back into the bright, wide-open halls of the house, I became conscious of having dropped something besides the candle. My match-box was gone—not my match-box, but my grandfather's which I had found lying on his table and carried off on this adventure, in all the confidence of irresponsible youth. To make use of it for a little while, trusting to his not missing it in the confusion I had noticed about the house that morning, was one thing; to lose it was another. It was no common box. Made of gold and cherished for some special reason well known to himself, I had often hear him say that some day I would appreciate its value, and be glad to own it. And I had left it in that hole and at any minute he might miss it—possibly ask for it! The day was one of torment. My mother was away or shut up in her room. My father—I don't know just what thoughts I had about him. He was not to be seen either, and the servants cast strange looks at me when I spoke his name. But I little realized the blow which had just fallen upon the house in his definite departure, and only thought of my own trouble, and of how I should meet my grandfather's eye when the hour came for him to draw me to his knee for his usual good-night.

"That I was spared this ordeal for the first time this very night first comforted me, then added to my distress. He had discovered his loss and was angry. On the morrow he would ask me for the box and I would have to lie, for never could I find the courage to tell him where I had been. Such an act of presumption he would never forgive, or so I thought as I lay and shivered in my little bed. That his coldness, his neglect, sprang from the discovery just made that my mother as well as my father had just fled the house forever was as little known to me as the morning calamity. I had been given my usual tendance and was tucked safely into bed; but the gloom, the silence which presently settled upon the house had a very different explanation in my mind from the real one. My sin (for such it loomed large in my mind by this time) coloured the whole situation and accounted for every event.

"At what hour I slipped from my bed on to the cold floor, I shall never know. To me it seemed to be in the dead of night; but I doubt if it were more than ten. So slowly creep away the moments to a wakeful child. I had made a great resolve. Awful as the prospect seemed to me,—frightened as I was by the very thought,—I had determined in my small mind to go down into the cellar, and into that midnight hole again, in search of the lost box. I would take a candle and matches, this time from my own mantel-shelf, and if everyone was asleep, as appeared from the deathly quiet of the house, I would be able to go and come without anybody ever being the wiser.

"Dressing in the dark, I found my matches and my candle and, putting them in one of my pockets, softly opened my door and looked out. Nobody was stirring; every light was out except a solitary one in the lower hall. That this still burned conveyed no meaning to my mind. How could I know that the house was so still and the rooms dark because everyone was out searching for some clue to my mother's flight? If I had looked at the clock—but I did not; I was too intent upon my errand, too filled with the fever of my desperate undertaking, to be affected by anything not bearing directly upon it.

"Of the terror caused by my own shadow on the wall as I made the turn in the hall below, I have as keen a recollection today as though it happened yesterday. But that did not deter me; nothing deterred me, till safe in the cellar I crouched down behind the casks to get my breath again before entering the hole beyond.

"I had made some noise in feeling my way around these casks, and I trembled lest these sounds had been heard upstairs! But this fear soon gave place to one far greater. Other sounds were making themselves heard. A din of small skurrying feet above, below, on every side of me! Rats! rats in the wall! rats on the cellar bottom! How I ever stirred from the spot I do not know, but when I did stir, it was to go forward, and enter the uncanny hole.

"I had intended to light my candle when I got inside; but for some reason I went stumbling along in the dark, following the wall till I got to the steps where I had dropped the box. Here a light was necessary, but my hand did not go to my pocket. I thought it better to climb the steps first, and softly one foot found the tread and then another. I had only three more to climb and then my right hand, now feeling its way along the wall, would be free to strike a match. I climbed the three steps and was steadying myself against the door for a final plunge, when something happened—something so strange, so unexpected, and so incredible that I wonder I did not shriek aloud in my terror. The door was moving under my hand. It was slowly opening inward. I could feel the chill made by the widening crack. Moment by moment this chill increased; the gap was growing—a presence was there—a presence before which I sank in a small heap upon the landing. Would it advance? Had it feet—hands? Was it a presence which could be felt?

"Whatever it was, it made no attempt to pass, and presently I lifted my head only to quake anew at the sound of a voice—a human voice—my mother's voice—so near me that by putting out my arms I might have touched her.

"She was speaking to my father. I knew from the tone. She was saying words which, little understood as they were, made such a havoc in my youthful mind that I have never forgotten the effect.

"'I have come!' she said. 'They think I have fled the house and are looking far and wide for me. We shall not be disturbed. Who would think looking of here for either you or me.'

"Here! The word sank like a plummet in my breast. I had known for some few minutes that I was on the threshold of the forbidden room; but they were in it. I can scarcely make you understand the tumult which this awoke in my brain. Somehow, I had never thought that any such braving of the house's law would be possible.

"I heard my father's answer, but it conveyed no meaning to me. I also realized that he spoke from a distance,—that he was at one end of the room while we were at the other. I was presently to have this idea confirmed, for while I was striving with all my might and main to subdue my very heart-throbs so that she would not hear me or suspect my presence, the darkness—I should rather say the blackness of the place yielded to a flash of lightning—heat lightning, all glare and no sound—and I caught an instantaneous vision of my father's figure standing with gleaming things about him, which affected me at the moment as supernatural, but which, in later years, I decided to have been weapons hanging on a wall.

"She saw him too, for she gave a quick laugh and said they would not need any candles; and then, there was another flash and I saw something in his hand and something in hers, and though I did not yet understand, I felt myself turning deathly sick and gave a choking gasp which was lost in the rush she made into the centre of the room, and the keenness of her swift low cry.

"'Garde-toi! for only one of us will ever leave this room alive!'

"A duel! a duel to the death between this husband and wife—this father and mother—in this hole of dead tragedies and within the sight and hearing of their child! Has Satan ever devised a scheme more hideous for ruining the life of an eleven-year-old boy!

"Not that I took it all in at once. I was too innocent and much too dazed to comprehend such hatred, much less the passions which engender it. I only knew that something horrible—something beyond the conception of my childish mind—was going to take place in the darkness before me; and the terror of it made me speechless; would to God it had made me deaf and blind and dead!

"She had dashed from her corner and he had slid away from his, as the next fantastic glare which lit up the room showed me. It also showed the weapons in their hands, and for a moment I felt reassured when I saw that these were swords, for I had seen them before with foils in their hands practising for exercise, as they said, in the great garret. But the swords had buttons on them, and this time the tips were sharp and shone in the keen light.

"An exclamation from her and a growl of rage from him were followed by movements I could scarcely hear, but which were terrifying from their very quiet. Then the sound of a clash. The swords had crossed.

"Had the lightning flashed forth then, the end of one of them might have occurred. But the darkness remained undisturbed, and when the glare relit the great room again, they were already far apart. This called out a word from him; the one sentence he spoke—I can never forget it:

"'Rhoda, there is blood on your sleeve; I have wounded you. Shall we call it off and fly, as the poor creatures in there think we have, to the opposite ends of the earth?'

"I almost spoke; I almost added my childish plea to his for them to stop—to remember me and stop. But not a muscle in my throat responded to my agonized effort. Her cold, clear 'No!' fell before my tongue was loosed or my heart freed from the ponderous weight crushing it.

"'I have vowed and I keep my promises,' she went on in a tone quite strange to me. 'What would either's life be worth with the other alive and happy in this world.'

"He made no answer; and those subtle movements—shadows of movements I might almost call them—recommenced. Then there came a sudden cry, shrill and poignant—had Grandfather been in his room he would surely have heard it—and the flash coming almost simultaneously with its utterance, I saw what has haunted my sleep from that day to this, my father pinned against the wall, sword still in hand, and before him my mother, fiercely triumphant, her staring eyes fixed on his and—

"Nature could bear no more; the band loosened from my throat; the oppression lifted from my breast long enough for me to give one wild wail and she turned, saw (heaven sent its flashes quickly at this moment) and recognizing my childish form, all the horror of her deed (or so I have fondly hoped) rose within her, and she gave a start and fell full upon the point upturned to receive her.

"A groan; then a gasping sigh from him, and silence settled upon the room and upon my heart, and so far as I knew upon the whole created world.

"That is my story, friends. Do you wonder that I have never been or lived like other men?"

After a few moments of sympathetic silence, Mr. Van Broecklyn went on, to say:

"I don't think I ever had a moment's doubt that my parents both lay dead on the floor of that great room. When I came to myself—which may have been soon, and may not have been for a long while—the lightning had ceased to flash, leaving the darkness stretching like a blank pall between me and that spot in which were concentrated all the terrors of which my imagination was capable. I dared not enter it. I dared not take one step that way. My instinct was to fly and hide my trembling body again in my own bed; and associated with this, in fact dominating it and making me old before my time, was another—never to tell; never to let any one, least of all my grandfather—know what that forbidden room now contained. I felt in an irresistible sort of way that my father's and mother's honour was at stake. Besides, terror held me back; I felt that I should die if I spoke. Childhood has such terrors and such heroisms. Silence often covers in such, abysses of thought and feeling which astonish us in later years. There is no suffering like a child's, terrified by a secret which it dare not for some reason disclose.

"Events aided me. When, in desperation to see once more the light and all the things which linked me to life—my little bed, the toys on the window-sill, my squirrel in its cage—I forced myself to retraverse the empty house, expecting at every turn to hear my father's voice or come upon the image of my mother—yes, such was the confusion of my mind, though I knew well enough even then that they were dead and that I should never hear the one or see the other. I was so benumbed with the cold in my half-dressed condition, that I woke in a fever next morning after a terrible dream which forced from my lips the cry of 'Mother! Mother!'—only that.

"I was cautious even in delirium. This delirium and my flushed cheeks and shining eyes led them to be very careful of me. I was told that my mother was away from home; and when after two days of search they were quite sure that all effort to find either her or my father were likely to prove fruitless, that she had gone to Europe where we would follow her as soon as I was well. This promise, offering as it did, a prospect of immediate release from the terrors which were consuming me, had an extraordinary effect upon me. I got up out of my bed saying that I was well now and ready to start on the instant. The doctor, finding my pulse equable, and my whole condition wonder fully improved, and attributing it, as was natural, to my hope of soon joining my mother, advised my whim to be humoured and this hope kept active till travel and intercourse with children should give me strength and prepare me for the bitter truth ultimately awaiting me. They listened to him and in twenty-four hours our preparations were made. We saw the house closed—with what emotions surging in one small breast, I leave you to imagine—and then started on our long tour. For five years we wandered over the continent of Europe, my grandfather finding distraction, as well as myself, in foreign scenes and associations.

"But return was inevitable. What I suffered on reentering this house, God and my sleepless pillow alone know. Had any discovery been made in our absence; or would it be made now that renovation and repairs of all kinds were necessary? Time finally answered me. My secret was safe and likely to continue so, and this fact once settled, life became endurable, if not cheerful. Since then I have spent only two nights out of this house, and they were unavoidable. When my grandfather died I had the wainscot door cemented in. It was done from this side and the cement painted to match the wood. No one opened the door nor have I ever crossed its threshold. Sometimes I think I have been foolish; and sometimes I know that I have been very wise. My reason has stood firm; how do I know that it would have done so if I had subjected myself to the possible discovery that one or both of them might have been saved if I had disclosed instead of concealed my adventure."

A pause during which white horror had shone on every face; then with a final glance at Violet, he said:

"What sequel do you see to this story, Miss Strange? I can tell the past, I leave you to picture the future."

Rising, she let her eye travel from face to face till it rested on the one awaiting it, when she answered dreamily:

"If some morning in the news column there should appear an account of the ancient and historic home of the Van Broecklyns having burned to the ground in the night, the whole country would mourn, and the city feel defrauded of one of its treasures. But there are five persons who would see in it the sequel which you ask for."

When this happened, as it did happen, some few weeks later, the astonishing discovery was made that no insurance had been put upon this house. Why was it that after such a loss Mr. Van Broecklyn seemed to renew his youth? It was a constant source of comment among his friends.

END OF PROBLEM VIII

PROBLEM IX

VIOLET'S OWN

"It has been too much for you?"

"I am afraid so."

It was Roger Upjohn who had asked the question; it was Violet who answered. They had withdrawn from a crowd of dancers to a balcony, half-shaded, half open to the moon,—a balcony made, it would seem, for just such stolen interviews between waltzes.

Now, as it happened, Roger's face was in the shadow, but Violet's in the full light. Very sweet it looked, very ethereal, but also a little wan. He noticed this and impetuously cried:

"You are pale; and your hand! see, how it trembles!"

Slowly withdrawing it from the rail where it had rested, she sent one quick glance his way and, in a low voice, said:

"I have not slept since that night."

"Four days!" he murmured. Then, after a moment of silence, "You bore yourself so bravely at the time, I thought, or rather, I hoped, that success had made you forget the horror. I could not have slept myself, if I had known—"

"It is part of the price I pay," she broke in gently. "All good things have to be paid for. But I see—I realize that you do not consider what I am doing good. Though it helps other people—has helped you—you wonder why, with all the advantages I possess, I should meddle with matters so repugnant to a woman's natural instincts."

Yes, he wondered. That was evident from his silence. Seeing her as she stood there, so quaintly pretty, so feminine in look and manner—in short, such a flower—it was but natural that he should marvel at the incongruity she had mentioned.

"It has a strange, odd look," she admitted, after a moment of troubled hesitation. "The most considerate person cannot but regard it as a display of egotism or of a most mercenary spirit. The cheque you sent me for what I was enabled to do for you in Massachusetts (the only one I have ever received which I have been tempted to refuse) shows to what extent you rated my help and my—my expectations. Had I been a poor girl struggling for subsistence, this generosity would have warmed my heart as a token of your desire to cut that struggle short. But taken with your knowledge of my home and its luxuries, it has often made me wonder what you thought."

"Shall I tell you?"

He had stepped forward at this question and his countenance, hitherto concealed, became visible in the moonlight. She no longer recognized it. Transformed by feeling, it shone down upon her, instinct with all that is finest and best in masculine nature. Was she ready for this revelation of what she had nevertheless dreamed of for many more nights than four? She did not know, and instinctively drew herself back till it was she who now stood in the semi-obscurity made by the drooping vines. From this retreat, she faltered forth a very tremulous No, which in another moment was disavowed by a Yes so faint it was little more than a murmur, followed by a still fainter, Tell me.

But he did not seem in any haste to obey, sweetly as her low-toned injunction must have sounded in his ears. On the contrary, he hesitated to speak, growing paler every minute as he sought to catch a glimpse of her downcast face so tantalizingly hidden from him. Did she recognize the nature of the feelings which held him back, or was she simply gathering up sufficient courage to plead her own cause? Whatever her reason, it was she, not he, who presently spoke saying as if no time had elapsed:

"But first, I feel obliged to admit that it was money I wanted, that I had to have. Not for myself. I lack nothing and could have more if I wished. Father has never limited his generosity in any matter affecting myself, but—" She drew a deep breath and, coming out of the shadow, lifted a face to him so changed from its usual expression as to make him start. "I have a cause at heart—one which should appeal to my father and does not; and for that purpose I have sacrificed myself, in many ways, though—though I have not disliked my work up to this last attempt. Not really. I want to be honest and so must admit that much. I have even gloried (quietly and all by myself, of course) over the solution of a mystery which no one else seemed able to penetrate. I am made that way. I have known it ever since—but that is a story all by itself. Some day I may tell it to you, but not now."

"No, not now." The emphasis sent the colour into her cheek but did not relieve his pallor. "Miss Strange, I have always felt, even in my worst days, that the man who for selfish ends brought a woman under the shadow of his own unhappy reputation was a man to be despised. And I think so still, and yet—and yet—nothing in the world but your own word or look can hold me back now from telling you that I love you—love you notwithstanding my unworthy past, my scarring memories, my all but blasted hopes. I do not expect any response; you are young; you are beautiful; you are gifted with every grace; but to speak,—to say over and over again, 'I love you, I love you!' eases my heart and makes my future more endurable. Oh, do not look at me like that unless—unless—"

But the bright head did not fall, nor the tender gaze falter; and driven out of himself, Roger Upjohn was about to step passionately forward, when, seized by fresh compunction, he hoarsely cried:

"It is not right. The balance dips too much my way. You bring me everything. I can give you nothing but what you already possess abundance— love, and money. Besides, your father—"

She interrupted him with a glance at once arch and earnest.

"I had a talk with Father this morning. He came to my room, and—and it was very near being serious. Someone had told him I was doing things on the sly which he had better look into; and of course he asked questions and—and I answered them. He wasn't pleased—in fact he was very displeased,—I don't think we can blame him for that—but we had no open break for I love him dearly, for all my opposing ways, and he saw that, and it helped, though he did say after I had given my promise to stop where I was and never to take up such work again, that—" here she stole a shy look at the face bent so eagerly towards her—"that I had lost my social status and need never hope now for the attentions of—of—well, of such men as he admires and puts faith in. So you see," her dimples all showing, "that I am not such a very good match for an Upjohn of Massachusetts, even if he has a reputation to recover and an honourable name to achieve. The scale hangs more evenly than you think."

"Violet!"

A mutual look, a moment of perfect silence, then a low whisper, airy as the breath of flowers rising from the garden below: "I have never known what happiness was till this moment. If you will take me with my story untold—"

"Take you! take you!" The man's whole yearning heart, the loss and bitterness of years, the hope and promise of the future, all spoke in that low, half-smothered exclamation. Violet's blushes faded under its fervency, and only her spirit spoke, as leaning towards him, she laid her two hands in his, and said with all a woman's earnestness:

"I do not forget little Roger, or the father who I hope may have many more days before him in which to bid good-night to the sea. Such union as ours must be hallowed, because we have so many persons to make happy besides ourselves."

The evening before their marriage, Violet put a dozen folded sheets of closely written paper in his hand. They contained her story; let us read it with him.

DEAR ROGER,—

I could not have been more than seven years old, when one night I woke up shivering, at the sound of angry voices. A conversation which no child should ever have heard, was going on in the room where I lay. My father was talking to my sister—perhaps, you do not know that I have a sister; few of my personal friends do,—and the terror she evinced I could well understand but not his words nor the real cause of his displeasure.

There are times even yet when the picture, forced upon my infantile consciousness at that moment of first awakening, comes back to me with all its original vividness. There was no light in the room save such as the moon made; but that was enough to reveal the passion burningly alive in either face, as, bending towards each other, she in supplication and he in a tempest of wrath which knew no bounds, he uttered and she listened to what I now know to have been a terrible arraignment.

I may have an interesting countenance; you have told me so sometimes; but she—she was beautiful. My elder by ten years, she had stood in my mother's stead to me for almost as long as I could remember, and as I saw her lovely features contorted with pain and her hands extended in a desperate plea to one who had never shown me anything but love, my throat closed sharply and I could not cry out though I wanted to, nor move head or foot though I longed with all my heart to bury myself in the pillows.

For the words I heard were terrifying, little as I comprehended their full purport. He had surprised her talking from her window to someone down below, and after saying cruel things about that, he shouted out: "You have disgraced me, you have disgraced yourself, you have disgraced your brother and your little sister. Was it not enough that you should refuse to marry the good man I had picked out for you, that you should stoop to this low-down scoundrel—this—" I did not hear what else he called him, I was wondering so

to whom she had been stooping; I had never seen her stoop except to tie my
little shoes.

But when she cried out as she did after an interval, "I love him! I love him!"
then I listened again, for she spoke as though she were in dreadful pain, and I
did not know that loving made one ill and unhappy. "And I am going to marry
him," I heard her add, standing up, as she said it, very straight and tall.

Marry! I knew what that meant. A long aisle in a church; women in white
and big music in the air behind. I had been flower-girl at a wedding once and
had not forgotten. We had had ice cream and cake and—

But my childish thoughts stopped short at the answer she received and all
the words which followed—words which burned their way into my infantile
brain and left scorched places in my memory which will never be eradicated.
He spoke them—spoke them all; she never answered again after that once,
and when he was gone did not move for a long time and when she did it was to
lie down, stiff and straight, just as she had stood, on her bed alongside mine.

I was frightened; so frightened, my little brass bed rattled under me. I
wonder she did not hear it. But she heard nothing; and after awhile she was so
still I fell asleep. But I woke again. Something hot had fallen on my cheek. I
put up my hand to brush it away and did not know even when I felt my fingers
wet that it was a tear from my sister-mother's eye.

For she was kneeling then; kneeling close beside me and her arm was over
my small body; and the bed was shaking again but not this time with my
tremors only. And I was sorry and cried too until I dropped off to sleep again
with her arm still passionately embracing me.

In the morning, she was gone.

It must have been that very afternoon that Father came in where Arthur and
I were trying to play,—trying, but not quite succeeding, for I had been telling
Arthur, for whom I had a great respect in those days, what had happened the
night before, and we had been wondering in our childish way if there would be
a wedding after all, and a church full of people, and flowers, and kissing, and
lots of good things to eat, and Arthur had said No, it was too expensive; that
that was why Father was so angry; and comforted by the assertion, I was
taking up my doll again, when the door opened and Father stepped in.

It was a great event—any visit from him to the nursery—and we both
dropped our toys and stood staring, not knowing whether he was going to be
nice and kind as he sometimes was, or scold us as I had heard him scold our
beautiful sister.

Arthur showed at once what he thought, for without the least hesitation he
took the one step which placed him in front of me, where he stood waiting
with his two little fists hanging straight at his sides but manfully clenched in
full readiness for attack. That this display of pigmy chivalry was not quite
without its warrant is evident to me now, for Father did not look like himself
or act like himself any more than he had the night before.

However, we had no cause for fear. Having no suspicion of my having been
awake during his terrible interview with Theresa, he saw only two lonely and
forsaken children, interrupted in their play.

Can I remember what he said to us? Not exactly, though Arthur and I often
went over it choked whispers in some secret nook of the dreary old house; but
his meaning—that we took in well enough. Theresa had left us. She would

never come back. We were not to look out of the window for her, or run to the door when the bell rang. Our mother had left us too, a long time ago, and she lay in the cemetery where we sometimes carried flowers. Theresa was not in the cemetery, but we must think of her as there; though not as if she had any need of flowers. Having said this, he looked at us quietly for a minute. Arthur was trying very hard not to cry, but I was sobbing like the lost child I was, with my cheek against the floor where I had thrown myself when he said that awful thing about the cemetery. She there! my sister-mother there! I think he felt a little sorry for me; for he half stooped as if to lift me up. But he straightened again and said very sternly:

"Now, children, listen to me. When God takes people to heaven and leaves us only their cold, dead bodies we carry flowers to their graves and talk about them some if not very much. But when people die because they love dark ways better than light, then we do not remember them with gifts and we do not talk about them. Your sister's name has been spoken for the last time in this house. You, Arthur, are old enough to know what I mean when I say that I will never listen to another word about her from either you or Violet as long as you and I live. She is gone and nothing that is mine shall she ever touch again.

"You hear me, Arthur; you hear me, Violet. Heed me, or you go too."

His aspect was terrible, so was his purpose; much more terrible than we realized at the time with our limited understanding and experience. Later, we came to know the full meaning of this black drop which had been infused into our lives. When we saw every picture of her destroyed which had been in the house; her name cut out from the leaves of books; the little tokens she had given us surreptitiously taken away, till not a vestige of her once beloved presence remained, we began to realize that we had indeed lost her.

But children as young as we were then do not long retain the poignancy of their first griefs. Gradually my memories of that awful night ceased to disturb my dreams and I was sixteen before they were again recalled to me with any vividness, and then it was by accident. I had been strolling through a picture gallery and had stopped short to study more particularly one which had especially taken my fancy. There were two ladies sitting on a bench behind me and one of them was evidently very deaf, for their talk was loud, though I am sure they did not mean for me to hear, for they were discussing my family. That is, one of them had said:

"That's Violet Strange. She will never be the beauty her sister was; but perhaps that's not to be deplored. Theresa made a great mess of it."

"That's true. I hear that she and the Signor have been seen lately here in town. In poverty, of course. He hadn't even as much go in him as the ordinary singing-master."

I suppose I should have hurried away, and left this barbed arrow to rankle where it fell. But I could not. I had never learned a word of Theresa's fate and that word poverty, proving that she was alive and suffering, held me to my place to hear what more they might say of her who for years had been for me an indistinct figure bathed in cruel moonlight.

"I have never approved of Peter Strange's conduct at that time," one of the voices now went on. "He didn't handle her right. She had a lovely disposition and would have listened to him had he been more gentle with her. But it isn't in him. I hope this one—"

I didn't hear the end of that. I had no interest in anything they might say about myself. It was of her I wanted to hear, of her. Weren't they going to say anything more about my poor sister? Yes; it was a topic which interested both and presently I heard:

"He'll never do anything for her, no matter what happens; I've heard him say so. And Laura has vowed the same." (Laura is our aunt.) "Besides, Theresa has a pride of her own quite equal to her father's. She wouldn't take anything from him now. She'd rather struggle on. I'm told—I don't know how true it is—that she's working in a department store; one of the Sixth Avenue ones. Oh, there's Mrs. Vandegraff! Don't you want to speak to her?"

They moved off, leaving me still gazing with unseeing eyes at the picture before which I stood planted, and saying over and over in monotonous iteration, "One of the department stores in Sixth Avenue! One of the department stores in Sixth Avenue!"

Which department store?

I meant to find out.

I do not know whether up till then I had had the least consciousness of possessing what is called the detective instinct. But, at the prospect of this quest, so much like that of the proverbial needle in a haystack, as I did not even know my sister's married name and something within me forbade my asking it, I experienced an odd sense of elation followed by a certainty of success which in five minutes changed me from an irresponsible girl to a woman with a deliberate purpose in life.

I am not going to write down here all the details of that search. Some day I may relate them to you, but not now. I looked first for a beautiful woman, for the straight, slim, and exquisite creature I remembered. I did not find her. Then I tried another course. Her figure might have changed in the ten years which had elapsed; so might her expression. I would look for a woman with beautiful dark eyes; time could not have altered them. I had forgotten the effect of constant weeping. And I saw many eyes, but not hers; not the ones I had seen smiling upon me as I lay in my crib before the days I was lifted to the dignity of the little brass bed. So I gave that up too and listened to the inner voice which said, "You must wait for her to recognize you. You can never hope to recognize her." And it was by following this plan that I found her. I had arranged to have my name spoken aloud at every counter where I bargained; and oh, the bargains I sought, and the garments I had tried on! But I made little progress until one day, after my name had been uttered a little louder than usual I saw a woman turn from rearranging gowns on a hanger, and give me one look.

I uttered a low cry and sprang impetuously, forward. Instantly she turned her back and went on hanging, or trying to hang up, gowns on the rack before her. Had I been mistaken? She was not the sister of my dreams, but there was something fine in her outline; something distinguished in the way she carried her head which—

Next minute my last doubt fled! She had fallen her length on the floor and lay with her face buried in her hands in a dead faint.

Oh, Roger, Roger, Roger! I had that dear head on my breast in a moment. I talked to her, I whispered prayers in her unconscious ear. I did everything I should not have done till they all thought me demented. When she came to, as she did under other ministrations than mine, I was for carrying her off in my limousine. But she shook her head with a gesture of such disapproval, that I realized I could not do that. The limousine was my father's, and nothing of his was ever to be used for her again. I would call a cab; but she told me that she had not the money to pay for it and she would not take mine. Carfare she had; five cents would take her home. I need not worry.

She smiled as she said this and for an instant I saw my dream-sister again in this weary half-disheartened woman. But the smile was a fleeting one, for this was to be her last day in the store; she had no talent as a saleswoman and was merely working out her week.

I felt my heart sink heavily at this, for the evidences of poverty were plainly to be seen in her clothes and the thinness of her face and figure. How could I help? What could I do? I took her to a restaurant for food and talk, and before she would order, she looked into her purse, with the result that we had only a little toast and tea. It was all she could afford and I, with a hundred dollars in bills at that moment in my bag, could not offer her anything more though she was needing nourishment and dishes piled with savoury meats were going by us every moment.

I think, if she had let me, I would have dared my father's displeasure and been disobedient to his wishes by giving her one wholesome meal. But she was as resolute of mind as he, and, as she said afterwards, had chosen her course in life and must abide by it. My love she would accept. It took nothing from Father and gave her what her heart was pining for—had pined for for years. But nothing more—not another thing more. She would not even let me go home with her; and I knew why when her eyes fell at the searching look I gave her. Something would turn up, and when her husband's health was better and she had found another position she would send me her address and then I could come and see her. As we walked out of the restaurant we ran against a gentleman I knew. He stopped me for a passing word and in that minute she disappeared. I did not try to follow her. I could get her street and number from the store where she had worked.

But when I had done this and embraced the first opportunity which offered to visit her, I found that she had moved away in the interim, leaving everything behind in payment of her rent, except such small things as she and her husband could carry. This was discouraging as it left me without any clue by which to follow them. But I was determined not to yield to her desire for concealment in the difficult and disheartening task I now saw before me.

Seeking advice from the man who has since become my employer, I entered upon this second search with a quiet resolution which admitted of no defeat. It took me six months, but I finally found her, and satisfied with knowing where she was, desisted from rushing in upon her, till I had caught one glimpse of her husband whom, in the last six months, I had heard described but had never seen. To understand her, it was perhaps necessary to understand him, and if I could not hope to do this offhand, I could not fail to get some idea of the man from even the most casual look.

He was, as I soon learned, the fetcher and carrier of the small ménage; and the day came when I met him face to face in the street where they lived. Did he disappoint me; or did I see something in his appearance to justify her desertion of her father's home and her present life of poverty? If I say Yes to the first question, I must also say it to the last. If handsome once, he was not handsome now; but with a personality such as his, this did not matter. He had that better thing—that greatest gift of the gods—charm. It was in his bearing, his movement, the regard of his weary eye; more than that it was in his very nature or it would have vanished long ago under disappointment and privation.

But that was all there was to the man,—a golden net in which my sister's youthful fancy had been caught and no doubt held meshed to this very day. I felt less like blaming her for her folly, after that instant's view of him as we passed each other in the street. But, as I took time to think, I found myself growing sorrier and sorrier for her and yet, in a way, gladder and gladder, for the man was a physical wreck and would soon pass out of her life leaving her to my love and possibly to our father's forgiveness.

But I did not know Theresa. After her husband's death, which occurred very soon, she let me come to her and we had a long talk. Shall I ever forget it or the sight of her beauty in that sordid room? For, account for it as you will, the loveliness which had fled under her sense of complete isolation had slowly regained its own with the recognition that she still had a place in the heart of her little sister. Not even the sorrow she felt for the loss of her suffering husband—and she did mourn him; this I am glad to say—could more than temporarily stay this. Six months of ease and wholesome food would make her—I hardly dared to think what. For I knew, without asking her, or she telling me, that she would accept neither; that she was as determined now, as ever that nothing which came directly or indirectly from Father should go to the rebuilding of her life. That she intended to start anew and work her way up to a place where I should be glad to see her she did say. But nothing more. She was still the sister-mother, loving, but sufficient to herself, though she had but ten dollars left in the world, as she showed me with a smile that made her beautiful as an angel.

I can see that shabby little purse yet with its one poor greasy bill;—a sum to her but to me the price of a luncheon or a gift of flowers. How I longed, as I looked at it to tear every jewel from my poor, bedecked body and fling them one and all into her lap. I had worn them in profusion, though carefully hidden under my coat, in the hope that she would accept one of them at least, But she refused all, even such as had been gifts of friends and schoolmates, only humouring me this far, that she let me hang them for a few minutes about her neck and in her hair and then pull them all off again. But this one vision of her in the splendour she was born to comforted me. Henceforth in wearing them it would be of her and not of myself I should think.

Well, I had to leave her and go home to my French and Italian lessons, my music-masters and all the luxuries of our father's house. Should I ever see her again? I did not know; she had not promised. I could not go often into the quarter where she lived, without rousing suspicion; and she had bidden me not to come again for a month. So I waited, half fearing she would flit again before the month was up. But she did not. She was still there when—

But I am going too fast. The meeting I was about to mention was a very memorable one to me, and I must describe it from the beginning. I had ridden in my own car as near as I dared to the street where she lived; the rest of the way I went on foot with one of the servants—a new one—following close behind me. I was not exactly afraid, but the actions of some of the people I had encountered at my former visit warned me to be a little careful for my father's sake if not for my own. Her room—she had but one—was high up in a triangular court it was no pleasure to enter. But love and loyalty heed nothing but the object sought, and I was hunting about for the dark doorway which opened upon the staircase leading to her room when—and this was the great moment of my life—a sudden stream of melody floated down into that noisome court, which from its clearness, its accuracy, its richness, and its feeling startled me as I had never before been startled even by the first notes of the world's greatest singers. What a voice for a place like this! What a voice for any place! Whose could it be? With a start, I stopped short, in the middle of that court, heedless of the crowd of pushing, shouting children who at once gathered about me. I had been struck by an old recollection. My sister used to sing. I remembered where her piano had stood in the great drawing-room. It had been carted away during those dreadful weeks and her music all burned; but the vision of her graceful figure bending over the keyboard was one not to be forgotten even by a thoughtless child. Could it be—oh, heaven! if this voice were hers! Her future was certain; she had but to sing.

In a transport of hope I rushed for the dim entrance the children had pointed out and flew up to her room. As I reached it, I heard a trill as perfect as Tetrazzini's. The singer was Theresa; there could be no more doubt. Theresa! exercising a grand voice as only a great artist would or could.

The joy of it made me almost faint. I leaned against her door and sobbed. Then when I thought I could speak quite calmly, I went in.

Roger, you must understand me now,—my desire for money and the means I have taken to obtain it. My sister had the makings of a prima-donna. Her husband, of whose ability I had formed so low an estimate, had trained her with consummate skill and judgment. All she needed was a year with some great maestro in the foreign atmosphere of art. But this meant money—not hundreds but thousands, and the one sure source to which we might rightfully look for any such amount was effectually closed to us. It is true we had relatives—an aunt on our mother's side, and I mentioned her to Theresa. But she would not listen to the suggestion. She would take nothing from any one whom she would find it hard to face in case of failure. Love must go with an advance involving so much risk; love deep enough and strong enough to feel no loss save that of a defeated hope. In short, to be acceptable, the money must come from me, and as this was manifestly impossible, she considered the matter closed and began to talk of a position she had been offered in some choir. I let her talk, listening and not listening; for the idea had come to me that if in some way I could earn money, she might be induced to take it. Finally, I asked her. She laughed, letting her kisses answer me. But I did not laugh. If she had capabilities in one way, I had them in another.

I went home to think.

Two weeks later, I began, in a very quiet way to do certain work for the man who had helped me in my second search for Theresa. The money I have earned has been immense; since it was troubles of the rich I was given to settle, and I was almost always successful. Every cent has gone to her. She has been in Europe for a year and last week she made her debut. You read about it in the papers, but neither you nor any one else in this country but myself knew that under the name she chosen to assume, Theresa Strange, the long forgotten beauty, has recovered that place in the world, to which her love and genius entitle her.

This is my story and hers. From now on, you are the third in the secret. Some day, my father will be the fourth. I think then, a new dawn of love will arise for us all, which will stay the whitening of his dear head—for I believe in him after all. Yesterday when he passed the wall where her picture once hung—no other has ever hung there—I saw him stop and look up, and, Roger, when he passed me a minute later, there was a tear in his hard eye.

THE END